CHARLIE BONE

AND THE

CASTLE OF MIRRORS

CHARLIE BONE

AND THE

CASTLE OF MIRRORS

CHILDREN OF THE RED KING

BOOK 4

JENNY NIMMO

ORCHARD BOOKS
AN IMPRINT OF SCHOLASTIC INC.
NEW YORK

Library of Congress Cataloging-in-Publication Data available

ISBN 0-439-54528-5

10 9 8 7 6 5 4   06 07 08 09

Printed in the U.S.A.
First Scholastic edition, July 2005

Cover illustration © 2005 by Chris Sheban
The text type was set in 11-pt. Diotima Roman.
The display type was set in Latino–Rumba.
Book design by Marijka Kostiw

For David,
who led me to the castle,
with love.
— J. N.

CONTENTS

THE ENDOWED CHILDREN

The endowed are all descended from the ten children of the Red King, a magician-king who left Africa in the twelfth century, accompanied by three leopards.

The Red King had already lived for several centuries, and he made a marvelous glass sphere, putting into it memories of his life and travels through the world. He used the sphere to twist through time, visiting the past and the future.

In any other hands, the Time Twister is dangerous and unpredictable.

Beatrice Bloor
b.1835
Witch.

**Bertram Babing-
ton Bloor**
b.1840
Having read Mary
Shelley's "Frankenstein,"
Bertram, a scientist-
magician, tried to make
a human being. He was
not successful.

m.

**Donatella da
Vinci**
b.1845
Daughter of an Italian
magician. She assisted
Bertram but was
electrocuted during one
of his experiments.

Gideon
b.1875
Mathematician. Knighted
for tutoring a royal prince.
Sir Gideon was not endowed
or interested in magic.

m.

Gudrun Solensson
b.1876
Amateur singer.

Ezekiel
b.1902
Spoiled, cunning, flawed
magician. Continued his
grandfather's experiments.

m.

Hilda Hansoff
b.1902
Botanist. Fatally
poisoned by a
rare plant.

Bartholomew
b.1930
Unendowed.
Mountaineer. Lost
in the Himalayas.

m.

Mary Chance
b.1930
Dancer. Danced herself
to death when Bart
disappeared.

Mais
b.
w

Harold
b.1955
Unendowed, but
interested in his
grandfather's
experiments.

m.

Dorothy de Vere
b.1957
Violinist.

Note:

Charlie Bone can hear
the voices of people in
photographs and
paintings. In certain
circumstances he can
meet them.

Manfred
b.1985
Hypnotist.

Yorath Yewbeam
b.1850
Shape-shifter.

m.

Vera Kuragina
b.1862
Hypnotist.

Grace Bloor
b.1885
Painter. Unendowed.
Lived with her son and
grandson, Paton, until
she died, aged eighty.

m.

Manley
b.1884
Soldier. Killed in 1918
in the Great War.

Yolanda
b.1900
Shape-shifter.
Inherited her father's
castle. Never married.

Henry
b.1905
Disappeared when
he was eleven.
Unendowed.

Daphne
b.1908
Clairvoyant. Died of
diphtheria in 1916.

James
b.1910
Unendowed.
Historian.

m.

Solange Sourzac
b.1912
French actress. Fell and broke
her neck in mysterious
circumstances while visiting
Yolanda's castle in 1964.

Monty Bone
b.1937
Pilot. Died 1963.

m.

Grizelda
b.1937
Unendowed.

Lucretia
b.1942
Matron.
Unendowed.

Eustacia
b.1947
Clairvoyant.

Venetia
b.1952
Designer
of magic
clothes.

Paton
b.1957
Power-
booster.

Amy Jones
b.1967
Store assistant.

m.

Lyell
b.1962
Pianist.
Disappeared in
1994.

Note:

When James Yewbeam's wife,
Solange, died, his four
daughters went to live with
their evil great-aunt,
Yolanda, who turned them
against their father. Yolanda
also tried to steal Paton, but
James resisted her.

Charlie
b.1992
Picture
traveler.

THE CHILDREN OF THE RED KING, CALLED THE ENDOWED

MANFRED BLOOR — Teaching assistant at Bloor's Academy. A hypnotist. He is descended from Borlath, elder son of the Red King. Borlath was a brutal and sadistic tyrant.

CHARLIE BONE — Charlie can hear the voices of people in photographs and paintings. He is descended from the Yewbeams, a family with many magical endowments.

IDITH AND INEZ BRANKO — Telekinetic twins, distantly related to Zelda Dobinski, who has left Bloor's Academy.

DORCAS LOOM — An endowed girl whose gift is the ability to bewitch clothes.

ASA PIKE — A were-beast. He is descended from a tribe who lived in the northern forests and kept strange beasts. Asa can change shape at dusk.

BILLY RAVEN — Billy can communicate with animals. One of his ancestors conversed with ravens that sat on a gallows where dead men hung. For this talent he was banished from his village.

LYSANDER SAGE   Descended from an African wise man. He can call up his spirit ancestors.

GABRIEL SILK   Gabriel can feel scenes and emotions through the clothes of others. He comes from a line of psychics.

JOSHUA TILPIN   Joshua's endowment is magnetism. His origins are, at present, a mystery. Even the Bloors are unsure where he lives. He arrived at their door alone and introduced himself. His tuition is paid through a private bank.

EMMA TOLLY   Emma can fly. Her surname derives from the Spanish swordsman from Toledo whose daughter married the Red King. The swordsman is therefore an ancestor of all the endowed children.

TANCRED TORSSON   A storm-bringer. His Scandinavian ancestor was named after the thunder god, Thor. Tancred can bring wind, thunder, and lightning.

PROLOGUE

The Red King and his queen were riding by the sea. It was that time of year when the wind carries a hint of frost. Evening clouds had begun to appear, and where the sun could find a way through the gathering dusk, it struck the sea in bands of startling light.

The king and queen urged their horses home, but all at once, the queen reined in her mount and in absolute stillness stared out across the water. The king, following her gaze, beheld an island of astounding beauty. Caught in shafts of sunlight, it sparkled with a thousand shades of blue.

"Oh," sighed the queen, in a voice of dread.

"What is it, my heart?" asked the king.

In the matter of their children the queen's intuition was greater than the king's, and when she saw the Island of a Thousand Blues, it was as if an icy hand had clutched her heart. "The children." Her voice was hardly more than a whisper.

The king asked his wife which of their nine children concerned her, but the queen couldn't say. Yet when they returned to the Red Castle and she saw her two sons, black-browed Borlath and blond Amadis, the queen had a terrible sense of foreboding. She saw black smoke rising from the blue island and flames turning the earth to ash. She saw a castle of shining glass appear in a snowstorm, and when her soul's eye traveled over the glass walls, she saw a boy with hair the color of snow climb from a well and close his eyes against the death that lay all around him.

"We must never let our children see that island," she told the king. "We must never let them tread on that blue, enchanted earth."

The king made a promise. But in less than a year the queen would be dead, and the king, bowed down with grief, would leave the castle and his children. The queen died nine days after giving birth to her tenth child, a girl named Amoret. A girl whom no one could protect.

A FATAL SNEEZE

At the edge of the city, Bloor's Academy stood dark and silent under the stars. Tomorrow, 300 children would climb the steps between two towers, cross the courtyard, and crowd through the great oak doors. But for now the old building appeared to be utterly deserted.

And yet, if you had been standing in the garden, on the other side of the school, you could not have failed to notice the strange lights that occasionally flickered from small windows in the roof. And if you had been able to look through one of these windows, you would have seen Ezekiel Bloor, a very old man, maneuvering his vintage wheelchair into an extraordinary room.

The laboratory, as Ezekiel liked to call it, was a long attic room with wide floorboards and a ceiling of bare rafters. Assorted tables, covered with bottles, books, herbs, bones, and weapons, stood against the walls, while beneath them, a stack of dusty chests protruded into the room, threatening to trip anyone who might pass their way.

Dried and faded plants hung from the rafters, and pieces of armor, suspended from the broad cross-beams, clunked ominously whenever a draft swept past them. They clunked now as Ezekiel moved across the floor.

The old man's great-grandson, Manfred, was standing beside a trestle table in the center of the room. Manfred had grown during summer vacation, and Ezekiel felt proud that this tall young man had chosen to work with him rather than go off to college like the other seniors. Mind you, despite his height, Manfred had a skinny frame, sallow, blotchy skin, and a face that was all bones and hollows.

At this moment, his face twisted into a grimace of concentration as he shuffled a pile of bones across the table in front of him. Above him hung seven gas jets set into an iron wheel, their bluish flames emitting a faint purr. When he saw his great-grandfather,

Manfred gave a sigh of irritation and exclaimed, "It's beyond me. I hate puzzles."

"It's not a puzzle," snapped Ezekiel. "Those are the bones of Hamaran, a warhorse of exceptional strength and courage."

"So what? How are a few measly bones going to bring your ancestor back to life?" Manfred directed a disdainful glance at Ezekiel, who instantly lowered his gaze. He didn't want to be hypnotized by his own great-grandson.

Keeping his eyes fixed on the bones, the old man brought his wheelchair closer to the table. Ezekiel Bloor was 101 years old, but other men of that age could look considerably better preserved. Ezekiel's face was little more than a skull. His remaining teeth were cracked and blackened, and a few thin strands of white hair hung from beneath a black velvet cap. But his eyes were still full of life; black and glittering, they darted about with a savage intensity.

"We have enough," said the old man, indicating the other objects on the table: a suit of chain mail, a helmet, a black fur cape, and a gold cloak pin. "They're Borlath's. My grandfather found them in the castle, wrapped in leather inside the tomb. The skeleton was gone." He stroked the black fur almost fondly.

Borlath had been Ezekiel's hero ever since he was a boy. Stories of his warlike ancestor had fired his imagination until he came to believe that Borlath could solve all his problems. Lately, he had dreamed that Borlath would sweep him out of his wheelchair and together they would terrorize the city. Then Charlie Bone and his detestable uncle would have to look out.

"What about electricity for the — you know — moment of life? There isn't any in here." Manfred looked up at the gas jets.

"Oh, that!" Ezekiel waved his hand dismissively. He wheeled himself to another table and picked up a small can with two prongs extending from the top. He turned a handle in the side of the can and a blue spark leaped between the prongs. "Voilà! Electricity!"

he gleefully announced. "Now get on with it. The children will be back tomorrow, and we don't want any of them getting in the way of our little experiment."

"Especially Charlie Bone," Manfred grunted.

"Charlie Bone!" Ezekiel almost spit the name. "His grandmother said he'd be a help, but he's the reverse. I thought I'd almost got him on my side last semester, but then he had to go whining on about his lost father and blaming me."

"He wasn't wrong there," Manfred muttered.

"Think what he could do with that talent of his," Ezekiel went on. "He looks into a picture and, bingo, he's there, talking to people long dead. What I wouldn't give . . ." Ezekiel shook his head. "He's got the blood of that infernal Welsh magician. And the wand."

"I have plans for that," said Manfred softly. "It'll be mine soon — just you wait."

"Indeed." Ezekiel chuckled. He began to propel himself around the room while his great-grandson concentrated on the delicate job of bone-gluing.

As Ezekiel moved into the deep shadows at the far end of the room, his thoughts turned to Billy Raven, the white-haired orphan who used to spy on Charlie Bone. Billy had become rebellious of late. He'd refused to tell Ezekiel what Charlie and his friends were up to. As a result, Ezekiel and the Bloors were in danger of losing control of all the endowed children in the school. Something would have to be done.

"Parents," Ezekiel mumbled to himself. "I'll have to get Billy adopted. I promised I'd find the orphan some parents and I never did. He's given up on me. Well, Billy shall have his nice, kind parents."

"Not too kind," said Manfred, who had overheard.

"Never fear. I've got just the couple. I don't know why I didn't think of them before." Ezekiel turned his head expectantly. "Ah, we're about to get help!"

A distant patter of footsteps could be heard, and a few seconds later, the door opened and three women walked into the room. The first was the oldest. Her iron-gray hair was piled atop her head in a giant bun; her clothes were black and so were her eyes. Lucretia Yewbeam was the school matron and one of Charlie Bone's great-aunts. "I've brought my sisters," she told Ezekiel. "You said you needed help."

"And where's the fourth?" asked Ezekiel. "Where's Grizelda?"

"She's best left out of things for now," said Eustacia, the second sister. "After all, she's got to live with our wretched brother — and the boy. She might blab, accidentally, of course."

Eustacia, a clairvoyant, walked over to the table. Her gray hair still held threads of black, but in most other respects she resembled her older sister. Her small black eyes darted over the objects on the table and she gave a crooked smile. "So, that's what you're up to, you old devil. Who is he?"

"My ancestor Borlath," Ezekiel replied. "Greatest of all the Red King's children. Most magnificent, powerful, and wise."

"Most vile and bloodthirsty would be more accu-rate," said the third sister, dumping a large leather bag on the table. Her greasy hair hung over her shoulders in sooty swaths, and dark shadows ringed her coal-black eyes. Compared to her sisters, she looked a mess. Her long coat was a size too large, and the gray-ish blouse beneath looked badly in need of a wash. No one would have guessed that this bedraggled creature had once been a proud and immaculately groomed woman.

"Venetia's been waiting for something like this," said Eustacia. "Ever since that hateful Charlie Bone burned her house down."

"I thought your brother did that," Manfred chimed in.

"So he did," snarled Venetia, "but Charlie was responsible, the little worm. I want him snuffed out. I want him trembling with fear — tortured, tor-mented, dead."

"Calm down, Venetia." Ezekiel spun quickly to her side. "We don't want to lose the boy entirely."

"Why? What use is he? Can you imagine what it's like to lose everything? To see your possessions — the work of a lifetime — go up in smoke?"

Ezekiel whacked the table with his cane. "Don't be so pathetic, woman. Charlie can be used. I can force him to carry me into the past. I could change history. Think of that!"

"You can't change history, Great-grandfather," Manfred said flatly.

"How do you know?" barked Ezekiel. "No one's tried."

An awkward silence followed. No one dared suggest that it had probably been tried several times, without success. Venetia chewed her lip, still thinking of revenge. She could wait, but one day she would find a way to finish off Charlie Bone — permanently.

"Because I've got the bones," snapped Ezekiel. "This horse, Hamaran" — he nodded at its remains — "was a magnificent creature, by all accounts. And a man mounted on a horse can be very threatening, don't you agree?"

The others agreed.

"The boy will be terrified," Ezekiel went on gleefully. "He'll do anything we ask."

Venetia said, "And how are you going to control this freak?"

Ezekiel had been hoping that no one would ask him this, because he didn't have a satisfactory answer yet. "He's my ancestor," he said with a confident grin. "Why wouldn't he help me? But first things first. Let's get it up and running. Ha-ha!"

While Lucretia sat on a moth-eaten armchair, her sisters unpacked the leather bag. Vials of liquid began to appear on the table; silver spoons; bags of herbs; small, twinkling pieces of quartz; a black marble pestle and mortar; and five candles. Ezekiel watched the proceedings with hungry eyes.

An hour later the leg bones of a galloping horse had been arranged on the table. The chain mail glistened with a foul-smelling liquid, and the fur cape had been covered with tiny seeds.

The five candles cast leaping shadows on the wall.

One had been placed above the helmet, one at the end of each of the chain-mail sleeves, and the last two stood in place of the horse's missing front hooves.

Venetia had enjoyed the work in spite of herself. It was good to sink her teeth into something destructive again. As she caressed the black fur, tiny flames crackled at the tips of her fingers. "Are we ready, then?" she asked.

"Not quite." With a cunning smile, Ezekiel put his hand beneath the rug on his lap and produced a small golden casket. In the center of the jeweled lid, a cluster of rubies, shaped like a heart, shone in the dim room with a dazzling brilliance. "The heart," said Ezekiel, his voice a deep-throated gurgle. "Asa the beast boy found it in the ruin. He was out there digging, as is his wretched habit, and he found a gravestone marked with a 'B.' He dug farther and found this" — he tapped the casket — "buried deep beneath the stone."

From her chair in the shadows, Lucretia asked, "Why wasn't it in the tomb?"

"Why? Why?" Ezekiel gave way to a bout of unpleasant bronchial coughing. "Secrecy, maybe. But it's his. I know it. Borlath was the only one of the king's children with the initial 'B'." He opened the casket.

"Aaaaah!" Eustacia stepped away from the table, for inside the casket lay a small heart-shaped leather pouch that did indeed appear to contain something.

"See? A heart," said Ezekiel triumphantly. "Now, let's get on with it." Scooping the pouch from its casket, he placed it on the suit of armor, just left of center, where he judged a heart might lie. Then he uncoiled a wire from his electric box and wrapped the end once, twice, three times around the pouch.

An expectant hush descended on the room as the old man began to turn the handle of the silver box. Faster and faster. His crooked hand became a flying blur, his black eyes burned with excitement. A spark leaped between the steel prongs and traveled down the wire to Borlath's heart. Ezekiel emitted a croak of triumph and his hand became still.

The three sisters were tempted to exclaim with rapture, but they knew that silence was essential at such a moment. The bones of Hamaran were beginning to move.

Ezekiel and the Yewbeams were watching the table so intently, they failed to notice Manfred pull out a handkerchief and press it to his nose. His face turned bright pink as he struggled to suppress a sneeze. It was no use.

"Achoo!"

Ezekiel recoiled as if from a blow. He covered his ears and rasped, "No," as Manfred tried to hold back yet another sneeze. The sisters watched in horror as the young man screwed up his face and, "Achoo!"

The bones stopped moving. Vile, black vapor rose from the fur, and the chain mail writhed under the smoldering pouch.

"Achoo!"

There was a thunderous bang, and a reeking pall of smoke filled the room. As the onlookers choked and sputtered, a huge form lifted from the table and vanished into the billowing black clouds. Hidden under one of the tables at the far end of the room, a short, fat dog trembled and closed his eyes.

A second violent bang shook the whole room, and Lucretia cried, "What happened?"

"That bumbling idiot sneezed," shrieked Ezekiel.

"Sorry, sorry. Couldn't help it," whined Manfred. "It was the dust."

"Not good enough," scolded Venetia. "You should have taken your wretched nose outside. The whole thing's ruined. A waste of time."

"Maybe not," Eustacia broke in. "Look at the table. The bones have gone."

The smoke was clearing rapidly due to a sudden rush of cold air, and they all saw that the bones of Hamaran had indeed vanished. But Borlath's armor, helmet, cape, and gold pin still lay where they were, rather worse from the spell they had been subjected to.

"Darn!" cried Ezekiel. He thumped the table with his fist, and the scorched garments shuddered. "It didn't work."

"My part did," said Manfred. "The horse is out there." He pointed to a gaping hole in the wall.

"Doggone it!" yelled Ezekiel. "My laboratory's wrecked, and there's a warhorse on the loose."

"A warhorse with a tyrant's heart," said Venetia. "See, it's gone!"

Where the heart had lain, there was now only a scorched black hole in the smoldering armor.

"What does it mean?" asked Manfred in a hushed voice.

Ezekiel stroked his long nose. "It means that all's not lost. But I'll need help. I think I'll call on a friend of mine, someone with a score to settle."

Everyone looked at him, waiting for a name, but the old man was not ready to enlighten them.

"A warhorse could be very useful," said Venetia thoughtfully, "providing one could ride it."

They all stared at the empty space left by the bones, as though willing it to speak, and then Manfred said, "Billy Raven's good with animals."

In a long dormitory, three floors beneath Ezekiel's attic, Billy Raven woke up, suddenly afraid. He turned to the window for a reassuring glimpse of the moon — and saw a white horse sail through ragged clouds, then disappear.

THE PHANTOM HORSE

On the first day of fall semester, Charlie Bone dashed down to breakfast with a comb sticking out of his hair.

"What do you think you look like?" said Grandma Bone from her seat beside the stove.

"A dinosaur?" Charlie suggested. "I pulled and pulled, but my comb wouldn't come out."

"Hair like a hedge," grunted his bony grandmother. "Smarten yourself up, boy. They don't like untidiness at Bloor's Academy."

"Come here, pet." Charlie's more tenderhearted grandmother put down her cup of tea and tugged at the comb. Out it came with a clump of Charlie's hair.

"Maisie! Ouch!" cried Charlie.

"Sorry, pet," said Maisie. "But it had to be done."

"OK." Charlie rubbed his sore head. He sat at the kitchen table and poured himself a bowl of cereal.

"You're late. You'll miss the school bus," said Grandma Bone. "Dr. Bloor's a stickler for punctuality."

Charlie put a spoonful of cereal into his mouth and said, "So what?"

"Don't speak with your mouth full," said Grandma Bone.

"Leave him alone, Grizelda," said Maisie. "He's got to have a good breakfast. He probably won't have a decent meal for another five days."

Grandma Bone snorted and bit into a banana. She hadn't smiled for three months, not since her sister Venetia's house had burned down.

Charlie gulped down a mug of tea, flung on his jacket, and leaped upstairs to fetch his schoolbags.

"Cape!" he said to himself, remembering his blue cape still hanging in the wardrobe.

Charlie pulled out the cape, and a small photograph fluttered to the floor. Charlie picked it up. "Benjamin Brown," he said with a smile. "Where are you?"

The photograph showed a fair-haired boy kneeling beside a large yellow dog. Charlie had taken the photo himself, just before Benjamin's tenth birthday. There was no point in Charlie using his endowment to visit the scene of the photo. It could tell him nothing that he didn't already know.

In his eagerness to use his strange talent, Charlie often forgot that the people he "visited" could see him, too. Wherever they were when Charlie looked at their photos, they would see his face floating somewhere nearby. So Benjamin, who was having a drink in Hong Kong, saw Charlie's smiling face in his orange juice.

Benjamin took Charlie's magical appearances in his stride, but Runner Bean, his dog, could never get used to them.

The big dog was about to have his breakfast in the Pets' Café when Charlie's face looked up from a bowl of cereal.

Runner Bean leaped in the air with a howl; this sent a black rat scuttling under a cupboard, and a blue snake slithering back into its basket, and caused a very tall woman named Onoria Onimous to drop a plate of freshly baked scones. But the three colorful cats lying on top of the fridge merely yawned and closed their eyes.

Charlie put the photo in his pocket, shoved the blue cape in his bag, and ran downstairs.

"Don't forget . . . ," Maisie shouted, but Charlie darted out the front door and ran to the top of Filbert Street.

A blue school bus was about to drive off, when the door suddenly opened and a boy with a mop of curly chestnut hair popped his head out. "I saw you coming," said the boy. "The driver said he couldn't wait, but I made him."

"Thanks, Fido." Charlie handed one of his bags up to his friend Fidelio and climbed the steps into the bus.

"Got your cape?" asked Fidelio.

Charlie pulled the rumpled garment out of his bag. "I hate wearing it when I walk up Filbert Street. People laugh. There's a boy at number twenty who always shouts, 'Here he comes, Little Boy Blue, off to Bloor's, like a cockatoo!' But I didn't ask to go to Bloor's, did I?"

"You're not a cockatoo," Fidelio said with a laugh. "I bet you forgot to comb your hair again this morning."

"I tried."

The bus had come to a halt, and the two boys joined the crowd of children jumping down into a cobblestoned square. They walked past a fountain of stone swans and approached the steps leading to Bloor's Academy.

As Charlie walked into the shadow of the Music Tower, he found himself looking up at the steep roof of the turret. It had become a habit of his and he scarcely knew why he did it. Once, his mother had told him that she felt someone watching her from the small window under the eaves. Charlie gave an involuntary shiver and followed Fidelio through the wide-arched entrance.

Surrounded by children in capes of blue, purple, and green, Charlie looked for Emma Tolly and Olivia Vertigo. He saw Emma in her green cape, her long blond hair in two neat braids, but he was momentarily baffled by the girl beside her. He knew the face, but . . . could it be Olivia? She was wearing a purple cape, like everyone else in drama, but Olivia's face was usually covered in makeup, and she always dyed her hair a vivid color. This girl had a scrubbed look: rosy cheeks, gray eyes, and short brown hair.

"Stop staring, Charlie Bone," said the brown-haired girl, walking up to him.

"Olivia?" Charlie exclaimed. "What's happened to you?"

"I'm auditioning for a part in a movie," Olivia told him. "Got to look younger than I really am."

They climbed another set of stone steps, and then they walked between two huge doors studded with bronze figures. As soon as all the children were safely inside, Weedon, the janitor, closed and locked the doors. They would remain locked until Friday afternoon, when the children were allowed home for the weekend.

Charlie stepped into the vast flagstoned hall of Bloor's Academy. "What's the movie?" he asked Olivia.

"Shhh!" hissed a voice from somewhere near Charlie's ear.

Charlie looked up into a pair of coal-black eyes and nearly jumped out of his skin. He thought Manfred Bloor had left the school.

"I hope you haven't forgotten the rules, Charlie Bone!" barked Manfred.

"N-no, Manfred." Charlie didn't sound too sure.

"Come on, then. . . ." Manfred snapped his fingers and glared at Charlie, who looked down at his feet. He didn't feel like fighting Manfred's hypnotizing gaze so early in the day.

"Come on, what are the rules?" Manfred demanded.

"Er . . . Silence in the hall, / Talking not at all, / Never cry or call, / Even if you fall . . . er . . ." Charlie couldn't remember the last line.

"Write it out a hundred times and bring it to my office after snack time!" Manfred grinned maliciously.

Charlie didn't know Manfred had an office, but he

had no intention of prolonging the unpleasant con-versation. "Yes, Manfred," he mumbled.

"You should be ashamed of yourself. You're in the second year now. Not a very good example for fresh-men, are you, Charlie Bone?"

"Nope." Charlie caught sight of Olivia rolling her eyes at him, and only just managed to stop himself from giggling. Luckily, Manfred had spotted someone without a cape and strode away.

Olivia had disappeared into a sea of purple capes whose owners were crowding through a door beneath two bronze masks. Beyond the open door Charlie glimpsed the colorful mess that was already building up inside the purple coatroom. He hurried on to the sign of two crossed trumpets.

Fidelio was waiting for him just inside the blue coatroom. "Whew! What a shock!" breathed Fidelio. "I thought Manfred had left."

"Me, too," said Charlie. "That was the one good thing about coming back to Bloor's. I thought at least Manfred wouldn't be here." What was Manfred's new role? Would he be permanently on their tails, watching, listening, and hypnotizing?

The two boys discussed the problem of Manfred as they walked to assembly. On the first day of every school year, assembly was held in the theater, the only space large enough for all 300 pupils. Charlie hadn't joined Bloor's Academy until midsemester last fall; it was a new experience for him.

"Yikes, I'd better hurry," said Fidelio, looking at his watch. "I should be tuning up."

Dr. Saltweather, head of music, gave Fidelio a severe nod as he climbed up to the stage and took his place in the orchestra. Charlie joined the end of the second row and found himself standing directly behind Billy Raven. He turned around with a worried frown.

"I've got to stay in the first year for another twelve months," he whispered to Charlie, "but I've already done it twice."

"Bad luck! But you are only eight." Charlie scanned the row of new children in front of him. They all looked fairly normal, but you could never tell. Some of them might be endowed like himself and Billy, children of the Red King.

For the rest of the morning, Charlie traipsed through the huge, drafty building, finding his new classroom, collecting books, and looking for Mr. Paltry, who was supposed to be giving him a trumpet lesson.

By the time the hunting horn sounded for lunch, Charlie was utterly exhausted. He slouched down to the cafeteria, averting his eyes from the portraits that hung in the dimly lit corridor — just in case one of them wanted a conversation — and arrived at the blue cafeteria.

Charlie joined the line. A small, stout woman behind the counter gave him a wink. "All's well, then, Charlie?" she asked.

"Yes, thanks, Cook," said Charlie. "But it'll take me a while to get used to the second year."

"It will," said Cook. "But you know where I am if you need me. Peas, Charlie?"

Charlie accepted a plate of macaroni and cheese

and peas, then wandered around the tables until he found Fidelio, sitting with Billy Raven and Gabriel Silk. Gabriel's floppy brown hair almost obscured his face, and there was a forlorn droop to his mouth.

"What's up, Gabe?" asked Charlie. "Are your gerbils OK?"

Gabriel looked up sadly. "I can't take piano this semester. Mr. Pilgrim's gone."

"Gone?" Charlie was unexpectedly dismayed. "Why? Where?"

Gabriel shrugged. "I know Mr. Pilgrim was peculiar, but — well, he was just — brilliant."

No one could deny this. Mr. Pilgrim's piano playing was often heard echoing down the Music Tower. Charlie realized he would miss it. And he would miss seeing Mr. Pilgrim staring into space, his black hair always falling into his eyes.

Fidelio turned to Billy. "So how was your summer, Billy?" he asked carefully. For how could anyone spend their whole summer vacation in Bloor's Academy without going mad?

"Better than usual," said Billy cheerfully. "Cook looked after Rembrandt like she promised, and I saw him every day. And Manfred went away for a bit so it was OK here, really, except . . . except" — a shadow crossed his face — "something happened last night. Something really weird."

"What?" asked the other three.

"I saw a horse in the sky."

"A horse?" Fidelio raised his eyebrows. "Do you mean a cloud that looked like a horse?"

"No. It was definitely a horse." Billy took off his glasses and wiped them on his sleeve. His deep red eyes fixed themselves on Charlie. "It sort of hung there, outside the window, and then it just faded."

"Stars can do that," said Gabriel, who had perked up a bit. "They can create the illusion of animals and things."

Billy shook his head. "NO. It was a HORSE." He replaced his glasses and frowned at his plate. "It wasn't far away. It was right outside the window. It reared up and kicked the air, like it was fighting to be free, and then it just — faded."

Charlie found himself saying, "As if it were receding into another world."

"That's right," said Billy eagerly. "You believe me, don't you, Charlie?"

Charlie nodded slowly. "I wonder where it is now?"

"Wandering around the castle ruins with all the other ghosts?" Fidelio wryly remarked. "Come on, let's get some fresh air. We might see a horse galloping around the garden."

Of course, he was only joking, but as soon as the four boys walked through the garden door, Fidelio realized that his words held a ghostly ring of truth. He was the only one of the four who was not endowed. Fidelio might be a brilliant musician, but his endowment was not one that could be classified as magical.

It was Charlie who noticed it first, a faint thudding on the dry grass. He looked at Gabriel. "Can you hear it?"

Gabriel shook his head. He could hear nothing, but there was a presence in the air that he couldn't define.

Billy was the most affected. He stepped back suddenly, his white hair lifting in a breeze that no one else could feel. He put up his hand as if to ward off a blow. "It went right past," he whispered.

Fidelio said, "You're joking, aren't you?"

"'Fraid we're not," said Charlie. "It's gone now. Maybe it just wanted us to know it was here."

They began to cross the wide expanse of grass that Dr. Bloor liked to call his garden. It was really no more than a field, bordered by nearly impenetrable woods. At the end of the field, the red stones of an ancient castle could be glimpsed between the trees: the castle of the Red King. The four boys almost instinctively made their way toward the tall red walls.

Charlie's uncle Paton had told him how, when Queen Berenice died, five of the Red King's children had been forced to leave their father's kingdom forever. Brokenhearted, the king had vanished into the forests of the north, and Borlath, his elder son, had taken the castle. He had ruled the kingdom with such barbarous cruelty, most of the inhabitants had either died or fled in terror.

"Well?" said Fidelio. "Do you think the phantom horse is here?"

Charlie looked up at the massive walls. "I don't know." He turned to Billy.

"Yes," he whispered. "It's here."

The others listened intently. They could hear the distant shouts and chatter of children on the field, the thump of a soccer ball, the call of wood pigeons, but nothing else.

"Are you sure, Billy?" asked Charlie.

Billy hugged himself. He was shivering. "I think it would like to speak, but it's caught on the wrong side."

"Wrong side of what?" asked Fidelio.

Billy frowned. "I can't explain."

Charlie became aware that someone was standing

behind them. He turned around, just in time to see a small figure dart away and join a group of new boys playing soccer together.

"Who was that?" asked Gabriel.

"New boy," said Charlie.

It was impossible to tell whether the boy was in art, drama, or music because he wasn't wearing a cape. Today, it was warm and sunny. Summer was not yet over.

The sound of the horn rang out across the field and the four boys ran back to school.

For Charlie, the afternoon was no better than the morning. He found Mr. Paltry at last, but too late for his lesson. "What's the point of coming to a lesson without your trumpet?" grumbled the old teacher. "You're a waste of time, Charlie Bone. Endowed, my foot. Why don't you use your so-called talent to locate your trumpet? Now get out and don't come back until you've found it."

Charlie left quickly. He had no idea where to look. "The Music Tower?" Charlie asked himself. Perhaps one of the cleaners had found his trumpet and put it in Mr. Pilgrim's room at the top of the tower.

The way to the Music Tower led through a small, ancient-looking door close to the garden exit. Charlie braced himself, opened the door, and began to walk down a long, damp passage. It was so dark he could barely see his own feet. He kept his eyes on a distant window in the small circular room at the end of the passage.

As he got closer to the room, he began to hear voices, angry voices — men arguing. There was a clatter of footsteps. Charlie stood still until whoever it was had reached the bottom of the long, spiraling staircase. A figure appeared at the end of the passageway. It loomed toward Charlie and raised its purple wings, blocking out the light.

Plunged into darkness, Charlie screamed.

THE BOY WITH PAPER IN HIS HAIR

"Quiet!" hissed a voice.

Charlie shrank against the wall as the person, or thing, swept past and whisked itself through the door into the hall.

Charlie didn't know what to do. Should he go back the way he had come or on toward the tower? The hissing person might be in the hall, waiting for him. He chose the tower.

As soon as he emerged in the round sunlit room at the end of the passageway, Charlie felt better. Those purple wings had been the arms of a cape, he reasoned. And the angry person was probably a member of the school's staff, arguing with someone. He began the long, spiral ascent to the top of the tower. Bloor's Academy had five floors, but Mr. Pilgrim's music room was up yet another flight.

Charlie reached the small landing where music books were stored on shelves, in boxes, and in untidy piles on the floor. Between the rows of shelving, a small oak door led into the music room. A message had been tacked to the center of the door:

Mr. Pilgrim is away.

Charlie rummaged in the boxes, lifted the piles of sheet music, and searched behind the heavy books on the shelves. He found a flute, a handful of violin strings, a box of oatmeal cookies, and a comb, but no trumpet.

Was there any point in trying the room next door? Charlie remembered seeing a grand piano and a stool, nothing else. He looked again at the note. *Mr. Pilgrim is away.* It looked foreboding, as though there were another message behind those four thinly printed words: "Do not enter, you are not welcome here."

But Charlie was a boy who often couldn't stop himself from doing what all the signs told him not to. This time, however, he did knock on the door before going in. To his surprise, he got an answer.

"Yes," said a weary voice.

Charlie went in.

Dr. Saltweather was sitting on the music stool. His arms were folded inside his blue cape, and his thick white hair stood up in an untidy, careless way. He wore an expression that Charlie had never seen on his face before: a look of worry and dismay.

"Excuse me, sir," said Charlie. "I was looking for my trumpet."

"Indeed." Dr. Saltweather glanced at Charlie.

"I suppose it isn't in here."

"Nothing is in here," said Dr. Saltweather.

"Sorry, sir." Charlie was about to go when something made him ask, "Where is Mr. Pilgrim, sir?"

"Where?" Dr. Saltweather looked at Charlie as if he'd only just seen him. "Ah, Charlie Bone."

"Yes, sir."

"I don't know where Mr. Pilgrim has gone. It's a mystery."

"Oh." Charlie was about to turn away again, but this time he found himself saying, "I bumped into someone in the passage; I thought it might be him."

"No, Charlie." The teacher spoke with some force. "That would have been Mr. Ebony, your new teacher."

"Our teacher?" Charlie gulped. He thought of the purple wings, the hissing voice.

"Yes. It's a little worrying, to say the least." Dr. Saltweather gave Charlie a scrutinizing stare, as though wondering if he should say more. "Mr. Ebony came here to teach history," he went on, "but he turned up with a letter of resignation from Mr. Pilgrim. I don't know how he came by it. And now this — man — wants to teach piano." Dr. Saltweather raised his voice. "He comes up here, puts a message on the door, tries to keep me out of a room in my own department. . . . It's intolerable!"

"Yes, sir," agreed Charlie. "But he was wearing a purple cape, sir."

"Ah, yes, that!" Dr. Saltweather ran a hand through his white hair. "It seems that Mr. Tantalus Ebony is in the drama department, hence the purple."

Charlie said, "I see," although by now he was very confused. He had never heard of a teacher being in three departments at once.

"They are Dr. Bloor's arrangements, so what can I do?" Dr. Saltweather spread his hands. "Better run along now, Charlie. Sorry about the trumpet. Try one of the art rooms. They're always drawing our musical instruments."

"Art. Thank you, sir," said Charlie gratefully. The art rooms could be reached only by climbing the main staircase, and Charlie had just put his foot on the first step when Manfred Bloor came out of a door in the hall.

"Have you finished writing out your lines?" asked Manfred coldly.

"Er, no."

Manfred approached Charlie. "Don't forget or you'll get another hundred."

"Yes, Manfred. I mean no."

Manfred gave a sigh of irritation and walked away.

"Excuse me," Charlie said suddenly, "but are you still, er, a pupil, Manfred?"

"No, I am not!" barked the surly young man. "I am a teaching assistant. And call me sir."

"Yes, sir." The word "sir" tasted funny when applied to Manfred, but Charlie smiled, hoping he'd said the right thing at last.

"And don't forget." Manfred marched back into the prefects' room and slammed the door.

Charlie still hadn't found Manfred's office. He was now torn between looking for his trumpet and writing out a hundred lines. But then he remembered that he didn't know the last line of the hall rules. "Emma will tell me," he said to himself, and he began to climb the stairs.

Emma was often to be found in the art gallery, a long, airy room overlooking the garden. Today, however, the room appeared to be empty. Charlie searched the paint cupboard and inspected the shelves at the back of the room, then he crossed the gallery and descended an iron spiral staircase that took him down into the sculpture studio.

"Hi, Charlie!" called a voice.

"Hey, come on over," called another.

Charlie looked around to see two boys in green aprons grinning at him from either side of a large block of stone. One had a brown face and the other was very pale. Charlie's two friends were now in their third year. They had both grown considerably during summer vacation, and so had their hair. Lysander now had a neat head of dreadlocks decorated with multicolored beads, while Tancred had gelled his blond hair into a forest of stiff spikes.

"What brings you down here, Charlie?" asked Tancred.

"I'm looking for my trumpet. Hey, I hardly recognized you two."

"You haven't changed," said Lysander with a wide smile. "How do you like the second year?"

"I don't know. I'm in a bit of a jam. I keep going to

the wrong place. I've lost my trumpet," said Charlie. "I'm in trouble with Manfred and there's an, er, um, thing in the garden."

"What do you mean, a 'thing'?" Tancred's blue eyes widened.

Charlie told them about the horse Billy had seen in the sky and the hoofbeats in the garden.

"Interesting," said Lysander.

"Ominous," said Tancred. "I don't like the sound of it." The sleeves of his shirt quivered. It was difficult for Tancred to hide his endowment. He was like a walking weather vane, his moods affecting the air around him to such an extent that you could say he had his own personal weather.

"I'd better keep looking for my trumpet," said Charlie. "Oh, what's the last line of the hall rules?"

"Be you small or tall," said Lysander quickly.

"Thanks, Sander. I've got to write the whole thing out a hundred times before dinner and give it to Manfred — if I can find his office. You don't happen to know where it is, do you?"

Tancred shook his head and Lysander said, "Not a clue."

Charlie was about to return the way he'd come when Tancred suggested he try somewhere else. "Through there," said Tancred, indicating a door at the end of the sculpture studio. "The new children are having their first art lesson. I think I saw one carrying a trumpet."

"Thanks, Tanc!" Charlie walked into a room he'd never seen before. About fifteen silent children sat around a long table, sketching. Each had a large sheet of paper and an object in front of them. They were all concentrating fiercely on their work, and none of them looked up when Charlie appeared.

"What do you want?" A thin, fair-haired man with freckles spoke from the end of the table. A new art teacher, Charlie presumed.

"My trumpet, sir," said Charlie.

"And why do you think it's here?" asked the teacher.

"Because there it is!" Charlie had just spotted a

trumpet exactly like his. The instrument was being sketched by a small boy with mousy hair and ears that stuck out. The boy looked up at Charlie.

"Joshua Tilpin," said the teacher, "where did you get that trumpet?"

"It's mine, Mr. Delf." Joshua Tilpin had small pale-gray eyes. He half-closed them and wrinkled his nose at Charlie.

Charlie couldn't stop himself. He leaped forward, seized the trumpet, and turned it over. Last semester he had scratched a tiny "cb" near the mouthpiece. The trumpet was his. "It's got my initials on it, sir."

"Let me see." Mr. Delf held out his hand.

Charlie handed over the trumpet. "My name's Charlie Bone, sir. See, they're my initials."

"You shouldn't deface musical instruments like this. But it does appear to be yours. Joshua Tilpin, why did you lie?"

Everyone looked at Joshua. He didn't turn red, as Charlie would have expected. Instead, he gave a huge grin, revealing a row of small, uneven teeth. "Sorry, sir. Really, really sorry, Charlie. Only a joke. Forgive me, please!"

Neither Charlie nor the teacher knew how to reply to this. Mr. Delf passed the trumpet to Charlie, saying, "You'd better get back to your class."

"Thank you, sir." Charlie clutched his trumpet and turned to the door. He took a good look at Joshua Tilpin as he went. He had an odd feeling that the new boy was endowed. Joshua's sleeves and hair were covered with scraps of paper and tiny bits of eraser. Even as Charlie watched, a broken pencil lead suddenly leaped off the table and attached itself to the boy's thumb. He gave Charlie a sly grin and flicked it off. Charlie felt as though an invisible thread were tugging him toward the strange boy.

He quickly left the room, and the thread was broken.

The sculpture studio rang with the sound of steel on stone. Tancred and Lysander weren't the only ones chipping away at lumps of rock. Charlie flourished his trumpet in the air. "Got it," he sang out.

"Knew it," said Tancred.

Charlie's next priority was the hundred lines. Where should he write them? He decided on his new homeroom. As he crossed the hall, he was swamped by groups of children, some coming in from games, others rushing down the stairs, still more emerging from the coatrooms. Everyone seemed to know exactly where they were going, except Charlie. Something had gone horribly wrong with his schedule. He hurried on, hoping to find at least some of his year's group in the classroom.

There was a note tacked to the classroom door. It was printed in the same, old-fashioned handwriting as the words on Mr. Pilgrim's door:

Tantalus Ebony
Music, Mime, and Medieval History

Charlie put his ear to the door. Not a sound came from the other side. He went in.

• • •

There were no children in the room, but there was a teacher. He sat at a high desk in front of the window, a teacher with a long, narrow face and black eyebrows that met across the bridge of his nose. His dark hair covered his ears, and heavy bangs ended just above his eyebrows. He wore a purple cape.

"Yes?" said the teacher, looking up from his book.

Charlie swallowed. "I've come to write out some lines, sir."

"Name?" The man's voice rumbled as though it came from underground.

"Charlie Bone, sir."

"Approach!" The teacher beckoned with a long, white finger.

Charlie walked to the desk. The man stared at him for a full minute. His left eye was gray and his right eye brown. It was most disconcerting. Charlie was tempted to look away, but he held his ground and looked first into one eye and then the other. An angry frown crossed the man's face and he leaned back, almost as though he feared that Charlie had seen some part of him that he wished to keep secret. Eventually, the teacher said, "I am Tantalus Ebony."

"I guessed that, sir."

"How presumptuous. Stand still."

Charlie was about to say that he hadn't moved, when Mr. Ebony went on, "Why are you not with the rest of your class?"

"I got a bit confused, sir."

"Confused? Confused is for freshmen. Not a very promising beginning for your second year, is it, Charlie Bone? And you say you have lines already. I wonder why."

"I was talking in the hall, sir."

Mr. Ebony's response was amazing. He roared with laughter. He rocked with unrestrained giggles.

"Ahem." The teacher gave a little cough. "Go and write your lines, then. And don't disturb me. I'm going to sleep." Mr. Ebony pulled his purple hood over his head and closed his eyes. Still sitting bolt upright, he began to snore.

Is it possible to be watched by someone who isn't

looking at you? Charlie had the impression that the strange teacher was still awake. Or rather that someone else, behind the sleeping face, was still on guard.

After waiting a few seconds, Charlie tiptoed to his desk, got out an exercise book, and began to write out the hall rules. He had just completed the last line when the horn sounded for snack time. Mr. Ebony opened his eyes, threw back his hood, and cried, "OUT!"

"Yes, sir." Charlie gathered up his papers and hurriedly left the room.

"Where on earth have you been?" asked Fidelio, when he saw Charlie in the cafeteria.

"Where have you been?" said Charlie.

"I had English, then games."

Charlie saw a weekend of detention looming ahead. Mr. Carp, the English teacher, wouldn't forgive him for missing a lesson. "I was writing out my lines for Manfred," he said gloomily. "And I still haven't found out where his office is."

Fidelio couldn't help, nor could Gabriel when he arrived at their table. "What's with him, then?" he said, munching a Choclix bar. "I mean, what's Manfred supposed to be? He's not head boy anymore, and he's not a teacher. So what is he?"

"He's a hypnotizer," said Charlie grimly. "Always has been and always will be. He'll probably stay here for ever and ever, perfecting his skills until he becomes a musty old magician like his great-grandfather."

"As long as he keeps out of my way, I don't care what he is." Gabriel swallowed the rest of his Choclix and wiped his fingers on his sleeve. "By the way, I've decided to take piano with Mr. Ebony. I can't give it up, and he's quite good, actually."

"I'd go to Miss Chrystal if I were you," Charlie advised Gabriel. "Mr. Ebony isn't — isn't what he seems. I think he's dangerous."

The others looked at him questioningly, but Charlie couldn't explain his feeling.

After snack time, Charlie took his trumpet to Mr. Paltry's room. The elderly teacher was having a quiet cup of coffee. "I can't give you a lesson now," he said irritably. "Put your trumpet on the shelf and leave me in peace."

"Yes, sir." Charlie placed his trumpet on the shelf with five others, hoping it wouldn't get lost or stolen again. "Excuse me, sir, but do you know where Manfred Bloor's office is?"

"I don't know every single room in the building, do I?" Mr. Paltry fluttered a freckled hand. "Now, shoo."

Children were advised to leave their capes indoors on sunny days. Believe it or not, it was colder inside the dark academy than it was outside. Leaving his cape in the coatroom, Charlie went into the garden and asked as many people as he could if they knew the whereabouts of Manfred's office. Nobody knew. Charlie ran indoors again. As he put on his blue cape, he slipped his fingers into his pocket. The three pages had vanished.

"No!" yelled Charlie, just as Gabriel walked in.

"What's up?" asked Gabriel.

Charlie told him, and for the next fifteen minutes

Gabriel helped Charlie search the coatroom, but the three pages were nowhere to be found. Fidelio appeared and joined in the hunt. They looked in empty classrooms and even went down to the cafeteria. And then the horn sounded for dinner.

"Someone's determined to get me into trouble," moaned Charlie. "I'm losing everything, my trumpet, my lines. . . . What's going on?"

"Come and eat," said Fidelio. "Food helps the brain."

"Huh!" Charlie grunted.

The three boys made their way to the long, cavernous dining hall and took their places at the end of the music table.

The academy's staff sat at a table on a raised platform at the end of the room, and Charlie noticed that Manfred was sitting next to his father. So he was now officially a member of the staff. *At least he won't be doing his homework with us*, thought Charlie.

Dinner was almost over when Dr. Bloor stood up and clapped his hands. There was instant silence. The

big man walked to the front of the platform and surveyed the lines of children below him. He was an
impressive figure in his black cape, his shoulders wide,
his gray hair neatly cropped, and his mustache as
straight as a ruler. His eyes were almost hidden
beneath thick folds of flesh, and it was difficult to tell
what color they were. Now they looked black, yet
Charlie knew they were gray.

It was some time before the headmaster spoke.
The children looked up at him expectantly. At last he
said, "A word to those of the new children who are
endowed. You know who you are, so I shall not mention you by name. You will do your homework in the
King's room. Someone will show you the way. Do
you understand?"

Charlie heard three thin voices utter the words,
"Yes, sir." He couldn't tell where they had come from,
but they certainly didn't belong to anyone at the music
table.

Dr. Bloor suddenly shouted, "DISPERSE!"

Children sprang into action like clockwork.

Benches squeaked on the tiled floor, plates were collected into piles, glasses clinked, cutlery clanged, and then everyone made for the doors. As Charlie climbed up to the first floor, he was joined by Gabriel and Billy. Emma Tolly was ahead of him, and Tancred and Lysander could just be seen flying up another flight to the second floor.

Emma waited for Charlie to catch up with her. "I found these on the floor of our coatroom," she said, holding out three crumpled sheets of paper. "I heard you were looking for them."

"My lines," cried Charlie, grabbing the paper. "Thanks, Em. But how did they get in the art coatroom?"

"Haven't a clue," said Emma.

Charlie shoved the pages into his bag. The sound of heavy footsteps behind him made him look back, and he saw Dorcas Loom trudging slowly up the stairs. She was a plump girl with fair curly hair and a healthy complexion. Dorcas was a fervent admirer of Charlie's great-aunt Venetia, and with her endowment, she could make clothes that had a deadly magic.

"What are you staring at?" she said sullenly.

"A cat may look at a queen," replied Charlie.

Dorcas gave a "Ha" of disgust, then continued to plod up the stairs.

Charlie and his friends stepped into the strange, circular King's room, with its round table and curving, book-lined walls.

Manfred was standing at the far side of the table, staring straight at the doors. Charlie's heart lurched, and then disappointment washed over him in a sickening wave as he saw a hunched figure sitting beside Manfred. It was Asa Pike, Manfred's devoted slave, the boy who could become a beast at dusk. He should have left school. Why was he still here? There were also three new children in the room. Joshua Tilpin was one of them.

"Come on, come on," ordered Manfred impatiently. "Stop crowding in the door. I have an important announcement to make."

Charlie pulled himself together and walked around

the table until he came to a place beside Tancred. From here, he could see the Red King's portrait: an old painting of a musty figure in a red cape and a slim gold crown. Gabriel, Billy, and Emma followed Charlie, while Dorcas stomped in and closed the door with her foot.

"Show some respect for my father's house!" barked Manfred.

Dorcas scowled, but didn't dare to look Manfred in the eye. "Someone's sitting in my seat," she muttered.

"Don't be stupid, Dorc," said Manfred.

Asa snickered. "'Dork.' That's good."

Manfred ignored him. "Just sit anywhere, girl, and hurry up about it."

If Dorcas had wanted to sit on Manfred's other side, she was out of luck. Squeezed in between Manfred and Joshua Tilpin were two extraordinary-looking girls. They both had very shiny black hair, cut just below the ears, long bangs, and complexions that were so pale and smooth, they looked like porcelain.

Twins, obviously, thought Charlie. *If they're real.* For the girls' faces were so blank, and their bodies so still, they could have been dolls.

Dorcas shuffled around the table and put her books next to Joshua's. He gave her one of his beaming crooked-teeth smiles, and Dorcas actually smiled back.

"Now that we're all here," said Manfred, glancing at Dorcas, "I want to explain a few things. First of all, you probably didn't expect to see me again. Well, you're stuck with me." No one made a sound except Asa, who snorted. "I'm now a teaching assistant," Manfred went on importantly. "My job description is to supervise your homework, monitor your progress, supervise during exams, and help with any personal or work-related problems." He paused to take a breath, and Charlie wondered who on earth would want to ask the ex–head boy for help.

"Now, for introductions." Manfred named everyone at the table until he came to the inscrutable girls beside him. "And these are the twins Inez and Idith Branko."

As soon as their names were mentioned, the twins bent their heads and stared at the books in front of them. With alarming speed, the books flew across the table. One pile landed in Charlie's lap and the other in Tancred's.

"Oh, no!" Tancred grunted. "Telekinesis." The sleeves of his cape ballooned out, his blond hair crackled, and a draft sent a shiver through the loose sheets of paper lying on the table.

"I see that your summer vacation didn't improve your self-control, Tancred," said Manfred in a mocking tone.

Tancred and Charlie stood up and handed the twins' books back across the table. The girls didn't say a word and their faces remained completely blank.

Charlie couldn't resist remarking, "It's polite to say thank you."

Idith and Inez remained silent, but one of them, who knows which, shot him a very nasty look.

"Try and be pleasant to the new girls, Bone," said Manfred. "The twins are related to Zelda Dobinski, who has left us. Apparently, she is a mathematical genius, so she's off to a university at a very early age. Unfortunately, Asa here is the opposite of a genius. He's still with us because he failed all his exams."

Frowning with embarrassment, Asa hunched even farther down in his seat, and Charlie felt a rare twinge of sympathy for him. To be ridiculed by someone he admired must have been very painful.

"Last, but not least, we have Joshua Tilpin," Manfred announced.

On hearing his name, Joshua leaped up and bowed. Anyone would have thought he was a prince. And yet he looked a mess. His green cape was covered in dust, there were leaves and grass in his hair, and a cobweb hung from one of his ears.

"Sit down, Joshua," said Manfred. "You're not a pop star."

Joshua beamed at him, and to everyone's amazement, Manfred smiled back. Getting a smile out of Manfred was like getting water out of a stone.

What next? thought Charlie. He was just about to

start his homework when Manfred said, "Charlie Bone, you didn't bring me your lines."

"Oh, sorry, Manfred. I've got them here." Charlie fumbled in his bag.

"I asked you to bring them to my office."

"But . . . I don't know where it is," Charlie confessed.

Manfred sighed. He looked at the ceiling and declared, "I am behind words . . . on the way to music . . . beneath a wing . . . and before trumpets, masks, and brushes." He paused for effect and brought his gaze back to Charlie. "Do I make myself clear?"

In any other circumstance, Charlie would have said, "Clear as mud," but as the situation was already pretty grim, he decided to say, "Yes, Manfred."

"Good. Then bring your lines to my office before bedtime, or it's detention for you."

DETENTION FOR CHARLIE

Charlie was lucky to have a friend like Lysander Sage. Lysander always finished his homework early, and today, as soon as his work was done, he applied himself to Manfred's riddle.

As Charlie was leaving the King's room, Lysander grabbed his arm. "I think I know where Manfred's office is," he whispered. "Let's go and find our dorms and I'll explain."

Billy Raven had crept up on them. "Can I come with you?" he asked Charlie.

"Billy Raven, I want a word with you." Manfred stood outside the King's room, looking at the three boys.

Billy gave a resigned shrug and walked back to Manfred.

"Poor kid," Lysander said under his breath. He began to explain how he had interpreted Manfred's riddle.

"I started at the end," he said, "'Trumpets, masks,

and brushes' must refer to the signs above our coat-rooms. So Manfred's office is 'before' you get to them. If it's 'on the way to music,' then it must be somewhere down that long passageway to the Music Tower, and that's 'beneath' the west 'wing' — get it?"

"Mm," said Charlie. "But what about the words, 'behind words'?" he said.

"Words are in books," said Lysander. "I figure if you can find a bookcase in that passageway, Manfred's office will be behind it. Bookcases are often used as doors to secret rooms."

"Wow! You've got it, Sander. I did see a bookcase down there. Brilliant! Thanks!"

"You're welcome. Hope it works."

They had reached the first dormitories and began to scan the lists of names tacked to each door. Lysander found that he was still sharing with Tancred, and to Charlie's relief he saw his own name on a list with Fidelio's. Billy's name was at the bottom.

Fidelio was already unpacking his bag. He'd saved a bed beside his for Charlie. The dormitory was almost exactly the same as last year's. Six narrow beds arranged on either side of a long bleak room, with a single dim lightbulb hanging in the center.

Charlie quickly shoved all his possessions in a bedside dresser and hung his cape on a hook. "I'm going to try and find Manfred's office," he told Fidelio. "Can you cover for me if the matron comes in?"

"I'll say you're in the bathroom," said Fidelio. "Good luck."

Charlie was halfway down the hallway when he met an excited Billy Raven coming the other way.

"I'm being adopted. Manfred just told me."

"That's great!" cried Charlie.

The small boy touched his white hair. "I wonder why they want me. I mean, they could have chosen any boy. Someone nicer-looking, someone different."

"Who are they?" asked Charlie, suddenly concerned for Billy.

"They're called de Grey. Mr. and Mrs. de Grey. They're a bit older than I expected, actually. Manfred showed me a photo. But he says they're nice and very kind. And they've got a lovely house. I'll have my own room with everything I could want, even a TV, he says. Imagine, my own TV."

Charlie would have liked to see the de Greys' photo. He might have been able to learn a little more about them if he'd heard their voices. "Did Manfred give you the photo?" he asked.

Billy shook his head.

"Well, it's great news, Billy."

Charlie was about to continue on when Billy suddenly asked, "Did you bring your wand to school with you?"

"Yes, I —" Charlie stopped. "Why do you want to know?"

"I just thought, you know, it would be good if you had it with you — to protect you, kind of thing. Do you keep it in your bedside dresser?"

"No." Charlie kept his precious wand under his mattress, but he wasn't going to tell Billy. He'd said enough already.

"No. It'd be too long for the dresser," said Billy. "Under the mattress, then?"

Charlie felt uncomfortable. Was Billy still spying for the Bloors? "I've got to run, Billy," he said quickly. "Got to get my lines to Manfred's office. See you later."

Charlie hurried on. All the activity in the school had shifted to the dormitories, and the great flag-stoned hall echoed with Charlie's solitary footsteps. For the second time that day, he opened the ancient door leading to the Music Tower. He stepped into the dark passageway and surveyed the rough stone walls. Halfway down, on his right, he saw a small recess. Charlie crept along in the gloom, until he came to a narrow set of shelves crammed with drab, serious-looking books.

"Hmmm. Are you a door, then?" Charlie pushed one side of the bookcase, then the other. Nothing moved. Perhaps it wasn't a door at all. One by one, Charlie began to remove the books, searching for a knob or a handle to open the supposed door. But there was nothing.

"What are you doing?"

Charlie almost jumped out of his skin. A figure in a purple cape came gliding toward him. "Why are you here?" asked Tantalus Ebony.

"I was looking for Manfred's office," stammered Charlie.

"I see." Mr. Ebony gave Charlie a look of such overwhelming hatred, Charlie had to step back, dizzy with shock. A suffocating brew of smells filled his nostrils: stale air, candle wax, rotting things, mildew, and soot.

"You do well to be afraid, Bone," said the teacher coldly. "You're a troublesome little devil, aren't you?"

Before Charlie could reply, the man's features seemed to dissolve, and an array of completely different expressions crossed his pale face. For a fraction of a second, Charlie felt that from behind the changing masks, someone gazed out at him with infinite tenderness. He was sure that he had imagined this, however, when the look of haughty indifference returned to the teacher's face.

"You wanted the office." Mr. Ebony pressed a knot

in the wood at the top of the bookcase. Immediately, it swung aside, revealing the dim interior of a small office.

"Thank you." Nervously, Charlie stepped inside.

"I'll leave you to it, then. Toodle-oo." The extraordinary teacher's voice changed completely. He waved his long fingers and rushed away, humming a slightly familiar tune.

Charlie looked around the room. It was very tidy. A photograph of a younger-looking Dr. Bloor with a small boy and a dark-haired woman hung above the mantelpiece. Manfred and his parents. Beneath the window, there was a desk and an adjustable leather chair that faced the courtyard beyond. Charlie stepped up to the desk and put his lines on a stack of papers. He was about to turn away when something caught his eye. A small print of a horse lay beside the papers. Charlie picked it up. There were other pictures beneath, prints of horses' skeletons.

At this point, Charlie should have left the room, but he had noticed a packet of photographs at the end of the desk. Charlie was not the sort of boy to hold back when he saw something interesting. And he was always interested in photographs. As he carefully lifted the packet, he failed to hear the soft *swish* behind him.

The photos were disappointing. There were only two people in them: a man and a woman. They were both middle-aged and rather ordinary. The man had thinning hair and wore glasses; the woman's face was round, her hair short and straight, and her teeth very long. In all the photographs, she was smiling. No, not smiling, Charlie decided. It seemed rather that she was holding something invisible between her teeth.

In most of the photographs, the couple sat side by side on a sofa, but there were two taken in a garden and two more in a kitchen. Charlie was scrutinizing the empty-looking kitchen when he suddenly heard the woman speak.

Smile, Usher. We want to put the boy at ease.

I don't like children. The man's tone was light, his voice slightly nasal. *Never have.*

It won't be for long.

How long?

*Until he does what they want. You'll have to use your talent —
you know — to stop him from getting out.*

Talent? said the man in a whiny voice. *What use . . .*

Charlie heard footsteps. He quickly put the photos
back into the packet and placed it back down at the
end of the desk. But when he went to the door, he
found that it was stuck. There was no handle, no key-
hole, no latch. He was caught.

Charlie banged on the door. "Hi! Anyone there? It's
me, Charlie Bone."

There was no answer.

Charlie banged again. "Hi, Mr. Ebony, sir. Are you
there? Manfred?"

Charlie continued to knock and call for several
minutes, and then he gave up.

It began to get dark. Charlie sat in the chair and
thought about the photographs. All at once, it came to
him. They were Billy Raven's new parents. Billy had

always longed to have nice, kind parents and a real home. How could Charlie tell him the truth?

As he sat in the gloom, wrestling with his dilemma, the lights across the courtyard went out one by one until Charlie was left in complete darkness. He made his way around the room, fumbling for a light switch. There didn't seem to be one. He pushed at the door. He knocked and called but no one came. The cathedral clock struck nine. Charlie sat on the floor and dozed.

A sound from the courtyard woke him up. *Clop! Clop! Clop!* Charlie shook his sleepy head. Hooves. There was a horse in the courtyard. Charlie stood up. He could just make out the window's pale rectangle of light, but it was impossible to see anything in the yard beyond.

The cathedral clock struck ten and the hoofbeats faded. Charlie was about to shout again when the door swung open and a fierce light beamed in his face.

"What the heck are you doing here?"

Charlie recognized Dr. Bloor's deep voice. "I came to give Manfred some lines, sir, and then the door closed."

"How did you get in?"

"Mr. Ebony let me in, sir."

"Did he, now?"

"Yes, sir." Charlie wished Dr. Bloor would shine the flashlight away from his eyes.

"Well, it's detention for you, Charlie Bone. You'll stay in school an extra night. Now get back to your dormitory."

Dr. Bloor hauled Charlie out of the room and gave him a push down the passageway. Charlie had almost reached his dormitory when the matron loomed around a corner and grabbed his shoulder.

"Ouch!" cried Charlie. "If you were going to give me detention, don't bother. I've already got it."

Charlie could hear Lucretia Yewbeam grinding her teeth. "Be quiet, until you're spoken to. Where have you been?"

"Stuck in Manfred's office," said Charlie with a sigh. "He asked me to give him my lines."

"Lines? On the first day of the semester? You're hopeless. I can't believe we're related."

"Nor I," Charlie mumbled.

"What did you say?"

"I said, forgive me for being related to you."

"Get to bed," growled Charlie's great-aunt Lucretia.

The next morning, on their way down to breakfast, Charlie told Fidelio everything that had happened the night before. His friend listened attentively until Charlie began to talk about the photographs.

"So you've been listening again," Fidelio said wryly.

"I couldn't help myself," Charlie admitted. "They were a nasty pair, Fido. But how can I tell Billy?"

"Let's just hope you're wrong, and those people weren't the de Greys."

The two boys walked into the cafeteria and took their places at the music table.

"Interesting about the horses," Fidelio said as he buttered a piece of toast.

Billy Raven looked up from his cornflakes. "Did you say horses?"

"Tell you later, Billy," said Charlie. "By the way, I've got detention this weekend, so I'll be keeping you company."

"My new parents are coming to fetch me on Saturday," said Billy.

"So soon?"

"I'll have my own home!" Billy bounced up and down in his seat. "Yippee!"

Charlie grinned. He didn't want to dash Billy's hopes, but he was sure that real adoptions didn't happen this way. How did the Bloors get away with it? They kept children hidden from their relatives, they moved orphans around without their having any say in the matter, they even made fathers disappear.

"Charlie!" Fidelio nudged him. "If you don't want your breakfast, I'll eat it."

Charlie spooned cornflakes into his mouth as

quickly as he could. "I suppose you don't feel like getting detention with me?" he asked.

Fidelio looked embarrassed. "Sorry. Can't. I've promised to play in my brother's band on Saturday morning."

"At least I might get a look at Billy Raven's parents. That should be interesting," said Charlie.

During the first break, Charlie saw Emma and Olivia running around the field.

"Hey, you two!" cried Charlie, as he panted beside the girls. "Are you, er . . . occupied on Saturday?"

"Bookstore!" said Emma. "It's Auntie Julia's busy day."

"Have you got detention again, Charlie?" asked Olivia, slowing her pace.

"Yep. So, are you busy?"

Olivia stopped running and Emma drew up beside her.

"Well?" asked Charlie, taking a deep breath.

"Actually," said Olivia solemnly, "Saturday is probably going to be the most important day in my whole life."

"Definitely," agreed Emma.

"I'm auditioning for a movie. It's a really big movie. There are at least three huge stars in it, and I'm going to be Tom Winston's daughter, or at least I think I will be."

"Tom Winston?" Charlie asked.

"Don't tell me you've never heard of Tom Winston," said Olivia, frowning. "He's a HUGE star!"

"Oh. OK. Well, good luck," said Charlie. "Hey, you might be famous, Livvy!"

"Bound to be," said loyal Emma.

"Might be," said Olivia with a confident smile.

"So, will you talk to us when you're famous?" asked Charlie.

"What do you think?" Olivia's smile grew wider.

The hunting horn blared and Charlie never got to answer Olivia, because the two girls tore off and reached the garden door long before him. Charlie decided they must have been in training during vacation.

"Guess what," Charlie said, leaping into the coat-room. "Olivia Vertigo's going to be a movie star."

Fidelio was sitting on a bench, changing his shoes. "How come?" he asked, dropping one of his sneakers.

Several other children stared at Charlie, and Gwyneth Howells, the harpist, said, "Olivia Vertigo thinks she's so brilliant."

"But she is," Rosie Stubbs said generously. "I mean, I bet she will be famous."

Gwyneth gave her best friend a withering look, and Rosie said, "Oh, come on, Gwyn, you must admit she's a fantastic actress."

"She's going to an audition on Saturday," Charlie told them. "It's for a part in a gigantic movie. She'll be Tom Winston's daughter."

"If she gets the part," said Gwyneth with a sniff.

"She will," said Fidelio. "No question."

Soon the whole school was buzzing with talk of Olivia Vertigo's imminent fame. And Olivia began to wish that she'd kept her audition a secret.

Somehow, Charlie managed to keep out of trouble for the rest of the week, and when Friday arrived, he found that he wasn't dreading his extra night in school as much as he expected. He went down to the main hall to wish Olivia good luck before she left, but she didn't thank him.

"I wish you hadn't told so many people," she grumbled. "It's bad luck." And she strode away without a backward glance.

"She's nervous," Emma explained. "Sorry about your detention, Charlie. We'll meet on Sunday, shall we?"

"Pets' Café at two o'clock," said Charlie.

"You're on." Emma dashed after Olivia, her long blond pigtails bouncing against her cape.

A familiar smell assailed Charlie when he walked into the dormitory, and he wasn't surprised to see Cook's dog, Blessed, sitting at the foot of Billy's bed. Today the old dog looked even more depressed than usual. Charlie assumed this was due to his old age and bad health (Blessed was extremely fat), but Billy quickly set him straight.

"He's upset," said Billy, who was trying to pack a

battered-looking suitcase. "Partly because I'm being adopted, but mostly because he saw a terrible thing happen."

"Oh?" Charlie sank onto the bed next to Billy's. "What did he see?"

Billy glanced at Blessed, who gave a small grunting sort of whine.

"It's difficult to explain. I keep thinking I've got it wrong and he means something different, but then he says, 'True! True! Horse fly through wall.'"

"What?" Charlie raised his eyebrows.

Billy stopped packing and sat on his bed. "He says he was at the top of the house in a long, long room. Manfred was there, and old Mr. Ezekiel, and your three great-aunts, Charlie. He says there were things on a table: fur and metal things and — very, very old bones."

Charlie's scalp tingled. "What sort of bones?"

"Horse bones."

Blessed gave a sudden, throaty growl.

"He said that the bones turned into a horse." Billy

spoke very slowly, as though he were waiting for Charlie to stop him. But Charlie just listened, open-mouthed.

"Two of your great-aunts did things to the stuff on the table," Billy went on, "and Mr. Ezekiel had a can that made sparks. There was a bang and a lot of smoke, and a horse jumped off the table and crashed through the wall."

"What the heck are they up to? I didn't know my aunts could do stuff like that."

"There were three of them, remember. Manfred and Mr. Ezekiel as well. Maybe that made their power stronger." Billy frowned and shook his head. "It must have been the horse that I saw in the sky."

Charlie realized that this strange spell explained a great deal: the pictures on Manfred's desk, for instance; the ghostly presence in the garden; and the hoofbeats Charlie had heard in the courtyard. "But what's the purpose of it all?" he muttered.

Billy shrugged. "Maybe we'll never know."

"Oh, I think we will. In fact, you can bet your life on it."

"If I could see the horse, I could talk to it," said Billy.

"Maybe you could talk to it anyway," Charlie suggested.

Billy stared at Charlie through the thick round lenses of his glasses. "Yes," he said thoughtfully. He jumped down from the bed and resumed his packing. The small pile of clothes laid out on the bed only half-filled the large suitcase.

"I haven't got any more. That's it." Billy closed the suitcase and heaved it onto the floor.

"Nothing else?" Charlie was concerned. Where were Billy's toys, books, games, sneakers, and weekend clothes? At home, the closet in Charlie's room was packed with stuff. Was this all that Billy owned in the world?

"There is something else." Billy pulled a plastic bag from his bedside dresser and emptied it on the bed.

Along with the five small books that Cook had given him, there was a deck of cards, a small one-eared bear, and something wrapped in yellowing tissue paper.

"The Bloors usually give me food for presents," said Billy, carefully unfolding the tissue paper, "so most of my possessions have been eaten." He gave a sheepish grin. "But I kept these." He peeled back the last piece of tissue, revealing four white candles. "I found them in my aunt's cupboard before I was sent to Bloor's. Her dog told me they came with a birthday cake, but she never put them on the cake, and I never knew who sent it to me."

Charlie stared at the four small candles in Billy's hand. Each one looked as though it had been made from a coiled feather. The delicate wax filaments curved around the candles in spirals that made them appear mysterious and magical.

"I never lit them," Billy said softly.

"I can see that." Charlie screwed up his eyes and bent closer to the candles. "I wonder who sent them."

"I wish I knew." Billy carefully folded the candles into the tissue paper and slipped them in his pocket.

It was just as well that he did, because the next minute, Lucretia Yewbeam marched into the dormitory and began to examine Billy's packing.

"This is a mess," she said, throwing everything out onto the floor. "Fold your clothes properly, Billy Raven. Your new parents won't accept slipshod packing."

"Who are Billy's new parents?" asked Charlie.

"None of your business," snapped his great-aunt.

"But it is Billy's business," argued Charlie. "He only knows their names, not where they're from or if they've got a family or if they live . . ."

"You don't need to know these things," said the matron. "Billy will know soon enough. Now brush your hair before dinner, boy. You look as though you've just crawled out of bed."

Charlie gave a grunt of disgust. Trust Lucretia Yewbeam to mention his hair. She'd probably guessed that he'd forgotten to pack his hairbrush.

When the matron had gone, Charlie helped Billy repack his suitcase. Not that it looked any neater the second time around.

"It'll have to do," said Billy cheerfully. "Just think, I've got a home to go to!"

Charlie wondered if the small boy was as happy as he sounded. That night Billy thrashed around in his sheets. Understandable — starting a new life with unknown parents was not exactly an everyday occurrence.

BILLY'S OATH

The de Greys arrived just before lunch on Saturday. Billy and Charlie had spent the morning doing their homework in the King's room. Luckily, Manfred wasn't there to watch them, so they hadn't worked too hard. Billy didn't mention the wand again, and Charlie felt that maybe Billy's questions had been innocent.

At twelve o'clock, Manfred stuck his head in the door and barked, "Billy, bring your suitcase down to the hall."

"Yes, Manfred." Billy's eyes were as big as saucers. He looked happy and scared all at the same time.

"I'll give him a hand," Charlie offered.

"No, you won't. This is Billy's business."

Charlie followed Billy upstairs when he went to fetch his suitcase.

"Good-bye," Billy said. His face was pink with excitement, but it was hard to know what he was thinking. "Maybe I'll see you on Sunday."

"Good idea. Get your parents to bring you to my house, and I'll take you to the Pets' Café," said Charlie.

"Oh." Billy put down his suitcase. "What's going to happen to my rat, Rembrandt? Do you think they'll let me bring him?"

"Maybe not. But don't worry. I'll get Cook to fix things for you. She'll take him to the café."

Billy smiled. "See you on Sunday, then."

A few minutes after Billy had left the room, Charlie heard voices in the courtyard. He looked out and saw a man and woman talking to Dr. Bloor. There was no doubt that they were the people in Manfred's photos. The headmaster led them through the main doors, but just before they disappeared from view, the man looked up at Charlie's window. Charlie stepped behind the curtain. He had learned that the endowed could very often sense each other, and from Mr. de Grey's unsmiling features, Charlie could tell that the man had a powerful endowment, a talent that meant trouble for Billy Raven. "But what is it?" Charlie asked himself.

At one o'clock, he wandered down to the cafeteria. There was no one there, not even Manfred. Charlie stood behind the empty counter. There wasn't a plate or a knife and fork to be seen.

Cook's small, round figure came bustling through the kitchen door. "Charlie, Charlie, Charlie!" she exclaimed. "I didn't know you were here. Do you want some lunch?"

"Yes, please," Charlie said fervently. "I'm starving."

Cook beckoned him into the kitchen. "If it's only you, Charlie, we'll eat together — at my place."

Charlie followed Cook through the swing door at the side of the counter, and in five minutes, he was drinking a bowl of delicious parsnip soup. "I made a gallon of it for the Bloors," said Cook. "I'm afraid there's no roast beef left, but there's chocolate meringue pie."

Cook's homemade rolls were warm and crisp, and Charlie was told to use as much butter as he wanted. After two bowls of soup, four buttered rolls, and a large slice of Cook's special pie, he felt he had eaten enough to keep him going until Sunday.

"This is Billy's favorite soup," Cook said wistfully. "We always had our lunch together on weekends." She pulled out a large white handkerchief and vigorously blew her nose.

"Cook, aren't you a bit worried about Billy being adopted so suddenly?" asked Charlie.

"You better believe I am. I don't like the look of those de Greys." She shook her head. "They're not the parenting type, Charlie. You can tell."

"Do you think they'll let Billy keep Rembrandt?"

"I doubt it. But I'll take the little fellow to the Pets' Café. The Onimouses will keep him safe, and Billy can visit him on weekends."

Cook was one of the few adults in the school whom Charlie knew for certain had inherited some of the mysterious powers of the Red King. As yet, the Bloors had no idea who she really was, and she was determined to keep it that way. She had chosen to spend her life watching out for the endowed children at Bloor's Academy, but she couldn't always protect them, and this upset her considerably.

All at once, Cook leaned closer to Charlie and confided, "I got a letter from someone close to Billy."

"Who?" asked Charlie earnestly.

Cook looked over her shoulder. "I can't tell you his name yet, Charlie. He's a distant relative of Billy's, and when the poor boy's parents died, this — person — tried to adopt him. But he and the Bloors, well, to put it mildly, they just don't get along. It's the same with your family. The Yewbeams almost succeeded in murdering the poor man, so he had to retreat, as it were."

Charlie's jaw dropped. "Murder? You're saying my family . . . ?"

"Are you so surprised, Charlie?"

"No," he confessed, thinking of his great-aunts. "I suppose I'm not. But why did the Bloors get Billy?"

"His aunt just signed him over — simple as that." Cook let out a scornful sigh. "A weak woman. They probably paid her off."

"But why did they want him so badly?"

"His endowment, Charlie. Although it wasn't revealed until he was six, they suspected it. The Ravens are a very gifted family. Billy's relative tells me that he is the rightful owner of the Castle of Mirrors."

"Castle of Mirrors?" Charlie asked eagerly. "Wow. Tell me more."

"Charlie, you've got that look in your eyes. Don't go poking into places that don't concern you."

"I just want to know where it is," said Charlie innocently.

"To tell the truth, I don't really know," Cook admitted. "Perhaps your uncle Paton can tell you. He's a very knowledgeable gentleman, by all accounts."

Charlie would have liked to hear more, but they were rudely interrupted by the janitor, Mr. Weedon. Sticking his shaved head in the kitchen door, he bellowed, "That's where you are, Bone. Five minutes is all you've got to get ready."

Charlie leaped up. "How come? I'm supposed to stay here till snack time."

"How come? How come?" Weedon repeated in a mocking tone. "Because it happens to be convenient for your auntie to pick you up — that's why. Perhaps you hadn't noticed that school buses don't run on weekends, and it appears that no one else in your family can drive, at least not in daylight."

"Oh." Charlie felt embarrassed on his uncle's behalf. "Good-bye, then, Cook. Thanks for lunch."

"Good-bye, Charlie. Be good." Cook winked at him.

Charlie followed Weedon past the kitchen counters, empty sinks, shelves of dishes, and rows of gleaming saucepans.

"Hurry up," said Weedon. "She won't wait forever."

"But my bag," said Charlie, hurrying after Weedon's burly figure. "I've got to pack my pajamas and stuff."

"Matron's done that," said Weedon.

They had arrived in the hall, where Charlie found his great-aunt Eustacia pacing before the main doors.

"Come on! Come on!" said Eustacia. "We've been looking for you everywhere."

A nasty, sick feeling churned in Charlie's stomach. Eustacia drove like a maniac. She was the only driver who could make him feel carsick. "I've got to get my stuff," said Charlie, thinking of the wand hidden under his mattress.

"It's here!" Eustacia kicked at the bag lying at her feet. "Aunt Lucretia kindly packed it for you."

"But . . . but . . . I've got work to put in it," Charlie said desperately.

"Hurry up, then." His great-aunt gave a huge, disgruntled sigh.

Charlie seized his bag and rushed up to the dormitory. Lifting the edge of the mattress, he felt beneath it. The wand wasn't there. With increasing desperation, he lifted both ends and both sides of the mattress. Eventually, he pushed it right off the bed. The wand was gone.

Charlie hauled the mattress back into place and tidied the covers. The lurching feeling in his stomach grew worse.

"What on earth have you been doing?" Eustacia demanded when Charlie finally dragged his bag down to the hall again.

"I couldn't find it," Charlie said miserably. "My work, that is."

"Tsk! I can't wait any longer." His great-aunt consulted her watch. "I told Venetia I'd be back by two. Come along and be quick about it."

Weedon, who had been lurking by the main door, said, "Are we ready, then? One, two, three."

Great-aunt Eustacia tut-tutted impatiently as Weedon lifted a bunch of keys that hung by a chain from his belt. He selected a huge iron key, fitted it into the lock, then drew back two long bolts. The doors swung open.

"Madame," said Weedon, bowing his head.

"Enough of that," snapped Eustacia.

As Charlie followed her out, he noticed Billy Raven's suitcase standing in a corner of the hall. So he was still in the academy. Could it be that he was being whisked away before he could take a closer look at the de Greys?

Eustacia's black car was badly parked beside the swan fountain. As soon as Charlie had climbed into the backseat, she was off, cutting corners, bumping over curbs, rattling the wrong way down one-way streets, honking at people on pedestrian crossings, dangerously overtaking cyclists, exceeding the speed limit, and narrowly missing parked cars (no, make that, hitting three sideview mirrors).

To Charlie's dismay, Eustacia drove to Darkly Wynd, a grim alley where his three great-aunts lived in adjoining houses, all numbered thirteen. The third house was covered in scaffolding, but behind the pattern of planks and steel, a blackened, roofless building could be glimpsed — all that remained of Great-aunt Venetia's home.

"Take a good look, Charlie," said Eustacia, screeching to a halt outside the middle house. "You're responsible for that ruin."

"Not exactly," Charlie objected.

"Not in the strictest sense," his great-aunt conceded, "but you were with my fiendish brother when he did this, egging him on, no doubt."

"What did you expect him to do?" said Charlie defiantly. "Aunt Venetia tried to kill Miss Ingledew."

Eustacia opened her door and swung her legs onto the pavement. "Get out," she snarled, slamming the door.

Charlie was only too happy to oblige. He shuffled out of the car, dragging his bag behind him.

"Now get going," said Eustacia, pointing down the alley. "You've got legs. You can walk home."

Charlie turned and made a run for the alley. He didn't bother to thank his great-aunt for bringing him halfway home. But when he heard her front door slam shut, he stopped and looked back at the ruined house. He remembered the piano that had been revealed at the very top, when the wall of the burning building fell away, and he recalled the instrument's terrible fall, the eerie tune it had played when it crashed onto the basement steps and broke into a thousand pieces.

Who had played that piano, hidden in the attic of Aunt Venetia's house? Was it Lyell Bone, his father, imprisoned, hypnotized? And if it were, where was he now?

"Come back, Dad!" Charlie's whisper echoed in the empty alley. "Please try."

While Charlie made his way home, Billy Raven was eating his first meal with Usher and Florence de Grey at the academy. They would rather Billy use their first names, Florence told him, as they felt it was too late for them to be called Mom and Dad. They would never get used to it. Billy had been looking forward to saying "Mom" to someone, but he decided to make the best of it.

The Bloors' dining room was two doors down from Dr. Bloor's office in the west wing. It was a narrow room with a long window overlooking the garden. The walls were covered in red-and-gold-striped paper, and the ceiling was so high that Billy could barely make out the strange shapes surrounding the light fixture. He thought they might be gargoyles.

A chandelier hung above the oval mahogany table, and although it was a warm day, a fire burned behind the grate of a dark marble fireplace. Even in summer,

Mr. Ezekiel wrapped himself in a woolen blanket. He was old and cold right through to his soul.

Today, the old man sat at the head of the table, with his back to the window. He chewed with his mouth open, and sometimes bits of food fell into his lap. At the other end of the table, Dr. Bloor kept up a loud nonstop conversation with the de Greys, in an effort to divert attention from his grandfather's unpleasant eating habits.

Billy was squeezed between the matron and Manfred, facing his parents-to-be. The steaming food on his plate had fogged up his glasses, and when he attempted to wipe them with his napkin, the matron hissed, "Handkerchief!"

Billy didn't have a handkerchief. He blinked at the oversize dishes piled with meat and vegetables. The Bloors were obviously trying to impress their visitors. Billy grew bored with the dreary conversation. He cast furtive looks across the table at his new "mother," and she returned his gaze with quick, toothy smiles that never succeeded in crinkling her eyes.

Smiling was too much of a struggle for Mr. de Grey. He could manage only a lopsided smirk. Billy wondered if he were a disappointment to his new "father." Perhaps this morose-looking man had hoped for a boy with shiny brown hair and a healthy complexion, a boy with ordinary eyes who didn't need to wear glasses.

If it were true that the de Greys had always wanted to adopt a child, as they said, then why had they only just now got around to it? And why hadn't it occurred to the Bloors before that Billy would be a suitable candidate?

"Eat up, Billy," said Lucretia Yewbeam. "We want our dessert."

Billy stuffed another piece of potato into his mouth and tried to swallow it. There seemed to be a wall inside his stomach that wouldn't let the food go down. He gave up and laid his knife and fork neatly across his plate.

The matron gave a sigh and removed his plate.

"He's excited," she told the de Greys. "Give him an egg tonight. He loves eggs."

Billy wondered what could have made the matron say such a thing. How did she know what he liked? They had never even sat at the same table.

Lucretia continued clearing the plates, and there was a murmur of pleasure as Mr. Weedon appeared with a large chocolate meringue pie. Billy loved chocolate, but he couldn't eat the pie. Not a bite. He gazed at the large portion the matron had plunked in front of him. He wished he could give it to Rembrandt, but he didn't dare mention the rat. He wasn't supposed to have one. The Bloors would have killed it.

The matron removed Billy's untouched pie with a look of irritation. And then the table was completely cleared. People got up and sat down while Billy stayed where he was, the wall in his stomach getting heavier by the minute.

Mrs. de Grey put a gray bag on the table. She drew out three sheets of paper and laid them before Billy.

"Now for your oath, Billy," said Dr. Bloor in a solemn tone.

"Oath?" said Billy weakly.

"Indeed," boomed Dr. Bloor. "Adoptions don't just happen. They have to be arranged. Promises must be made."

Ezekiel leaned forward, his elbows resting on the table, his fists bunched into his cheeks. "Mrs. de Grey is an oath-keeper, Billy. Know what that is?"

Billy shook his head.

"She keeps the papers!" Ezekiel chortled unpleasantly. "Before you go to this nice new home of yours, you must sign an oath to do certain things that are spelled out on those forms in front of you. Understand?"

"Yes, sir."

"Check the boxes marked 'Yes' and sign your name at the bottom," said Mrs. de Grey in a businesslike tone. With a long fingernail, she touched a dotted line at the bottom of one of the forms, and then she remembered to smile.

"Do I have to?" Billy asked boldly.

"If you want to be adopted," said Manfred, his dark eyes fixed on Billy's face.

Mrs. de Grey handed Billy a pen and he began to read the first form.

NO   YES

❏   ❏ 1. I PROMISE ALWAYS TO TELL THE TRUTH.

❏   ❏ 2. I PROMISE TO BE SILENT AFTER SEVEN O'CLOCK
(MY PARENTS NEED TEN HOURS' SLEEP).

❏   ❏ 3. I PROMISE TO WEAR THE CLOTHES CHOSEN FOR
ME (AND VERY NICE THEY ARE, TOO).

❏   ❏ 4. I PROMISE NEVER TO ASK FOR FOOD (BECAUSE I
WILL BE GIVEN PLENTY).

❏   ❏ 5. I PROMISE NEVER TO DISCUSS WITH OTHER
CHILDREN WHAT OCCURS IN THE PASSING HOUSE.

❏   ❏ 6. I PROMISE TO ANSWER TRUTHFULLY ANY
QUESTIONS CONCERNING THE CHILDREN OF THE
RED KING, ESPECIALLY CHARLIE BONE.

Billy looked up. "Why?" he asked. "Why do I have to answer questions about Charlie, specifically?"

"It's a condition, Billy," said Dr. Bloor. "Check the box."

Billy checked it.

NO   YES

❑   ❑ 7. I PROMISE TO BATHE ON FRIDAY, SATURDAY,
           AND SUNDAY.

"You don't have to read the whole list," said Mrs. de Grey. "Just check off the boxes . . . dear."

The paper had an odd feel to it. The edges were hard and almost hot to the touch.

Billy completed his task and pushed the papers away from him. Florence de Grey quickly put them into her bag, which Billy saw was already stuffed with forms just like his. She patted the bag with satisfaction. "Safe and sound," she said, and then leaning forward, she told Billy, "I keep the oaths, / And thus they are kept. / No breaking of oaths, / Of which I am the keeper."

And this time the smile did crinkle her eyes.

"You'd better watch out, Billy," said Ezekiel with a snicker. "People have tried to break the oaths kept in that bag, and oh my, how they suffered for it."

"Really?" Billy said nervously.

Events moved swiftly after that. Everyone stood up except Ezekiel, who insisted on shaking Billy's hand and congratulating him. "Off you go, my boy," he said, giving Billy a push.

Dr. Bloor led the way down to the hall, where he patted Billy on the back and told him he was extremely fortunate to have found such good parents. Weedon opened the main doors, and Manfred lifted the large suitcase and gave it to Billy, who followed his new parents across the square to a small gray car.

Billy climbed into the back of the car with his suitcase, and as soon as Florence was in the passenger seat, Mr. de Grey drove off. Usher was a careful driver and Billy's journey across the city was a lot more comfortable than Charlie's had been.

They parked at the bottom of a dark cobblestoned alley, and Billy was told to get out. A thick mist had fallen, and he almost lost sight of the de Greys as they walked briskly up the steep alley. Billy hurried after them. He passed a rusty sign that said CROOK'S PASSAGE. Farther on, a large notice tacked to a doorway said VAGRANTS ARE ADVISED NOT TO LINGER.

Crook's Passage became steeper and steeper. Occasionally, Billy tripped over a shallow step, and the large suitcase bumped on the cobblestones. It seemed much heavier now, and Billy began to drag it behind him — *thump, thump, thump!* The de Greys appeared not to notice.

The wall inside Billy's stomach had moved up to his chest. He had imagined his new home to be a sunny house with a wide lawn, not somewhere dark and secret like this. A wooden sign creaked above his head and he stepped back to read it. The words "PASSING HOUSE TEN METERS" had been painted in black on a red background. Those ten meters were the steepest of all. Billy's breathing turned into a quiet groan as he heaved his suitcase up to a door, where his new parents stood watching him.

"Here we are, Billy," said Florence.

Above the door the words "THE PASSING HOUSE" had been carved in the stone. Usher fitted an enormous iron key into an equally enormous lock. There was a loud clunk and the door swung inward. Billy climbed two steps and walked into the house.

The hall was surprisingly large for a house that began in a dark alley. It was tiled in black-and-white marble, and its gray walls were decorated with plaster figures. A huge gilt-framed mirror hung above an empty glass cabinet, but when Billy looked into the mirror, he saw only a blob of white. His hair? The rest of him was swallowed up in a gray fog. Had the mist followed them in or was it always here?

"Come on, Billy!" called Florence, beckoning from a stone staircase.

Billy pattered across the marble tiles. His suitcase slithered and squeaked behind him. He walked between two tall marble columns and began to climb the staircase. One, two, three. He paused for breath, clinging to the iron railing. Usher de Grey had vanished through a door on the ground floor.

"Come on, come on!" Florence called from the landing. "You'll just love your room."

Billy puffed up the remaining steps and followed Florence down a long corridor. When they had reached the very end, she opened a door, saying, "Here we are!"

Billy stepped into his room: the very first room that had ever been truly his and no one else's. It was even better than he had expected. He put down his suitcase and gazed around him.

The bed was much larger than the narrow beds at Bloor's Academy. It had a blue checkered duvet and pillowcase and a pine headboard. There was a tall pine wardrobe and a matching chest of drawers, but Billy barely took in these details. He was staring at a TV on its black stand, and then at a computer, sitting on a pine desk. His?

"Mine?" asked Billy breathlessly.

"All yours," said Florence. She was still carrying the bag, and she tapped it briefly while she gave Billy one of her strange smiles. "As long as you keep your promises."

"My oaths?" said Billy.

"Exactly. Now, you make yourself at home, Billy. There's a sink in your room. See, behind that screen?" She pointed to a white screen in the corner. "So there's no excuse to come to meals with dirty hands. Understood?"

Billy nodded.

"Dinner is at six." She indicated a clock above the computer. "So, no excuses for being late, either." Florence turned on her heels and walked out, closing the door behind her.

Billy sat on his bed. It was too much to take in. He wanted to tell someone about it. Charlie. Maybe Charlie could come over. He would be so surprised.

It was only four o'clock. There would be plenty of time before dinner. Billy decided to ask Florence if he could have a friend over. He ran downstairs and looked into the rooms on the ground floor: a kitchen, a dining room, a very fancy living room, and an office. The de Greys were nowhere to be seen.

"Excuse me!" called Billy.

There was no reply.

Billy crept toward the front door. Maybe he should just go out and find Charlie. As he drew level with the hall mirror, something very odd happened. He found that he couldn't move any farther. An invisible barrier held him back. Again and again, Billy tried to slide his feet forward, but they met a solid wall of — nothing. It was impossible to reach the front door. He attempted to push his hands through the unseen barrier, but it was like pushing against a wall of iron.

Billy retreated and sat on a chair beside the empty cabinet. He couldn't believe what was happening. He wondered if he waited a few minutes, the ghostly barrier would melt away.

As he gazed around the hall, he noticed that there were no coats hanging on the hall stand; there were no hats on the pegs, no walking sticks, umbrellas, boots, or bags tucked into the space beneath the pegs. It was almost as if no one lived in the Passing House. And then Billy became aware of something black at the foot of the stand.

He got up and went to take a look. It was a very small cat with a gray muzzle and a thin tail. At last, something that Billy could talk to. He knelt beside the little creature and said, "Hello! I'm Billy. I've come to live here."

"Welcome, Billy," said the cat in a frail voice. "I am Clawdia. For myself, I am happy that you are here, but for you, I am very sorry."

ALICE ANGEL

When Charlie left Darkly Wynd, he didn't go straight home but instead turned onto a road that led to Ingledew's bookstore.

Ingledew's stood in a row of old, half-timber buildings that bordered the cathedral square. As Charlie walked over the ancient cobblestones toward the bookstore, he heard the sound of an organ being played deep inside the huge, domed building. His father had been the cathedral organist, until one day he had vanished from this very place. Maybe Charlie was standing exactly where his father had last been seen. Lyell Bone had tried to stop the Bloors from kidnapping Emma Tolly, and for this he had been horribly punished: hypnotized, trapped, hidden, and lost to his wife and child. They said that Lyell was dead, but Charlie knew better.

He gave a big shrug, told himself not to have

too many gloomy thoughts, and marched over to the bookstore.

Emma stood behind the counter, examining a pile of large leatherbound books. She looked up when the shop door tinkled and Charlie walked in.

"Hi, Charlie. You got out of detention early."

"They didn't want me around," said Charlie. "It's Billy's adoption day."

"Oh, of course. Did you see his new parents?"

"Yes, and I don't like the look of them. They don't really want Billy. I saw some photos on Manfred's desk and . . . well . . . I'm worried, Em. I'm sure it's not normal, the way those people just turned up and took Billy away."

"The Bloors do a lot of abnormal things," said Emma grimly. "But they get away with it because they're the oldest family in the city, and everyone's scared of them, even the mayor and the councillors."

"They think Manfred and Ezekiel can do anything, but they're wrong," Charlie muttered. "By the way, someone stole my wand."

"What?" Emma dropped a book. "Charlie, what are you going to do?"

"I don't know yet. I shouldn't have taken it to school, but I thought I might need it to kind of help me learn things."

"But still . . . " Emma shook her head. "Oh, Charlie, this is serious."

"You're telling me, but it's mine, Em. Truly mine. It's got nothing to do with the Yewbeams or the Bloors, and it won't work for them."

"But if they can't use the wand, they'll destroy it."

"That's what I'm afraid of."

Before Charlie could say any more, a very tall man with black hair and dark glasses walked through the curtained door behind the counter.

"Ah, Charlie, I thought I heard your voice." He suddenly looked at the light hanging over the counter, said, "Oh, darn," and began to back out.

Emma rushed to the light switch beside the curtain, but it was too late. There was a loud *pop*, and the lightbulb shattered, sending a shower of glass onto the antique books.

"Oh, Paton, really!" came an exasperated female voice from behind the curtain.

"Sorry, Julia! Sorry!" said Paton Yewbeam. "How was I to know the light was on? The sun's shining in there."

"I put it on to see the books better," Emma said plaintively. "Don't worry, I'll clean it up." She reached under the counter for the dustpan and brush, which had been kept handy ever since Paton's first visit to the bookstore.

Emma's aunt, Julia, now appeared behind the counter. "It could have been worse, I suppose."

Charlie was very surprised to see his uncle in the store so early in the day. As a rule, Paton never went out in daylight. He was embarrassed about his talent and afraid that he would be seen accidentally exploding traffic lights or the illuminations in store windows — even lights in private houses were at risk.

There must have been something very urgent to summon Uncle Paton to the bookstore. Unless, of course, it was Julia Ingledew. She was a very beautiful woman and Uncle Paton had fallen under her spell the moment he first saw her.

"Can I help?" offered Charlie, as he watched Emma and Miss Ingledew sweep up the tiny fragments of glass.

"Just go and talk to your uncle," said Miss Ingledew, "and keep him out of mischief." She gave a wry smile.

Charlie made his way past the curtain into Miss Ingledew's back room. Here, shelves crammed with books lined every wall. Books were piled on tables, on the floor, on chairs, and on Miss Ingledew's large mahogany desk. The whole room glowed with the warm colors of old bindings and gold tooling; it smelled of leather and very old paper. Candles had been lit on every spare surface because the small window let in very little light, and today Julia didn't want to put the table lamps at risk.

Uncle Paton sat on a small sofa surrounded by newspapers, folders, and yet more books. When Charlie appeared, his uncle removed his dark glasses and rubbed his eyes. "No darn use," he said in a troubled tone. "Although, I swear these glasses have prevented a few accidents." He put the glasses in the top pocket of his black corduroy jacket. "So, Charlie, your mother tells me you got detention again."

"Yes, and Aunt Eustacia had to pick me up," Charlie said reproachfully.

Paton shrugged. "Sorry, dear boy. But you know I can't drive in daylight."

"At least I'm still alive," said Charlie. "I'm surprised to find you here, Uncle P."

"Ah! I came before sunrise," said Uncle Paton, avoiding Charlie's eyes. "Julia phoned me last night. Someone put a letter through her door, addressed to me. All very intriguing. So I came by as soon as I decently could. As a matter of fact, the letter concerns a pal of yours, Charlie."

"Which one?" Charlie sat beside his uncle.

"Billy Raven. It's very odd." Uncle Paton pulled a crumpled envelope out of his pocket. It was addressed to Mr. Paton Yewbeam in frail, rather elegant handwriting. "I'd like to know what you make of it, Charlie."

Paton withdrew two sheets of paper. As he did so, a small candle fell out. Charlie caught it and held it up. "This is exactly like the candles Billy has. He doesn't know where they came from."

"Obviously from the man who wrote this letter. It proves their connection." Paton peered at the candle. "It's beautiful."

At that moment, Emma walked in. She was told to sit down and listen. Uncle Paton cleared his throat and began to read the mysterious letter.

"Dear Mr. Yewbeam,

Forgive me for insinuating myself into your life in this unconventional manner, but truthfully, I had no choice. Should a certain person in your household chance upon the contents of this letter, it would be nothing short of a disaster."

"He means Grandma Bone," said Charlie.

Paton nodded grimly and continued.

"*Your name, Mr. Yewbeam, was given to me by one of the few people in this city whom I know I can trust. And the lady whose mailbox I had to make use of is also a friend to the children, so I am told. You know the children of whom I speak? Yes, the endowed descendants of the Red King, those vulnerable children who are trying to use their talents in a manner that honors the name of their ancestor, his most esteemed majesty, the magician-king himself. There are others, I know, who defile his name and abuse their inherited talents. Alas, the child who is my greatest concern is neither on one side nor the other. I am Billy Raven's guardian. When the boy's father, Rufus Raven, and his pretty wife (they were both Ravens, you know, second cousins) realized that there was no escape from the Bloors and your malevolent (forgive the adjective) sisters, they begged me to become Billy's guardian, to watch over him, to protect and guide him; in short, to save him from becoming like the Bloors. But when Billy was orphaned, he was sent to an aunt who had little interest in nurturing the essentially good heart that he was born with. Instead, she chose to ignore the boy until he revealed his endowment, and then it was off to Bloor's for poor Billy.*

"Mr. Yewbeam, you must be wondering why I have so seriously neglected my duty. Where has this would-be guardian been for six years? you must be asking yourself.

"In prison, Mr. Yewbeam."

At this point, there was a gasp from Miss Ingledew, who had just entered the room. "Prison?" she said. "Paton, you didn't tell me he'd been in prison!"

"A detail I previously omitted for your peace of mind, Julia," said Paton.

Miss Ingledew perched on the arm of the sofa. "Your uncle has only read half of this letter to me," she told Charlie. "I'd better hear the rest."

Paton gave her a tender smile. "We shall benefit from your opinion, Julia."

"Oh, please, go on," begged Charlie.

"Where was I?" Paton ran his finger down the page in a maddeningly casual way.

"Prison!" cried Charlie. "He said he'd been in prison."

"Ah, yes. Here we are." Paton jabbed the paper with his finger and continued.

> "In prison, Mr. Yewbeam.
>
> "Let me assure you — I was not guilty. I was tricked by that wretch Weedon, on his master's orders, of course. The dreadful brute tried to murder me (a blow to the head in the dark while I was putting the cat outside). But having failed, he framed me as an armed robber. Me, of all people! I am a printer. I deal in fine paper, precious inks, a pure line. I deal in words, engravings, letterheads, pamphlets, et cetera. Nevertheless, I was caught at the scene of a vicious robbery and eventually sent to prison. Last week, I was released early — for good behavior.

"My first thought was of Billy, and so I contacted a loyal friend at Bloor's Academy. To my horror, I discovered that Billy was to be adopted by Florence and Usher de Grey. I cannot stress how disastrous this would be for Billy.

"Mr. Yewbeam, will you help me? Could you arrange for me to meet Billy, clandestinely? I know that your great-nephew, Charlie, has been a good friend to the boy, and perhaps he could be involved in the enterprise. Ultimately, we must get Billy away from the de Greys, but such a venture will have to be planned with the utmost care, the utmost secrecy.

"I will contact you again soon, Mr. Yewbeam. In the meantime, I look forward to our future collaboration.

"Yours, in hope,

C. Crowquill"

"Well!" exclaimed Miss Ingledew. "How extraordinary."

"It must have been Cook," said Charlie thought-fully. "Cook is Mr. Crowquill's friend at the academy, I bet. She told me she'd heard from one of Billy's relatives. And she said something about a Castle of Mirrors. Do you know where it is, Uncle P.? Billy's ancestor came from there, and it might be kind of important to him."

"Never heard of it," said Uncle Paton. "Charlie, have you seen these de Grey people?"

"Yes, I've seen them," said Charlie, "and I've, er, you know — heard their voices. Mr. de Grey said he didn't like children. So, obviously, he didn't want to adopt Billy."

"Is he with the de Greys now?" asked Miss Ingledew.

"They came to get him today," said Charlie. "But he's coming to my place on Sunday so we can go to the Pets' Café together. I'll tell him about Mr. Crowquill, shall I, Uncle P.?"

"No." Uncle Paton held up his hand. "Not yet,

Charlie. I shall have to give this meeting a great deal of thought. For now, it would be best if Billy didn't know about his guardian. If he inadvertently let the cat out of the bag, Mr. C. Crowquill would be in grave danger once again."

"OK. I won't tell him yet. The de Greys might not be very good parents, but at least Billy has got out of Bloor's Academy."

"Out of the frying pan and into the fire, if you ask me," said Emma gravely.

On Sunday morning, while Charlie waited for Billy to arrive, Grandma Bone came downstairs wearing her Sunday best: a hat made of black feathers, a voluminous charcoal-gray coat, and a stole in the form of two dead minks. The minks' tails hung down her back, while their heads met each other under her chin. The animals' reproachful glass eyes always gave Charlie the shivers, and he tried not to look at them when he met his grandmother in the hall.

"Grandma, do you . . . ?" Charlie began.

"Out of my way," she barked. "Eustacia's picking me up."

Sure enough, there was a horrible squeal of brakes as Aunt Eustacia's car hit the curb outside number nine Filbert Street.

"I just wanted to ask if you knew where my friend Billy Raven is living now?" Charlie persisted.

"Of course, I know," snapped Grandma Bone. "But I'm not telling you." She pushed Charlie out of the way, opened the front door, and slammed it shut behind her.

A few seconds later, Charlie heard the familiar screech of tires and a loud thump as Eustacia backed into a lamppost. There was a muffled shriek from Grandma Bone, and the car sped off.

Charlie slouched back into the kitchen muttering, "Old bat. She won't tell me where Billy lives."

"Don't worry, Charlie," said Maisie. "I expect your little friend is having a nice lunch with his new parents. He'll turn up later."

"I suppose," said Charlie.

Almost every Sunday afternoon, Charlie and his friends met at the Pets' Café. Today, Charlie waited for Billy until four o'clock, and then he left the house by himself. When he reached Frog Street, he could hear the noise from the café echoing down the narrow alley: barking, howling, yelping, twittering, and squawking.

The café stood beneath the rocks of a huge, ancient wall; in fact, the place was built right into the rock and looked as if it had been part of the wall for hundreds of years. The words "PETS' CAFÉ" had been painted above a large window, and to emphasize that this was strictly a café for animals accompanied by humans, pictures of tails, paws, whiskers, wings, and claws decorated each letter of the sign.

Charlie walked through a green door and came face-to-face with a large man wearing a T-shirt decorated with parrots.

"Ah, Charlie Bone," said Norton, the bouncer. "About time, too. Your friends have almost given up on you, and as for your dog, he's going berserk."

"Got held up," said Charlie. "And Runner's not my dog."

"He is while that friend of yours is in Hong Kong."

There was a joyful bark from behind the counter, and a large yellow dog rushed at Charlie, almost knocking him to the floor.

"Hi, Runner!" Charlie gave the dog a hug and looked for his friends. Emma and Gabriel sat at a corner table, sharing a plate of cookies. They were both drinking glasses of a bright pink liquid, and three of Gabriel's gerbils were lapping up the spillage.

"Cherry Blossom Cordial," Gabriel explained as Charlie led Runner Bean up to the table. "Gerbils love it!"

"I'll say," Charlie observed as he sat between his friends. "One's keeled right over."

"Oops, so it has." Gabriel scooped up the prostrate gerbil and put it in his pocket. "It'll recover," he said confidently. "It's Mrs. Onimous' new recipe. Powerful stuff. Want a sip?"

"No, thanks, but I'll have a cookie." Charlie took two cookies, one for himself and one for Runner Bean.

The big dog crunched it gratefully and then laid his chin in Charlie's lap, hoping for more.

"Where are the others?" Charlie asked, feeding Runner Bean another cookie.

"Tanc and Sander couldn't wait," said Emma. "You took ages, Charlie. I thought you were bringing Billy."

"He never showed. What about Olivia? Have you seen her? Did she get the part?"

Emma shrugged. "I phoned her house twice but no one answered. She promised to meet me here but — I don't know, something must have come up."

"Maybe by now she's a star and won't talk to the likes of us," said Gabriel.

"Not Livvy." Emma shook her head. "She's not like that. She'll show up."

But Olivia never appeared. Nor did Billy. Eventually, the three friends got tired of waiting. Emma and Gabriel went home and Charlie took Runner Bean for a walk. The boy and the dog were just approaching Frog Street after a good half-hour jog when Runner Bean gave a loud bark and tugged his leash.

On the other side of the road, Charlie saw Olivia darting into an alley. She threw Charlie a quick, furtive glance and then disappeared. Curious about her strange behavior, Charlie ran across the road. By the time he reached the alley, Olivia had disappeared, but Runner Bean tugged Charlie down the alley, across a cobblestoned square, and then into an area of small shops.

In the distance, a girl in a white T-shirt and black jeans looked back at Charlie and began to run again. But she was no match for the dog. Pulling his leash out of Charlie's hand, Runner Bean raced up the street and soon caught up with Olivia. Leaping up at her, he began to bark excitedly.

"Get off! Go away!" shouted the girl.

"Hold on, Liv," cried Charlie. "It's only Runner. What's the matter with you?"

Olivia slumped against the wall while Charlie ran

up and grabbed the dog's collar. "He wouldn't hurt you, Liv. He was just pleased to see you." Charlie stopped. "What is it? You look awful."

"Thanks very much!" Olivia grimaced.

"I don't mean 'awful,' I just mean . . . different," said Charlie quickly.

Olivia's face was streaked with tears, her eyelids were swollen, and her hair was a mess. She was wearing sneakers, and her T-shirt looked crumpled. Gone were the bright colors and wild clothes that she usually wore. Charlie had never seen his friend look so normal and yet so distressed. He felt he should ask about the audition; it would be worse to avoid such an important question.

"Did you get the part?"

Olivia's lips formed a tight line. She kicked the ground with the toe of her shoe and, through gritted teeth, replied, "No!"

"Oh, wow, I'm sorry." This seemed inadequate, but what else could Charlie say?

"Don't be," Olivia said furiously. "I don't want people to feel sorry for me."

"OK. But what happened? Do you want to talk about it?"

Olivia thought for a moment and then decided that she very much wanted to talk. She wanted to talk and talk until the whole shameful, humiliating experience was out in the open, being shared by at least one other human being — and a dog.

The day had begun well. Olivia had ended up on the list of finalists with five other girls. "They were all smaller than me," she said with a frown, "but Mom said that didn't mean anything. There was this girl sitting next to me; she had pigtails and freckles and a silly, high voice. She was thirteen, Charlie, but she was TINY." Olivia's frown deepened. "She kept saying that I was bound to get the part because my mom is famous."

"That's not a very nice thing to say," Charlie remarked.

"No, but I was too confident to realize that. I went into that room and did my monologue — acted my socks off. I was really good, I KNOW I was. And I was so sure I'd got the part. There were four of them sitting at the table, two men and two women. They didn't even take notes. And when I finished, the director, a friend of Dad's actually, smiled at me and said, 'Thank you, Olivia. That was very good, but not quite what we're looking for.'" A tear made its way down Olivia's cheek. "Pigtails got the part," she said grimly.

"No!" exclaimed Charlie. "I don't believe it."

"The worst of it is that I took it out on Mom. We had a terrible fight and I said it was all her fault. Now she's more upset than me. I said I was meeting you guys at the Pets' Café, but I couldn't face telling everyone. I thought I'd buy Mom some flowers to make up, and someone told me there was a flower store open, somewhere down here."

"It's right there!" Charlie nodded across the street. It was so distinctive, he wondered why he hadn't noticed it before. The door and window frame were deep green, and the words above the window were printed in curling gold letters: ANGEL FLOWERS.

"They're all white!" Olivia observed, her grim expression beginning to soften.

It was true. Every flower in the window was white: lilies, roses, daisies, and strange plants that Charlie had never set eyes on before.

"Let's see if the store's open." Charlie stepped off the pavement but Olivia hung back.

"Come on." Charlie grabbed her hand. Runner Bean was already dragging him across the street, and eventually the straggling three made it over to the flower store.

Peering between the white blooms in the window, Charlie said, "It's open. I can see someone." He approached the door.

"No," said Olivia. "I've changed my mind."

"Why?"

"I don't want to go in there." She stood rooted to the spot, her eyes fixed on a bunch of lilies.

"Come on. Just one lily," said Charlie. "It won't cost much."

"How do you know?" Olivia demanded.

Charlie couldn't understand her sudden reluctance to enter the store. "I don't know, but I can lend you some money if it's too expensive. In fact, I'll buy it for you." He tried the door. It opened into a store filled with the scent of flowers.

"Mmm!" Charlie sniffed the air. "It's fantastic."

"Isn't it!" said a voice.

A woman had appeared at the back of the store. Runner Bean ran up to her, his tail wagging wildly.

"What a lovely dog." She rubbed Runner Bean's ears, and he sat down, grunting with pleasure.

"We'd like some, er, lilies, I think," said Charlie.

"We?" said the woman. She had white hair and large green eyes.

"Yes, we. My friend wants some for her mom." Charlie looked behind him and saw Olivia slowly entering the shop.

"Ah, there you are," said the woman. "I'm so glad you've come at last."

"What do you mean?" Olivia froze. "I don't know you."

"But I know you," said the woman. "I'm Alice Angel." She held out her hand. "And you are Olivia."

Olivia still didn't move, so Charlie shook Alice Angel's hand. "Come on, Liv. It's OK." He looked back at Olivia, who was now wearing a dark scowl.

Alice Angel smiled. "There's no hurry. How many lilies would you like?"

Olivia wouldn't even open her mouth.

"How much are they?" asked Charlie.

Alice didn't reply. She placed a thoughtful finger on her chin and said, "Ten would be nice. One for each of the king's children. Though some don't deserve the thought. Yes, ten with a few sprigs of green." Her eyes were as green as the flowers' stalks. And how did she know about the king and his ten children?

"How much are they?" Charlie said anxiously.

"They're free," said Alice, skillfully arranging the lilies on her counter. She wrapped them in silver tissue and tied the bouquet with a white satin ribbon. "There!" she held out the flowers.

Charlie took the bouquet. "Are you sure they're free?"

"Absolutely." Alice looked across to Olivia. "You will come again soon, won't you? We have so much to discover together."

Olivia turned and quickly left the store.

Charlie had begun to feel very uneasy. There was something odd about Alice Angel. Her name, for a start, and her hair was the same shade of white as the lilies. He said, "Thanks very much for the flowers, Mrs. — Ms. Angel. I'm sorry my friend isn't . . . well, she's had a bit of a shock. She's not normally like this."

"I know. Would you like some apples? I grow them myself and they're very good." Alice smiled encouragingly.

"No, thanks," said Charlie a little suspiciously. "Mom works at a market."

"Of course," said Alice. "Good-bye, Charlie."

"Good-bye." Charlie walked out with Runner Bean at his heels. It was only when he was outside the store that he realized Alice Angel had used his name.

"How did she know my name?" he asked in a puzzled tone.

"How did she know mine?" Olivia took the flowers from Charlie. She looked both shocked and confused. "That woman can see right inside me," she said, almost in a whisper. "She knows things about me that I don't even know myself."

THE BOOK OF AMADIS

When Charlie took Runner Bean back to the Pets' Café, he asked the Onimouses if they knew of a shop called "Angel Flowers."

"Rings a bell," said Mr. Onimous. "It's one of those places that comes and goes, if you know what I mean."

Charlie didn't know.

"There's more going on in this town than anyone would believe," said Mrs. Onimous.

"Oh, I'd believe anything now," said Charlie. "In fact, I wouldn't be surprised if you told me that Runner Bean was a thousand-year-old fairy."

This made Mr. Onimous laugh so much he went bright red in the face and had to sit down very quickly on the floor.

Charlie gave Runner Bean a parting hug, said good-bye to the Onimouses, and hurried home. It was now six o'clock and his mother would be getting anxious.

"Where have you been?" cried Charlie's mother, Amy Bone, as he walked into the kitchen.

"We phoned the Gunns but Fidelio said he hadn't seen you," added his grandmother Maisie.

Charlie told them about his visit to the flower store. "That Alice Angel knows me, Mom, but how? Have either of you been to Angel Flowers?"

"I've never heard of it," said Maisie.

"Nor me," echoed Amy. "Oh, Charlie, I wish you wouldn't go wandering into strange parts of town by yourself."

"I was with Runner, and anyway Olivia was there, so I wasn't alone."

"But still." Amy sighed. "I can't help worrying, Charlie. If only your father was . . . There are people out there who don't wish you well. If you were to . . . disappear like Lyell, I don't know what I'd do."

"I won't disappear, Mom. My father wasn't endowed. But I am!"

"Exactly," Amy said softly. "Come and have your tea."

Charlie sat down, feeling guilty, and Maisie poured him a cup of tea. "We can't help worrying," she said. "Your great-aunt Venetia was here."

"Venetia!" Charlie's knife clattered onto his plate. "Did Grandma Bone let her in?"

"Nope. She must have a key. I opened the kitchen door, and there she was, standing in the hall. She looked dreadful, hair all over the place, clothes a mess. She used to be so put together. I think she's losing her mind. That fire in her house has driven her over the edge."

"She was carrying an armful of clothes," said Charlie's mother. "Wanted to know if we'd like them."

"As if!" snorted Maisie. "She'd probably poisoned them."

"We told her to leave, and then I locked all the bedroom doors just in case. Here's your key, Charlie." Amy Bone pushed a key across the table. "Lock your door when you go to school tomorrow, and give Maisie the key."

Charlie groaned. As if there weren't enough to remember, now they all had to lock their doors.

"It can't be helped," said Maisie. "We don't want to end up with poison in our pants or snakes up our sleeves, do we?"

When snack time was over, Charlie sat back to watch his favorite TV show, *The Barkers*, a story about dog people. Against Grandma Bone's wishes, Maisie had insisted on having a small TV on top of the kitchen cupboard. She didn't want to miss her soaps, she told Grandma Bone, and if she were to spend all her time slaving away in the kitchen, she could at least be permitted a little enjoyment while she did it. Unless, of course, certain people would like to do a bit of slaving themselves.

Grandma Bone was horrified at the thought of slaving and gave in.

Charlie's show had just begun when Uncle Paton looked in and said, "I've got it!"

"Got what?" asked Charlie, hoping the gleam in his

uncle's eye didn't mean that one of the aunts had given him a nasty disease.

"The Castle of Mirrors, dear boy," said Uncle Paton. "Come upstairs and I'll show you."

"But my show's just started," said Charlie, wriggling uncomfortably in his seat.

"Oh, well, if TV takes precedence — so be it!" Uncle Paton backed out, slamming the door behind him.

Charlie watched *The Barkers* for another five minutes, but he couldn't concentrate. Nothing was funny today. Maisie and his mother were giggling over a magazine article. It was horribly distracting. Charlie gave an audible sigh, turned off the TV, and left the kitchen. He ran upstairs and tapped on his uncle's door.

"What?" called Paton.

"You said you've got something to show me — about the Castle of Mirrors."

"Did I? Then you'd better come in," said Paton a little grudgingly.

Charlie went in. His uncle's room was in its usual

state of chaos. Books on the floor, papers on the bed, and shelves bending under the weight of manuscripts and encyclopedias. Paton sat at his desk. He was wearing his half-moon glasses and reading one of the oldest-looking books Charlie had ever seen. The pages were a dark mustard color and their edges rough and curling. The leather cover was soft and worn and could hardly restrain the coarse paper that appeared to spill out of it.

"Clever Julia found this among her treasures. She has an astounding memory, and when you mentioned a castle of mirrors, she knew she had seen the name before." Uncle Paton gingerly closed the book, and Charlie read the title, *The Book of Amadis,* printed in faded gold on the cover.

"Amadis?" said Charlie.

"The Red King's second son." Paton tapped the ancient book. "This tells it all. Amadis was forced to flee his father's castle when Borlath, the eldest, set out on his deadly pursuit of power. He destroyed everyone who got in his way, and in this he was helped by four of his siblings. The other five, including Amadis, tried to prevent the terrible slaughter that was going on in the surrounding countryside. But Borlath and his followers were strong, and eventually the more honorable siblings fled the castle in fear for their lives."

"And is Amadis Billy's ancestor?" asked Charlie.

"It would seem so."

"Then who is our ancestor? The one who began the Yewbeams. Was he good or evil?"

"From what I can find out, she was Amoret, Amadis' favorite sister."

"A girl?" Charlie hadn't even considered this.

"Yes, Charlie, a girl." Paton opened the ancient book again. "She fled with Amadis, but traveling north they became separated. Amoret was lost and Amadis sailed to an island in the northwest. He was well loved, and many who lived on the king's estates left their homes and followed Amadis rather than suffer Borlath's murderous tyranny. . . . "

Charlie broke in, "But Amoret? You said she was lost. Don't you know what happened to her? Doesn't anyone? I mean, could I find out . . . maybe on the Internet?"

Paton gave a sigh of impatience. "You wouldn't find Amoret in your computer, Charlie. Her history is too secret for that. No one knows the whole truth. It is we who must uncover it. And that's what I've been trying to do for the past twenty years." He swept out an arm, indicating the shelves of books and worn papers. "When I met Julia Ingledew, it was like finding a treasure — someone else who was fascinated by the past, who thought nothing of spending a whole week pursuing one tiny, elusive fact in order to complete a puzzle. To me such a person is a jewel, Charlie, even if she were not the most congenial and lovely person I have ever met."

Charlie had never heard his uncle speak so passionately. "Are you going to marry her?" he asked.

Paton blinked and then said quietly, "I dare not even think about that."

"Why not? It seems like a good idea to me," he said bluntly.

Uncle Paton gave a delicate cough. "Our subject was the Castle of Mirrors, not the future of Paton Yewbeam," he said in a flat tone. "Are you interested in this book or not?"

"You bet," said Charlie earnestly. "Could I sit down, please? It's been kind of a long day."

"Help yourself." Paton motioned his head, and Charlie, having pushed several books aside, made himself comfortable on Paton's large, untidy bed.

Paton swiveled his worn leather chair around to face Charlie and began to read. As evening drew in and an early moon appeared in the darkening sky, Charlie was swept away by the story of Prince Amadis and the Castle of Shining Glass. The clutter of his great-uncle's room faded and, through half-closed eyes, he began to see a castle rising in the center of a blue island set in a glittering sea.

"They said it was the fairest castle in the world."

Uncle Paton was the perfect storyteller. He made the written words his own, and his deep, melodious voice filled the room with bright images: splendid knights, horses, golden cups, shining swords and shields, flying pennants, the raging surf — and fire.

"When Amadis and his followers had built their fine castle, there followed fifteen years of peace. The land was fertile and they prospered. The prince married one of his followers and they had four children. The youngest was called Owain."

"And the other three?" Charlie asked, tentatively.

"Not relevant," said his uncle. He proceeded to explain why those three poor children had no part in the story.

"It was inevitable that Borlath should hear of the island castle and want it for himself. With a thousand savage mercenaries, he crossed the sea and surrounded the castle, demanding that Amadis give it up."

"And Amadis refused?" Charlie threw in.

"Of course. He knew that if he surrendered the

castle, his family would be slaughtered. But it was a heartbreaking decision to have to make. Amadis was well aware of Borlath's terrible talent."

Charlie leaned forward eagerly. "That's what I was going to ask, Uncle P. All the Red King's children were endowed, right? So what could Amadis do? And what about Borlath?"

"Amadis knew the language of birds and beasts. He could talk to any creature in the world, but this didn't count for much when he had to defend his people against Borlath."

Charlie waited expectantly, until at last his uncle told him, "Borlath had fire. When he put his mind to it, he could burn anything in his way. But he didn't want to destroy such a fine building; he wanted it for himself, so he laid siege to the castle. That didn't mean that he sat around waiting for Amadis to surrender. Oh, no! First, Borlath's army tried to scale the walls. The archers on the battlements soon put a stop to that. Then the mercenaries tried to force the great oak door with a battering ram. But a cloud of bats swooped down and all but blinded them. At the end of the tenth week, Amadis and a hundred men left the castle in the dead of night and attacked Borlath's sleeping army. Surprise gave Amadis an advantage, but eventually his small force was overcome by Borlath's bloodthirsty warriors, experts in killing who relished every severed head and limb."

Charlie shuddered. "So was Amadis killed?"

"He was fatally wounded," Uncle Paton replied. "A spear in his shoulder." He referred to the book and added, "Most of his men were killed, but the few who survived managed to get the prince back to the castle and he lived — until the end.

"Perhaps, in his heart, Amadis had always known that Borlath would find him one day. So within the castle, he had stored a huge supply of grain and provisions. They also had a very deep well. When the stores began to get low, Amadis talked to the animals." Paton smiled to himself. "An army of rats invaded Borlath's stores. Wolves attacked the sentries, birds pecked holes in the tents, and at night the bats came again, screeching out of the sky and making sleep impossible. The lives of Borlath's soldiers became intolerable. The weather was turning cold. It began to rain. The army had had enough. They wanted to go home."

"And that's when Borlath used fire, isn't it?" said Charlie.

Paton nodded. He looked down at the book. "At the base of the castle, there was an outer and inner wall of thick wooden stakes. But within the wood and rising above it was a wall of yellow stone. In a gesture of fury and contempt, Borlath raised his fists and called for fire. The wooden stakes burst into flame. Those inside the castle were immediately engulfed in a ring of fire. Some threw themselves from the battlements. Others were overwhelmed before they could climb that far. Every man, woman, and child, every creature within the castle perished — except one."

"Who?" exclaimed Charlie, jolted out of the dreadful world of flames that his uncle had conjured up. "I mean, how could anyone . . . ?"

"Wait!" his uncle commanded.

Charlie fell silent.

"The intense heat of those burning stakes caused the stones to vitrify; in other words, the walls turned to glass, a thick, black glass." Paton's dark eyes took on an animated gleam. "Now, this is the really interesting part, Charlie. I believe it might hold a clue to the other side of your family." Paton turned a page. "During his travels, Amadis had made friends with a Welsh magician, a man called Mathonwy. This magician lived on the mainland far south of the prince's island. But the blaze that Borlath created was so fierce, it lit up the sky for miles around. Clouds turned to fire, birds became black, and the bloodred sea boiled like a cauldron.

"From far away, Mathonwy saw the conflagration. He guessed what had happened. Was it too late to save his friend, Prince Amadis? Mathonwy did the only thing he could. He caused a snowfall. A blanket of snow swept toward the burning castle. When it reached the island, the snow fell, and where it touched the scorched walls, a strange thing happened. The vitrified stones began to shine."

"A castle of shining glass," breathed Charlie. "But, Uncle P., what's the connection to my family?"

"Mathonwy," said Paton brusquely. "Remember the name on the family tree that Maisie gave you? Your Welsh ancestor?"

"Oh," said Charlie slowly. "But the date is wrong."

"The name is enough. The Welsh used their ancestors' names over and over."

"Oh," Charlie said again, and thinking of his Welsh ancestor, he remembered the wand. "Uncle Paton, I've lost the . . . you know . . . the wand."

"What!" Paton's glasses slid to the end of his nose.

"I took it to school. It was stupid of me. I put it under my mattress and now it's gone."

"Do you suspect anyone?"

"Yes. And if it's who I think it is, I'll probably get it back. Please go on with the story."

Uncle Paton shook his head. "Sometimes, your carelessness astounds me, Charlie."

He looked down at the book. "The castle walls became so smooth and so bright that Borlath's soldiers beheld an army looking out at them. What a hideous and terrifying sight it was. Believing that Prince Amadis and his men had survived the fire and were, therefore, supernatural, the mercenaries ran for their boats. Only Borlath realized that the glimmering army was his own, but he didn't attempt to take the castle. For some reason, the shining walls appalled him and he too left the island."

"So they were all dead in there," said Charlie, "except for one. It must have been like a great shining tomb. I wouldn't like to have been the one to survive. Who was it, Uncle P.?"

Paton referred to the book again, turning several pages before he reached a place almost at the end. "There was one survivor, the prince's youngest son, white-haired Owain, who was an albino and knew the language of the beasts and birds. So Owain, being without home or family, departed from the island on the advice of a raven. And the raven traveled with him."

"He sounds like Billy," said Charlie in astonishment. "Exactly like Billy."

"Exactly," Paton agreed. "Odd how the same features pop up through the generations. Unfortunately, it doesn't say how the boy managed to survive, but I'll just read the ending because this is really interesting. 'It is said that Prince Amadis will be seen again in the Castle of Shining Glass by one of Owain's bloodline.'"

"Billy?" said Charlie.

Paton looked over his glasses. "Maybe." He returned to the book. "And Owain traveled to the Holy Roman Empire and had two sons. The elder became a scribe — in other words, a person who wrote out documents or copied manuscripts — and the younger could speak the language of the beasts and birds. The latter was banished from his village for consorting with ravens that perched upon a gallows where dead men hung."

Charlie shivered. "Horrible. But it was mean to banish him."

"Unusual habits were considered the work of the

devil in those days," said Uncle Paton. "And now for the end." He put a finger on the last paragraph. "The first son of Owain was called Crowquill in that he used such for his work. And these words, being the truth to the best of my knowledge, were written down by a descendant of that Crowquill, in the year of our Lord, 1655."

"So . . . ," said Charlie thoughtfully, "they were connected even then — the Ravens and the Crowquills. There are so many strange things going on in this city, Uncle P."

"Indeed," said his uncle.

"It's as if the city is drawing them all back, all the people whose stories began right here, on the ground under our feet, under all the houses and streets and parks."

"Even this house," added Paton.

"Even us. Like threads being pulled tighter and tighter together."

"How eloquent you're becoming, Charlie," said Uncle Paton with a smile.

"Today," Charlie went on, "I went into a flower shop, and the woman there knew my name. And she was really interested in my friend Olivia. But Livvy would hardly come into the shop. She said the woman knew more about her than she did herself."

"Is this girl endowed?"

"No, not in the least. But she's a brilliant actress. Only she just failed an audition and she's really — I can't describe it — she's kind of different, desperate, furious!"

"Sounds like trouble, Charlie. Desperate women can be dangerous."

"Can they?" Charlie yawned in spite of himself. "Thanks for reading me the book, Uncle P. It's been like putting things in a frame, so you can begin to see them better. I wonder what's going to happen next."

"I wonder, Charlie," said Uncle Paton. "I wonder." He closed the book and pushed it carefully into one of the cubbyholes on his desk. "You'd better find that wand before it gets into the wrong hands."

Charlie was thinking that perhaps it already had.

THE WHITE MOTH

Manfred Bloor was losing his power. He'd been aware of it for a year now, ever since Charlie Bone had managed to resist him. Charlie had conjured up pictures of his lost father, a man whom Manfred had found easy to hypnotize when he was nine years old. When Manfred was nine, he had been at the height of his powers; now they were waning.

No one had guessed what was happening to him. Manfred was still capable of scaring children when he gave them a nasty glare. And the horse experiment had almost restored his confidence, since it was his part in the procedure that had been the most successful. Or had it been? Maybe it had been Venetia Yewbeam's foul-smelling potions that had done the trick.

Another thing. Where was the horse now? And how were they going to control it? Manfred was secretly fearful of that "undead" horse and its brutal heart. He needed something to protect himself.

It was easy to persuade Billy Raven to steal Charlie's wand. Afraid that his one chance of happiness might be snatched away at the last minute, Billy had found the wand and handed it over.

A lot of good it had done little Billy. He was now trapped in the Passing House, and the kind parents he had longed for were nothing more than coldhearted villains with extremely unpleasant powers.

"Oh, what a Silly Billy," Manfred chanted as he paced around his office, twirling the slim white stick. "And now for the test. What are you going to do for me, little stick?" He noticed a fly crawling across his desk and touched it with the wand's silver tip. "Turn into a frog," he demanded.

Manfred felt a sharp sting on his palm and he dropped the wand. The fly was still a fly. It flew up to the ceiling where it stayed, upside down and very still. Manfred had a bad feeling it was laughing at him.

"Turn into a frog," he cried, throwing the wand at the ceiling. As the white stick left his hand, a searing pain traveled down Manfred's arm. "Oooow!" he yelled.

The wand hit the fly and fell to the ground. The fly, unharmed, sailed over to the window.

"Turn that thing into a frog!" screeched Manfred, seizing the wand and hurling it at the window. This time, the pain that struck his hand felt like a red-hot poker. Indeed, there was a large red welt across his palm.

As Manfred screamed, the fly buzzed behind the curtain, and once more the wand fell to the ground. There was now no doubt in Manfred's mind that the wand would not work for him. In fact, the more he attempted to use it, the more it would punish him for daring to try.

"You . . . you . . ." Swearing horribly, Manfred scooped up the wand and pitched it into the empty fireplace. He then gathered as much scrap paper as he could find and flung that into the fireplace. Manfred's final act was to strike several matches and drop them onto the paper.

The flames that roared up the chimney were very gratifying, but there was a moment of panic for

155

Manfred when they began to leap into the room. He tore off his black cape and tossed it over the fire, smothering the flames. The cape smoldered and a cloud of smoke billowed out. Coughing and choking, Manfred staggered to the window and flung it open.

At the same moment, Tantalus Ebony walked into the room, chuckling merrily. "What are we up to, young man?"

Manfred whirled around, still coughing. He pointed to the fire. "Wand . . . ugh . . . Charlie Bone's . . . I'm . . . ugh . . . burning it." He cleared his throat with a hoarse, grating sound. "It wouldn't work for me, so I've finished it off. At least the little wretch can't use it now."

"Oooo! Temper, temper." Tantalus giggled. "You'll have to learn to control that, my old pal."

"I am not your old pal," Manfred retorted. "And I wish you could decide who you were."

"Today, I'm . . ." Tantalus gazed up at the ceiling. "I'm a bit of Vincent Ebony, the postman — he called everyone his old pal — but then I'm also partly the hitchhiking headmaster, Tantalus Wright. I haven't had so much fun in years."

"I hope you haven't forgotten why you're here," Manfred said sourly.

"Oh, THAT!" Tantalus narrowed his mismatched eyes and licked his thin lips. "No, I haven't forgotten THAT."

The fire in the grate was by now a glowing pile of ash, and the two men watched with satisfaction as the remains of the charred wand finally crumbled to dust. A sudden draft from the open window lifted the ashes, and a tiny cloud of them fluttered into the room. Gradually, the cloud assumed the shape of a white moth with delicate silver-tipped wings.

"Catch it!" roared Tantalus.

Manfred leaped, but too late. The moth floated out of the window, closely followed by the elusive fly.

In the bathroom of number nine Filbert Street, Charlie Bone, wearing pajamas, stood beside the sink feeling very ill. His whole body seemed to be on fire.

Was it the flu? He sensed that something awful had happened. But what? Perhaps one of his friends had been in an accident.

Charlie held his hands under the cold tap. Steam rose from his fingers, almost as though they were the prongs of a red-hot iron. "Ow!" Charlie quaked. "Ooo, what's happening?"

"Indeed what?" said a grouchy voice from the doorway. Grandma Bone stood, glaring in at Charlie. "You've been in this bathroom for twenty minutes. Other people have needs too, you know."

"Yessss!" Charlie gritted his teeth as another cloud of steam hissed off his fingertips. "But I'm very hot, you see, Grandma. Look! Steam!"

"Wickedness made manifest," growled his grandmother. "Take your nasty hands elsewhere."

Charlie left the bathroom, flapping his steamy fingers in the air. He went into his bedroom, opened the window as wide as he could, and held his hands out in the cool air. It was a strange evening. An autumn mist was creeping through the town, muffling the sound of traffic and softening the contours of walls and fences. There was a strong scent of flowers in the air.

A shining speck of dust floated out of the sky. As it drew nearer, Charlie could make out two white wings tipped with silver, a white moth. The little creature flew down to Charlie's outstretched hand and settled on his index finger.

"Wow!" said Charlie. "You're amazing." He carried the moth inside and let it walk onto his bedside table, where it spread its wings and sat perfectly still. Charlie got the impression that the moth felt at home in his room. He realized that his hands no longer burned and that his fever had stopped. He was perfectly well again.

In a house not far from Charlie's, Olivia Vertigo sat on the edge of her bed, peeling an apple. It was the fifth apple she had tried to peel that day. And this attempt was proving to be as unsuccessful as the others. Every time she thought she'd reached the end, another inch of peel appeared, and yet the strand that hung from the apple was at least a meter long.

In a sudden fury, Olivia dropped the knife and flung the apple across the room. She buried her face in her hands and sobbed, "What's happening to me?"

The door opened and her mother looked in. Vivienne Vertigo (or Viva Valery, as she was known in the movies) might have been a film star, but this had never prevented her from being a kind and considerate mother. She had always managed to help her daughter through her little "spells of temperament," as she put it. But Olivia's mood over the last twenty-four hours was beginning to defeat her.

"The flowers are beautiful, Olivia, thank you!" said Vivienne.

Olivia didn't look up.

"Oh, poor Livvy." Mrs. Vertigo went over to her daughter and sat beside her on the bed. "I failed my first audition too, you know. It just wasn't the right part for you. There'll be another chance. You mustn't be so downhearted."

"I'm not," growled Olivia.

"Then what is it?"

"Something's happening to me, Mom."

"You're growing up, darling."

"It's not THAT!" yelled Olivia. "It's something else. It's making me . . . oh, I don't know. I hate it. I don't want it to happen."

Mrs. Vertigo stopped herself from making a dramatic gesture. Instead she gave a modest shrug and said, "I don't quite understand, my darling."

Olivia gave a huge sigh. "When I came in with the flowers, I felt like eating an apple. So I took one from the bowl in the kitchen. But I couldn't peel it. I tried four more, but . . . but the peel never comes to an end."

"Can't you eat the peel, darling?" asked Mrs. Vertigo. "It's supposed to be good for the hair."

"I don't like the peel," cried Olivia, exasperated by her mother's lack of understanding. "But that's not the point. Why does the peel never end? I go around and around and around, and it NEVER ENDS."

At last Mrs. Vertigo said, "Those apples come from the tree at the end of the garden. I've never had any trouble with them before."

Olivia gave up on the apples. "And then there's the flowers."

"They're beautiful," gushed her mother. "But where on earth did you find them? I thought you were at the Pets' Café. I was so worried when Mr. Onimous told me you hadn't been there."

"That's the thing, Mom. The flowers found me. There was this alley that I'd never seen before, and I felt I had to go down there. And then I found this flower shop, Angel Flowers. When I went in, the woman inside said she knew me, and that was scary because I don't know her. Her name is Alice Angel."

"Alice Angel, Alice Angel," Mrs. Vertigo repeated the name very slowly. "Of course," she said at last. "Alice Angel does the flowers — weddings, christenings, celebrations. She decorated the house for your christening party, Livvy. I haven't seen her since, but she lives just down there."

"Where?" Olivia jumped off the bed and followed her mother's pointing finger to the window. "Where? Where?"

"On the other side of the wall there's a garden. It backs onto ours. Alice Angel lives in a house at the far end. At least she used to."

"Mom, I'm going to take a look right now."

"OK, Livvy." Mrs. Vertigo was pleased to see her daughter's sad face come to life once more. "But please don't climb over the wall. The house could belong to a stranger."

"Never fear," Olivia said brightly. She ran downstairs and out into the garden.

A white September mist lay over the grass, and the air was warm and filled with scents. Olivia approached the shrubbery at the bottom of the garden. She could see the wall rising above it, but before she could reach it, she stumbled over a fallen apple. There were others lying nearby. In fact, the ground was covered with them. But there were no apple trees in the Vertigos' garden. The fruit came from a long branch that hung over the wall. The tree grew on the other side.

Olivia pushed her way through the dense shrubbery. She wasn't tall enough to see over the wall, so she hauled herself up and sat on the top. When she looked down into the garden beyond, she thought there'd been a sudden snowfall, for it was filled with white flowers. They climbed into trees, crowded the borders, and crept across the narrow stone path. White petals lay everywhere, like patches of snow.

At the end of the path, a very small house stood under a blanket of white roses. Only the door and one window could be glimpsed. Even the chimney was wrapped in greenery.

Olivia had hardly taken in this extraordinary scene when her eyes were drawn to a rounded wooden structure that she could just make out above the sea of flowers. Olivia squinted into the dusk. It was a caravan, a real gypsy caravan.

Just then the door of the house opened and light

flooded onto the path. A figure stepped out. It was small and very thin; it wore a long, hooded coat, and it shuffled up the path, head bent and shoulders hunched. And then it left the path and waded through the flowers until it reached the caravan. Olivia heard feet dragging up the wooden steps. She squinted her eyes and leaned farther over the wall, trying to see whether the strange figure was a man or a woman.

A voice called, "Sleep well, my dear." Framed in the doorway of the rose-covered house stood a woman with shining white hair. Alice Angel.

"Bless you!" replied the hooded figure. It went into the caravan and closed the door.

Alice remained where she was for a moment. And then she called, "Is that you, Olivia?"

Olivia shuddered and dropped down into her own garden.

A MAN TRAPPED IN GLASS

On Monday morning, Charlie expected to see Billy Raven on the school bus, but there was no sign of him.

Charlie finally caught up with Billy in assembly. The small boy appeared to be exhausted. There were dark shadows under his eyes, and his face wore a hungry, pinched look.

"How are things at home, Billy?" Charlie whispered as the orchestra tuned up.

"Fine," said Billy. "It's great. Really."

"I waited for you. I thought your parents would bring you to the Pets' Café."

"No. I . . . you see . . . we were busy," Billy said solemnly.

A hundred blue-caped children launched into the first hymn, and Charlie gave up temporarily, but after the first break, he found Billy in the blue coatroom.

"Billy . . . ," Charlie began.

Billy cried, "Stop!"

Charlie stared at Billy in surprise. "OK."

"Please don't ask me about my home or my parents or anything like that, because I won't tell you." Lowering his voice, he added, "I can't."

For a moment, Charlie was at a loss. The de Greys had obviously threatened Billy, and Charlie didn't want to make trouble for him. "OK. Maybe you can tell me if you stole my wand?"

Billy's pale face turned scarlet. "I . . ." He struggled with his answer. At last, he said quietly, "I'm sorry, Charlie. Really sorry."

"I suppose you gave it to Manfred."

Silently Billy nodded.

"Let me guess. He threatened you in some way. Maybe he said you wouldn't go to a new home after all."

Billy gave another mute nod.

Charlie sighed. "I wish you hadn't done that, Billy,

but I suppose I can't blame you." He left the coatroom and hurried on to his classroom. The sound of laughter echoed toward him as he approached Tantalus Ebony's room. When he walked in, he found half the class in fits of giggles.

Tantalus Ebony sat behind his desk with his chin resting on his chest. His purple hood was pulled over his head, his eyes were closed, and he was snoring very loudly.

Charlie took his place next to Fidelio, who was sprawled across his desk, shaking with helpless laughter. Charlie couldn't stop himself from giggling, although he kept an eye on the teacher.

Suddenly, Mr. Ebony's head shot up and he bellowed, "Quiet!" His voice sounded completely different. Last week, he had a high-pitched whine, but now his voice sounded as though it were rumbling up from a deep cavern. It was such a shock, the whole class immediately fell silent.

Mr. Ebony looked a bit shaken by the deep voice

that had come booming out of him. "Ahem," he said, clearing his throat. "Hmmm! Hmmm!"

It was difficult to keep a straight face while the extraordinary teacher worked his way through a series of coughs, wheezes, whistles, and puffs, but none of the children in the classroom allowed a glimmer of a smile to cross his or her face. They feared detention.

At last, the teacher found a suitable voice for his lesson, and in a pleasant but commanding tone, he announced, "Medieval history. Open your books to page forty-three. The Plantagenets."

For forty minutes, the class listened to Tantalus Ebony's description of the reign of Henry II and the murder of Thomas à Becket. It was the most interesting lesson Charlie had ever had. The lesson had almost reached its end when, to their surprise, Mr. Ebony asked, "And where was the Red King when these battles, murders, and intrigues were taking place?"

No one knew what to say.

Mr. Ebony looked directly at Emma Tolly and said,

"You should know, Emma the Endowed, should you not? You who have the king's blood in your veins, the king's gift in your fingers"— he leaned over the desk and whispered hoarsely — "in your wings."

Everyone looked at Emma, who stammered, "I . . . don't know, sir."

"He was right here, you silly girl. Living very comfortably in that old ruin you can see at the edge of the grounds. Who would have thought a gloomy old castle like that could have been a nice family home? But it was. The king and queen and their ten children lived there happily until one day the queen died — hey-ho, it happens. So the king went off to mope in the woods, deserting his children, even the baby." Mr. Ebony shook his head. He had an odd, satisfied grin on his face now. "Of course, there were plenty of servants to look after them, but it's not the same, is it? Not the same as having a mommy and daddy, is it, Emma?"

"No, sir." Emma looked close to tears.

Charlie wondered why Tantalus Ebony had picked

on Emma. There were two other endowed children in the room: he and Gabriel, who was sitting at the back, nervously pulling at his hair. Without thinking, Charlie asked, "Are you endowed, sir?"

Ignoring the question, Mr. Ebony turned his gray-brown gaze on Charlie and asked, "How's the wildlife on Filbert Street, Mr. Bone?"

Charlie was completely dumbfounded. "What?" he croaked.

"The wildlife, Charlie. Come on. Seen any unusual butterflies lately? Any moths? And how about a horse?"

Charlie's mouth dropped open but not a sound came out. "No," Charlie mumbled.

"No, what?"

"No, sir," said Charlie.

"Stupid boy. I meant which. No moths or no horse?"

Charlie's mind raced. Was it a trick question? Before Charlie could make up his mind, Fidelio said, "He hasn't seen either of them."

"And who asked you, insolent boy?" yelled the

teacher. All at once, his mood changed. Locking his fingers together, he stretched out his arms, turning his palms toward the class. A horrible crunch of bones could be heard, and Mr. Ebony said cheerily, "Class dismissed."

Hardly believing his luck, Charlie gathered his books and made for the door. As he left the room, he heard Mr. Ebony whistling a familiar tune.

"Is that man weird or what?" said Fidelio.

"It's like he's two different people," said Charlie.

"Three," put in Gabriel, who had just caught up with them. "When he's teaching piano, he's completely different — calm and serious and his playing is fantastic."

Emma and Olivia were walking ahead of the boys, but just before they reached the hall, Olivia turned to Emma and shouted, "Oh, shut up! I don't want to talk about it," and she ran across the hall to the drama coatroom.

"What's up with her?" asked Fidelio.

Emma hung back until the boys reached her. "I

suppose everybody knows by now that she failed her audition. It'll be all over the school."

"I'd forgotten about it," Gabriel admitted.

"Poor thing," said Fidelio. "She must feel awful."

Charlie confessed that he'd seen Olivia since the audition. He told the others about the woman in Angel Flowers, who seemed to know Olivia and him.

Asa Pike, who was prowling around the hall, called, "You bunch, stop lurking in corners. You're supposed to be getting ready for lunch."

Observing the rule of silence, the four children walked into the hall and went to their respective coatrooms.

Billy Raven was standing at the back of the lunch line when Charlie and his friends walked into the cafeteria. "Can I sit at your table?" he asked Charlie.

"I suppose." Charlie grinned. Billy looked so nervous, it was impossible to remain angry with him.

Today, it was tomato soup and rolls. While the others hungrily spooned up the soup, Billy just sat staring at it.

"Not well, Billy?" asked Fidelio.

"Oh, yes, I'm very well," gushed Billy. "My parents are great. They give me wonderful things to eat. I had such a gigantic breakfast, I just can't eat any more."

The others stared at him, surprised by his enthusiastic speech. But after that, Billy said nothing until the end of the meal. They were piling up their plates, ready to take them to the counter, when Billy asked shyly, "Gabriel, could you tell me about something? It's a thing that's been worn by someone, but it's not a usual kind of thing."

"Show it to me outside," said Gabriel, interested by an object that wasn't usual.

The object turned out to be a button. Billy pulled it out of his pocket, muttering, "It's not as if I'm telling you anything, is it? I mean I'm not talking about home, am I?"

"'Course not," said Gabriel, taking the button.

The four boys were sitting on the grass at the edge of the grounds, with the red walls of the ruined castle behind them.

"Where did you find it, Billy? And what's so unusual about it?" asked Fidelio.

"Can't say." Billy clamped his mouth shut.

The button was quite ordinary. It was large and black, the sort of button that might come from a suit or a coat.

"I need to know a bit more about it," said Gabriel. "Did you find it in your new home? In a wardrobe? On the floor? Do you know who wore the clothes it came from?"

Billy gave two nods and then shook his head twice.

"OK, so we're a bit closer." Gabriel turned the button over. "I guess I'll have to work with what I've got." He placed the button in different positions down the middle of his body and then on each side. "It's difficult," he said. "You see, I can't actually put it on, so I don't think it's going to work . . . ugh!" Gabriel's long thin body jerked backward, and he looked down at the button, which he held over the left pocket of his shirt. A quiet, rhythmic beating could be heard when he pressed the button closer to his heart.

Billy gazed with round eyes at Gabriel's face, as the older boy uttered a series of shocked gasps.

"It's amazing." Gabriel closed his eyes, and the other three listened in absolute silence as he said, "There's glass everywhere. Walls of glass. No, it's mirrors . . . mirrors with . . . with a dark man looking into them. And there's music, piano music, but I can't see a piano. I think the man is trapped . . . inside the mirrors."

All at once, the silence was broken by an inhuman scream. Hoofbeats thundered around the circle of boys, and they cowered down, bowing their heads, terrified they'd be crushed by angry hooves. Only Fidelio remained upright, completely unaware of the sounds that were frightening his friends.

Gabriel, his face drained of color, flung the button into the long grass by the ruin, and the invisible animal seemed to follow it. Charlie looked up quickly, and an image flashed across his vision: a white horse with a flying tail. And then it was gone. Whether it went into the ruin or just vanished into thin air, he couldn't be sure.

"What's going on?" asked Fidelio.

Before anyone could reply, Billy Raven groaned and clutched his stomach. Doubled up in agony, he rolled over and lay moaning in the grass.

"What's up, Billy?" Charlie gingerly touched his shoulder.

"I didn't tell," moaned Billy. "I didn't tell about the Passing House . . . ow . . . ooo . . . did I? The button wasn't telling, was it? I didn't break my oath. I didn't. Mmmm . . . aaah . . . I think I'm dying."

Charlie rushed over to Miss Chrystal, who was on break duty. "It's Billy Raven," he cried, grabbing her arm. "He says he's dying."

Miss Chrystal sprinted across the grounds faster than Charlie would have thought possible. Bending over Billy, she said, "Oh, poor boy. What is it, love? Your tum? Oh, dear, dear. Can you get up, Billy?"

By now, Billy was in so much pain he couldn't

speak. Helped by the other boys, Miss Chrystal managed to get Billy to his feet, but he was still doubled up in pain. Very carefully, they helped support him across the grounds and into the hall.

Mr. Weedon, sitting by the door, looked up from his newspaper and asked, "What's wrong with the kid?"

"He's not at all well, Mr. Weedon," said Miss Chrystal. "Can you help me get him to the infirmary?"

"No problem," grunted the janitor. He swung Billy off his feet and carted him off.

That evening, Charlie asked the matron if he could visit Billy.

"Out of the question," said Lucretia Yewbeam. "He's far too ill."

"But what is it?" asked Charlie. "Did he eat something?"

The matron gave him a cold smile. "He's not strong. Things can get him down. Now, go to bed and don't interfere."

Charlie wasn't going to give up that easily. The next

day, while he was in the lunch line, he leaned over the counter and asked Cook if she'd seen Billy.

"Took the poor boy some broth, Charlie. But he couldn't eat it," she replied.

"What's wrong with him, Cook?"

"No idea. He wouldn't say a word. Just lay there, looking terrified."

"Well, I know where he lives now, Cook. Somewhere called the Passing House."

"The Passing House?" Cook's eyebrows arched, but before she could say any more, Gwyneth Howells, standing behind Charlie, gave his ankle a kick.

"Get a move on," Gwyneth whined. "I want my fries."

Charlie was obliged to move on.

No one saw Billy for the rest of the week, and Charlie had a sickening feeling that he'd been taken back to the unpleasant parents who had no love for him. And what did he mean about breaking his oath? Did the de Greys have some mysterious hold over Billy? Were they aware of everything he said and did?

Charlie resolved to find out more about the black button. During every break for the rest of the week, he walked down to the long grass surrounding the castle. Fidelio joined him whenever he could get away from his music practice, and sometimes Gabriel came to help, kicking the grass from side to side and mumbling, "I'd rather we didn't find it, actually. It's trouble — really it is." And he would look over his shoulder, half expecting a wild stallion to leap out of nowhere and crush him to death.

One afternoon, when Charlie was searching alone, he sensed someone watching him, and looking up, he saw Olivia, her gaze fixed on the ground by his feet.

"What are you doing?" she asked sullenly. She looked even worse than usual. Her hair was greasy, her shirt was dirty, and the white sneakers she'd taken to wearing were now a grayish brown.

"Liv, why don't you do your hair anymore?" asked

Charlie. "You know, like you used to. All those great colors."

"It's none of your business," Olivia retorted. "I asked you what you were doing."

Charlie sighed. "Looking for a button," he said. "Want to help?"

Olivia began to push at the undergrowth with the toe of her sneaker. "Why do you want it? Can't you get another one?"

"No. Billy found it in his new home, and Gabriel, you know . . . found its story. But I want to know more."

"All that psychic nonsense," said Olivia sulkily. "You guys never give up, do you?"

Charlie was shocked. "Liv, you used to help us. You liked to be involved. What on earth is the matter with you?"

"If you really want to know, I can't peel apples, and I'm sick of all this endowment. . . ." She stopped and stared at the ruin. "What was that?"

"What was what?"

"I thought I heard a sort of grunt, like a horse!"

"You heard it? Liv, that means . . ."

"I don't want to know what it means," cried Olivia. She ran off, leaving Charlie with a lot to think about.

When the hunting horn blared, Charlie was reluctant to give up the search. Finding the black button had become enormously important to him. Gabriel had described a dark man trapped within mirrors, with piano music in the background. Could the dark man be his father, Lyell Bone? Gabriel had already seen Lyell before, that time when Charlie had given him his father's tie. So he desperately needed Gabriel to "look" again and tell him if the two images matched.

Charlie trudged across the grass, the last one to leave the grounds. As he stepped into the hall, Manfred Bloor came out of the prefects' room.

"Ah, the very person," said Manfred. "I want a word with you, Charlie Bone."

"It's bedtime," Charlie objected. "I'll be late and get detention."

"This is more important." Manfred walked over to the door of the Music Tower and beckoned Charlie. "Don't worry, I'll give you a note for Matron."

Charlie grudgingly followed Manfred down the passage to his office. When they reached the dusty bookcase, Manfred said, "I suppose you know my secret entrance, by now." He pushed his finger on the wood between two books on the top shelf, and the bookcase swung inward.

"After you, Charlie." Manfred ushered Charlie into the room, and the bookcase swung into position behind them.

Charlie felt trapped. What awful surprise did Manfred have in store for him? Looking around the office, he noticed a pile of ash in the grate. The smell of burned paper still lingered in the room, and Charlie wondered why Manfred needed a fire in such warm weather. Something made him say, "I believe you've got something of mine, Man — sir."

"And what would that be?"

"A white cane. Billy Raven gave it to you."

"Oh, you mean your wand. Don't be coy, Charlie. Everyone knows it's a wand. Well, it's been confiscated."

"You can't do that!" cried Charlie.

"Don't be stupid. Of course, I can. Wands are forbidden. It's a new rule."

Charlie was speechless. A string of rude words sprang to his mind, but he knew that if he used them, it would only give Manfred an excuse to punish him.

The new teaching assistant motioned Charlie to sit at the desk while he paced the room, self-consciously stroking the meager growth of beard on his chin. Eventually, he took a breath and said, "There is a portrait of our illustrious ancestor in the King's room."

"Yes." Charlie felt nervous with Manfred moving behind him, just out of sight.

"I've noticed you looking at it," Manfred went on.

"Have you?"

"Don't play innocent," said Manfred curtly. "Of course, you look at it. We all do from time to time. But you, Charlie Bone, you have a motive, don't you?"

"Do I?"

"Come off it, Bone," snapped Manfred. "You want to 'go in,' don't you? And you probably could if it weren't for something in that picture blocking you."

"Oh?" Charlie was intrigued. So Manfred knew about the dark shadow behind the king's shoulder, the person, or thing, who was preventing Charlie from entering the painting.

"Have you ever heard anything from that picture, Charlie?" Manfred's tone became soft and persuasive, and Charlie found himself responding to the sudden gentleness in that normally cold voice.

"Yes, I've heard trees rustling, horses, the clink of a harness. Sometimes steel clashing, and rain."

"Never the king's voice?"

"No, never."

Manfred came and stood on the other side of his desk. Placing his hands on the edge, he leaned close to Charlie and asked, "Do you know why you can't hear the king, Charlie?"

"It's the shadow," Charlie replied quietly.

"More than a shadow, Charlie. That dark form is my ancestor Borlath, the elder son of the king. And, Charlie, he's come back!"

"What?" Charlie sat up. "What do you mean?" A wave of fear washed over him.

"My great-grandfather conducted a most interesting experiment. He was helped by your great-aunts and, of course, me. We found the bones of Borlath's horse, you see, and most important of all, his heart."

"Borlath's heart?" breathed Charlie.

"His heart." Manfred brought his face so close, Charlie could see the deep-blue veins that threaded the hypnotist's eyelids. "It was in a casket, beneath a gravestone marked with a 'B.' To tell the truth, it was Asa who found it. He likes to do a bit of digging when he's — not himself — if you get my meaning."

"I do." Charlie looked away from Manfred's looming face.

"The horse came to life," Manfred continued, "in my great-grandfather's attic laboratory. And so did the heart. They became fused, as it were, and crashed through the wall — you can see the hole from outside if you look up. So now there's a horse on the grounds, with a savage heart, and it's after you."

"Me?" Charlie jumped to his feet, and his chair crashed onto the floor.

"I just thought you ought to know." Manfred spread his hands. "Because if you step out of line, the horse will be only too willing to punish you. By that, I mean that hooves can inflict very nasty injuries."

Charlie refused to give Manfred the satisfaction of seeing how scared he was. He shrugged his shoulders and said, "I think I ought to go to bed now."

"Of course." Manfred swung the bookcase open and Charlie hurriedly left the room. He could still feel Manfred's mocking gaze as he stepped into the hall and hastened up to the dormitories without once looking behind him.

Up on the fourth floor, Billy Raven lay on a narrow white bed at the end of the infirmary. It was a very long room, and not one of the other fifteen beds was occupied. The awful stomach cramps had receded, but Billy was left with no doubt that they would return if he so much as whispered about his new home. Had he really broken an oath by giving the black button to Gabriel? And how did the oaths know?

Matron looked in and told Billy that tomorrow he would be returning to the Passing House. "A little break from your friends is desirable," she said in her chilly voice. "It'll help you to sort things out, Billy." She left without giving him a word of comfort or even a sooth-ing glass of milk.

Billy stared into the gathering darkness, unable to sleep. A full moon sailed into the sky, its brilliance fall-ing through the uncurtained window. Billy heard nails clicking across the floorboards toward him. A familiar voice said, "Billy sick?"

"Blessed." Billy put his hand down and stroked the dog's wrinkled head. *Did it count,* he wondered, *if you told a dog the things you could tell no one else?*

"Horse," grunted Blessed. "In garden."

"Horse?" Billy sat up.

"Ghost horse," said Blessed.

Billy got out of bed and ran to the window. The horse stood right below him, not a disappearing, shadowy creature this time, but very real. Its coat was a dazzling white in the moonlight, and every hair of its thick mane and tail shimmered like threads of silver.

Billy opened the window and looked down at the horse. It met his gaze and spoke. "Child," it said. "My child."

"Help me," said Billy.

THE JAILBIRD

Charlie found the black button on Friday at the end of lunch break. Gabriel had thrown it farther than they had thought, because it was lying between two stones paving the inside of the great arch into the castle.

As Charlie thrust the button into his pocket, a voice said, "What's that, Bone?" Asa Pike was peering around the side of the arch.

"What's what?" asked Charlie innocently.

"You picked something up."

"Oh, that!" Charlie put his hand in his pocket and found that by a stroke of luck he'd left a marble in it. "It's just a marble." He pulled it out and held it up to the light. "See! We were playing here yesterday and it rolled into a crack. I thought I'd never get it out."

Asa eyed the marble suspiciously. "Where did you get it?"

"Can't remember. I've had it for ages. It's a kind of mascot."

"Hmmm." Asa turned away. The prefect's strange stride always gave Charlie the creeps, and he had an unpleasant vision of Asa's beast shape digging away in the ruins. *Where did he find the heart?* Charlie wondered. And did they know for certain that it was Borlath's?

Charlie gave an involuntary shiver and left the ruin. As he slipped the marble into his pocket, his fingers touched the black button, and it brought him a surge of hope. Maybe, at last, he was getting close to finding his father.

While they were standing in line for the school bus that afternoon, Charlie asked Gabriel to meet him at the Pets' Café on Saturday. "I've found the button," whispered Charlie. "Can you try it again, Gabriel?"

Gabriel gave one of his enigmatic shrugs. "I'm not sure I want to meet that horse again."

"The button's got nothing to do with the horse," said Charlie. "Trust me. I'll explain tomorrow."

"You'd better," said Fidelio. "And you still haven't told us why you were late for bed last night."

"All will be revealed," Charlie promised.

• • •

Uncle Paton had lately acquired the habit of ordering delicious food from a fancy store in the city. An inheritance from one of his mother's wealthy French relatives had made this possible, but he made sure that everyone at number nine should benefit from his good fortune.

Of course, it only gave the Yewbeam sisters yet another reason to hate their brother. But while Grandma Bone privately seethed, she couldn't help enjoying the delicacies. Grizelda Bone loved good food, especially foie gras and caviar. Today, while Paton, Maisie, and Julia Ingledew sat in the kitchen, eating venison pie, Grandma Bone reclined in the living room with her own jar of caviar, a plate of melba toast, and a glass of port. She didn't like eating with visitors, especially Miss Ingledew, whom she imagined was chasing her brother, though anyone could have told her that it was the other way around.

"Wow!" exclaimed Charlie when he entered the

kitchen. "What a fantastic smell. Can I have some of whatever it is that's making it?"

Uncle Paton cut him a large slice of pie, and Maisie pushed a pot of chutney in his direction.

"Try some. It beats the usual stuff," said Maisie with a wink. "It's got rum in it."

Charlie noticed that his uncle was wearing a new jacket. "Are you going somewhere special?" he asked.

Paton put a finger to his lips. "Shhh! We don't want a certain person to know about it."

"Actually, we planned to take you with us," said Julia under her breath.

No more was said on the subject, and although Charlie was burning with curiosity, he realized that everyone was waiting for Grandma Bone to fall asleep. A few minutes later, Amy Bone got back from work and joined everyone in the kitchen. Charlie was asked to take the bottle of port into the living room.

"Charlie — how nice — s'more port?"

Charlie found it hard not to smile at Grandma

Bone's slurred speech. She had clearly drunk more than one glass of port already. He carefully refilled her glass and asked if she'd like some venison pie.

"Pie — mmm — nice." Grandma Bone smacked her lips and lifted her feet onto the sofa.

Charlie returned to the kitchen, put a slice of pie on a plate, and covered it with lots of rum and apricot chutney. "She's nodding off," he said softly.

Ten minutes later, they heard loud snores coming from the living room.

"She'll be out for hours," said Maisie. "I'd go now if I were you."

"Where are you going?" asked Amy.

"Ah . . . to a house quite near here," Paton told her. "And we'd like to take Charlie."

"Why?" asked Amy. "It's . . . it's not dangerous, is it?"

"Oh, Mom. Of course not," said Charlie, who had no idea whether it was dangerous or not.

"How do you know?" his mother gave Paton a wary look.

Paton scratched his head. "Well, it shouldn't be

dangerous." He consulted a note that he'd pulled out of his top pocket. "It's only a few blocks away, and as far as I know, it's a very quiet neighborhood."

"As far as you know," muttered Amy. "Paton, you're always going somewhere dangerous."

"Mom, please," Charlie begged.

"We have to meet a relative of Billy Raven's," explained Miss Ingledew. "The poor man's in a bad way. He has to send Paton's letters to me in case they get into the wrong hands."

Amy gave a grudging smile. "All right, Charlie."

It was still not dark enough for Uncle Paton to risk an appearance outside, but after waiting for another half hour, an obliging black cloud began to cover the sky. By the time the small expedition left number nine, heavy raindrops fell into the street.

Uncle Paton opened a large blue umbrella, which covered him and Miss Ingledew but left Charlie catching most of the drops. Unconcerned, Charlie ran ahead. Following the road down to the park, he turned left as he'd been instructed. Here, an avenue of tall plane trees gave him some protection from the rain, which had become very heavy. He walked on for another half a kilometer until Uncle Paton shouted, "Take a right, Charlie. It's number fifteen."

Charlie rounded a corner onto a road that could almost have been described as a country lane. Leafy boughs swept over the pavement, and most of the houses were hidden behind tall hedges or overgrown shrubs.

The gate of number fifteen was badly in need of a coat of paint, and one hinge was missing. Charlie could hardly see the house — it was covered in ivy and white roses. A delicious scent wafted out from the garden, and Miss Ingledew declared that it was the most wonderful aroma in the world.

"I'll have to get it bottled for you," said Uncle Paton fondly.

They pushed open the rickety gate and walked up the path to a white door. There was no bell or knocker, so Charlie pulled a brass chain that hung at the side of the door. A chime could be heard, sounding inside the house.

The next moment, Alice Angel was standing on the doorstep. "Charlie, you came, too," she said. "Oh, I'm so glad."

Charlie was speechless. No one had told him they were going to see Alice Angel. He was rather confused. But Uncle Paton and Miss Ingledew stepped into the house and introduced themselves as though Alice were a perfectly normal person, so Charlie decided to follow them.

Alice took their damp coats and jackets and led them into a pretty living room. Because so much greenery covered the windows, the room was rather dark, and Alice immediately reached for the light switch.

"Stop!" cried Paton.

His cry came too late. The lights in the small chandelier hanging in the center of the room exploded one by one, and a shower of glass fell onto the carpet, missing Alice by centimeters.

"I'm so, so sorry," Paton apologized. "I should have warned you. How thoughtless. How remiss. Oh dear!"

"My fault entirely," said Alice. "It's too dark in here. I'll get the dustpan while you talk to Christopher."

Charlie stared into the gloom, trying to locate Christopher, while Uncle Paton and Miss Ingledew argued with Alice about who should sweep up the broken glass. Alice insisted that her visitors should make themselves comfortable while she fetched a dustpan.

As they took their seats, a quiet chuckle came from a corner of the room, then a voice said, "So, Mr. Yewbeam, you're a power-booster. I've always wanted to meet one."

Everyone peered into the corner and eventually made out a small scrawny man with thinning hair and ill-fitting clothes. The stranger got up and came toward them, extending his hand. "Christopher Crowquill," he said. "I know who you are."

While they all shook hands, Alice came back with

a dustpan and brush, which Paton immediately grabbed. He began to sweep the floor, and Alice returned to the kitchen for cake and candles. When they were all sitting comfortably in the candlelit room, the cakes were passed around and Christopher Crowquill questioned Charlie about Billy Raven.

"Billy's ill, Mr. Crowquill," said Charlie.

"Ill?" Christopher looked alarmed.

"He'd just shown us a button he'd found, and then suddenly he was rolling about in agony. He kept mumbling about an oath and how he hadn't broken it. He was taken to the infirmary and I haven't seen him since."

"The oaths are deadly!" Christopher declared. "Florence keeps a bag full of them. They're mostly signed by people who've borrowed money. Unfortunately, once an oath has been signed Florence never returns it, even when the money has been repaid. If anyone breaks an oath, they experience a torturous pain. Sometimes, the agony is so great the victim is crippled for life. The paper is dipped in poison and then imbued with what I've been led to believe is a vicious spirit. They've made Billy sign an oath, I'll bet my life on it."

"So that's why he was too scared to tell me anything," said Charlie thoughtfully. "But I think I know the name of his new home. He called it the Passing House."

"The Passing House!" Christopher clapped his hand to his forehead. "Dear me. The Passing House could never be described as a home. The Bloors use it for occasional guests: people who need somewhere to hide or others whom the Bloors want to hide. If Usher de Grey is involved, then Billy won't be able to leave the place until Usher chooses to let him go. Oh, the poor child. I must help him."

"But how can Usher keep the boy a prisoner?" asked Miss Ingledew indignantly.

"My dear, he can create a force field." Christopher gazed at his knotted, careworn hands and shook his head. "He is powerfully endowed, that man, and most unpleasant. Poor Billy will never be able to break away. Usher's invisible wall is stronger than iron."

This information made everyone feel so gloomy, there was utter silence in the room until Uncle Paton suddenly said, "The button, Charlie. What's its significance?"

Charlie explained that Billy had found the button in the Passing House and was curious to know if it could tell him anything. "We've got this friend, Gabriel," he told Alice and Christopher, who were both looking puzzled. "Gabriel can feel things. He can see things too if he wears someone else's clothes. It gives him a lot of grief, so he steers clear of old clothes and stuff most of the time. At first, we didn't think it would work with a button, because you can't put it on, can you? But then it did work."

There was an expectant hush, eventually broken by Uncle Paton, who said, "And . . . ?"

"And . . ." Charlie was unexpectedly embarrassed.

"He saw a man with dark hair, trapped inside walls of glass — mirrors — and he heard a piano, but he couldn't see it. And then . . . and then . . ." Charlie described the terrifying experience of the ghost horse and the dreadful experiment in Ezekiel's laboratory.

The room was immediately filled with exclamations of horror and consternation. In fact, the outraged voices became so loud and fierce, Charlie felt overwhelmed and he begged to be allowed out for a breath of air.

Alice showed him the back door, and Charlie stepped into a calm ocean of flowers. It had stopped raining at last and a wonderful steamy scent filled the garden.

"Phew! And I never told them the horse was after me," Charlie murmured.

The sight of a real gypsy caravan took his mind off his immediate problems, and he waded through the flowers until he reached a set of wooden steps leading up to the caravan door. He was about to climb the steps when a movement at the end of the garden caught his eye. To his surprise, he saw Olivia staring at him from the top of a high wall.

"Liv!" he called. "Olivia. What are you doing here?"

Olivia dropped down on the other side.

"Be like that, then!" called Charlie. Leaping over the rain-soaked plants, he came to the wall and called again, "Liv, are you there? What are you doing?" Charlie hauled himself up to the top of the wall and looked into another garden, this one rather bereft of flowers. The smooth green lawn swept up to a large white house that Charlie immediately recognized. The house belonged to the Vertigos. Alice Angel was Olivia's neighbor. How odd that Olivia didn't know her.

There was no sign of Olivia, so Charlie dropped down from the wall, picked up a shiny red apple, and went back inside the house.

"Ah, you've found an apple." Alice beamed at Charlie when he walked in. "Those apples are so good."

Things had calmed down a bit, although Uncle Paton and Christopher Crowquill were now discussing something in a quiet but agitated way.

"I saw my friend Olivia," Charlie told Alice. "I didn't know she lived on the other side of your wall. She wouldn't speak to me."

"She's having a crisis," Alice said gravely. "It sometimes happens when people fight against their true nature. I hope she accepts things soon. It will make such a difference — to all of you."

"Really?" Charlie was baffled. "How do you . . . I mean, are you endowed, Miss Angel?"

"Alice, please." Her green eyes twinkled. "Yes. I am endowed."

Charlie would have liked to ask her a few questions, but at that moment, Uncle Paton stood and, brushing the cake crumbs off his trousers, said, "We must go!"

As they took their leave, Christopher Crowquill thanked his visitors and warmly shook their hands. "I can't tell you what your visit means to me," he said. "I have few friends left in this ill-starred city. And being a jailbird has taught me who they are. Alice Angel is true to her name. She has been an angel. Not one week passed during my long incarceration that she didn't visit me. She gave me hope and now she has given me shelter. But I beg you to keep my whereabouts a secret or she will be in as much danger as I am."

They swore never to tell a soul about their visit, Uncle Paton more vehemently than anyone. "We'll be in touch," he said to Christopher. "Don't give up hope."

The white door closed firmly behind Paton as he followed Charlie and Miss Ingledew down the path. The street was deserted, but Christopher was taking no chances.

The streetlights had come on, and although it had stopped raining, Uncle Paton took the precaution of hiding his head under the umbrella, just in case he had another accident. The umbrella covered Julia as well, so neither of them saw the odd gray shape that darted into the shrubbery on the other side of the park railings. Charlie wasn't sure that he'd seen it either, but he became more and more convinced that he had seen it, and that it wasn't a fox or a dog but a gray misshapen beast. Spying was Asa Pike's favorite occupation, so if he had followed them, number fifteen Park Avenue was now a marked house.

Charlie told himself that Asa couldn't possibly have guessed why he and his uncle were visiting Alice Angel. By the time they had reached Filbert Street, he felt reassured, but there was something he needed to know, and he asked his uncle why Mr. Crowquill had called the city ill-starred.

"I imagine that for him the place is ill-starred because he was sent to prison," said Uncle Paton. "That's a terrible thing to happen when you're innocent."

"No, it's more than that," said Julia quietly. "Think of all the tragedies that have happened on this ground, right from the start when the Red King's children began to kill each other. I've more than a hundred ancient books that describe the eternal struggle that has been going on here through the centuries. Good people struck down and evil prevailing." She smiled. "But I still love the city. I think it's because, to survive among all those dark deeds, the good have to be that much brighter and that much stronger."

Charlie thought of his father, struck down and lost because he tried to fight the Bloors. "You found *The Book of Amadis*," he said. "Do you think it was my father who Gabriel saw caught in the Castle of Mirrors? I know he had dark hair, and I know he's trapped somewhere, and then there's the piano music."

"I can't say, Charlie," Julia said gently. "But it's possible."

They had reached number nine, and Paton folded the umbrella while Charlie ran ahead to turn off the hall light and any others that might be at risk.

Grandma Bone had woken up. "Where've you all been?" she called from the living room.

"Walking," said Paton.

"Walking? Is that woman here again?"

"If you mean Julia, yes, she's here," said Paton angrily. "We're going to have a cup of tea, and then I'm walking her home."

"You'd better watch out for the lights." His sister gave a nasty cackle.

"I don't think I'll have any tea," Julia said quickly.

"Emma went home with a friend, but she'll be back soon."

As Uncle Paton escorted Miss Ingledew down the steps, she called back, "Emma's got a new pet, Charlie."

"What is it?" he asked.

"You'll find out tomorrow," said Miss Ingledew, taking Paton's arm. "When she brings it to the Pets' Café."

THE PASSING HOUSE

Charlie ran almost all the way to the Pets' Café. He had Runner Bean's leash in his pocket and an excellent plan in his head. The city was full of Saturday shoppers and this slowed Charlie down.

He turned onto Frog Street at the same time as Dorcas Loom and her two older brothers. Albert and Alfred Loom were broad, pugnacious-looking youths. They enjoyed robbing backpacks, tormenting cats, and tripping up skateboarders. They were also the proud owners of four rottweilers, which gained them admission to the Pets' Café. Dorcas usually waited on a bench outside. She was afraid of animals, and Charlie often wondered how she managed to live with two such aggressive creatures — not to mention the rottweilers.

With a quick "Hi!" Charlie dashed ahead of the Looms and bounded into the Pets' Café.

"What's up, Charlie?" said Norton. "Are you being chased by the headless horseman or what?"

"You'll find out in a minute," said Charlie.

He saw Emma's blond head in the distance, and leaving Norton to face the Looms, he made his way over to her. He was surprised to find that the table was full. Lysander and his parrot, Homer, had turned up. Tancred sat beside him with one of Gabriel's gerbils, and Gabriel was feeding Billy's black rat, Rembrandt.

"Charlie, sit here!" Fidelio made space for Charlie, as his deaf cat clung to his shoulder.

As soon as Charlie sat down, Runner Bean, who'd been asleep under the table, leaped onto his lap, giving the table such a shake it tipped to one side, sending several plates and glasses crashing to the floor.

There were cries of "That dog!" "Can't you control him, Charlie?" "I was enjoying that cake!" "There goes my juice!" while Charlie yelled, "No one told me Runner was under the table."

Almost simultaneously, the Loom boys arrived,

causing an even greater commotion with their rottweilers. The four big dogs began snapping at any small creature that had the bad luck to be within biting range.

The noise in the café was so loud that Mr. Onimous had to jump on a table and shout, "Quiet, please! Unruly behavior is not acceptable in this establishment."

Homer, Lysander's parrot, squawked, "Well said, sir!"

At which Alfred Loom shouted, "What's your problem, darling?"

Mr. Onimous stared at the youth in disbelief. "I beg your pardon?" he said.

"I said, 'What's your problem?'" Alfred repeated.

Pulling himself up to his full height of four feet eleven inches (plus the table, which made him six feet five inches), Mr. Onimous replied, "Consider the smaller animals, sir. You can see how frightened they are. Your dogs create mayhem every time they bring you in here."

"It wasn't us, it was him." Albert Loom pointed at

Charlie. "Him and that crazy yeller dog. He's bigger than ours."

Runner Bean gave a deep-throated bark and rushed at the rottweilers, while Homer squawked, "Get 'em!"

A terrible fight ensued. Several other dogs couldn't resist joining in and the uproar was deafening. Screeching birds flew up to the ceiling, cats shrieked, snakes practically strangled themselves, donkeys jumped on strangers, and an iguana ran out the door. Anything smaller just hid.

Norton was badly bitten when he tried to separate the dogs, and Charlie was knocked to the ground by a terrified Shetland pony, just as he grabbed Runner Bean's collar.

Mrs. Onimous jumped up beside her husband (thus making herself eight feet six inches) and began to bang an empty cookie tin. Her head was now touching the ceiling, and you might have thought the sight of such a huge person would subdue the mob. Not today. Only the sound of an approaching siren made any impact. As soon as the Looms heard the siren, they pulled their dogs out of the fight and left the café. Two minutes later, Officer Wood and Officer Singh arrived on the scene. Things had calmed down considerably by then, but Mr. and Mrs. Onimous were still standing on the table.

Officer Singh crunched his way over the broken dishes and addressed the proprietor. "Could we have a word, sir?" he asked Mr. Onimous. "In private."

Mr. Onimous jumped off the table, and when he had helped his wife down in as dignified a manner as possible, the couple disappeared into the kitchen with the two policemen. Norton, whose hands were bleeding profusely, limped after them.

"The Looms were off like lightning when they heard that siren," Tancred remarked.

"And they caused all the trouble," added Emma. "It's not fair."

Charlie had managed to haul Runner Bean back to the table, and everyone made a great fuss over him for being so brave. Homer even shouted, "Croix de Guerre!" although no one knew what it meant.

"It's a French medal for bravery," Lysander explained. "He learned that from Mom."

They shared the cookies that were left on the table while they waited for Mr. and Mrs. Onimous to reappear. Several of the noisier animals had left, and it was now quiet enough for Charlie to hear a distinct and persistent quacking coming from somewhere. He looked down and saw a white duck sitting under Emma's chair. "So it's a duck," he said. "Your aunt told me you'd got a new pet."

"She flew into our yard yesterday," said Emma. "I named her Nancy, after my mother. She died, you know."

"Yes, of course. She's a very nice duck." Charlie couldn't think what else to say.

"No Olivia again," Fidelio observed. "What's the matter with her, Em?"

Emma shrugged. "I don't know. She hardly talks to me now, and when she does, she's always in a bad mood."

"She looks a mess," said Lysander.

"And she used to look fantastic," Tancred added sadly.

Charlie thought it was about time he told them about Alice Angel and the flower store. "I think Olivia's endowed," he said. "But she won't admit it. She even heard the ghost horse, and as far as I know, only the endowed can hear it."

Fidelio agreed. He had never seen, heard, or sensed the horse, even while the others were cowering away from it.

Lysander demanded to know more about the ghost horse, so Charlie brought him up to date, adding the details of Ezekiel's horrible experiment.

"A heart!" cried Tancred, when Charlie had finished. "That is so gross!"

"There's more." Without mentioning Christopher Crowquill, Charlie went on to tell his friends about Billy Raven and the dreadful talents of his new parents.

"So now you're going to risk your life, and maybe

ours, trying to rescue Silly Billy, is that it?" asked Tancred.

"That's about it," said Charlie. "But Billy isn't silly. He's just had a lot of bad luck."

"I'll say," Gabriel muttered grimly.

It seemed a good time to mention the button again. Charlie held it out to Gabriel and begged him to "visit" the world of mirrors just once more. "Maybe if you listen to the piano again, you'll recognize the music. Anything that could tell me a bit more about that place — and the man trapped there!"

Gabriel took the button with a sigh and, once again, held it over his heart. He closed his eyes, and they all watched in silence as his brow furrowed and his long face took on a look of solemn concentration. Now and again, a shudder passed through his body, and his mouth gave a small twitch. After five minutes had passed, Gabriel opened his eyes and dropped the button onto the table.

"Rachmaninoff," he said. "*Prelude in C.* And it's a record — one of those old 78s that scratch."

"And the man?" asked Charlie.

"His face was all distorted. There were so many mirrors — details kept breaking up. Sorry, Charlie."

But Charlie wasn't too disappointed. He had the name of the music now. It was something to go on.

Chatter in the café sank to a whisper as Officer Singh and Officer Wood came out of the kitchen and left the café. A few moments later, Mr. Onimous appeared and announced that they were closing for the day. Norton had to be taken to the hospital for stitches and a tetanus shot.

When Charlie and his friends got up to leave, Mr. Onimous came over to their table. "Sorry, kids," he said. "We won't be open tomorrow. Norton's in a bad way and my poor wife has got the shakes. The police have warned us that our precious café might be closed down. Those Loom boys make trouble whenever they come here and people are complaining."

"You should ban the dogs, Mr. Onimous," said Lysander. "My father would advise it."

"Your father might be a judge, but he doesn't know anything about running pets' cafés," said Mr. Onimous gravely. "I can't start banning dogs, young Lysander. Owners maybe, but not dogs." He leaned over the table and picked up the black rat. "I'd better take him back to the kitchen. He misses Billy something terrible, you know."

"Billy's coming to visit him very soon." Charlie sounded more confident than he felt. "Thing is, Mr. Onimous, I need to find a place called the Passing House."

"Whatever for?" Mr. Onimous asked, looking surprised.

Charlie told him about Billy's adoption, and as he listened, Mr. Onimous' wise, whiskery face became furrowed with concern. "Grief! Grief! And more of it," he declared. "What's happened to the world when a boy can't lead a carefree life? The Passing House is in Crook's Passage, Charlie. Up by the cathedral in the old part of the city. But look out! I wouldn't want to cross swords with those de Greys."

"I'll take Runner," said Charlie, fastening the leash to Runner Bean's collar.

"You're not going without me," said Fidelio.

"And I'll be walking that way, too." Emma tucked Nancy into a lidded basket.

Gabriel, Tancred, and Lysander lived in the opposite direction, on a wooded hill called the Heights. But they all wanted to be contacted if help were needed. Tancred's blond hair was sizzling with electricity, and little breezes kept whipping around their ankles as they walked up Frog Street.

"I've got a nasty feeling about all this," Tancred said. "Storm's on standby, Charlie."

"And that goes for my ancestors," said Lysander.

When they reached High Street, the three older boys turned right, while Charlie, Fidelio, and Emma took a left turn toward the cathedral. Once again, a heavy mist had begun to thread its way through the city. But this was not the gentle mist of yesterday. It was more like vapor that came from deep under the earth: Chilly and sinister, it thickened with every step that the three friends took closer to the cathedral.

As they passed Ingledew's bookstore, Emma went in and put Nancy's basket by the counter. Her aunt was talking to a customer, so Emma gave a cheerful wave and said, "Back soon!" then hopped out again. At this point, Fidelio ran in and laid his elderly cat on top of the basket.

"Won't be long," Fidelio told the bemused Miss Ingledew.

When Fidelio came out of the store, he noticed three bright creatures approaching through the mist. "Did you know the Flames were following us?" he asked Charlie.

Charlie looked back at the three gleaming cats. "They must have a reason," he said. "They always do. Hi there, Aries! Hi, Sagittarius and Leo!"

The cats replied to his greeting with deep, friendly meows. Runner Bean gave a warning bark but the cats didn't take offense. When the small party set off again, they followed at a discreet distance, respecting the big dog's instincts.

Beyond the cathedral, the city became a maze of narrow passages and damp, shadowy steps. The street signs were cracked and faded, some of them almost illegible. To find Crook's Passage, Charlie had to take several steps into the darkest alley he'd yet come across.

"It's here," he said in a low voice.

"Gloomy place," Fidelio remarked, following cautiously.

"It smells awful." Emma wrinkled her nose.

They began the steep ascent, stumbling over sudden steps as they peered into the dimness ahead. Runner Bean kept up a continual whine, which put everyone's nerves on edge. The cats bounded past the children and led the way, their bright coats glowing in the mist.

After walking under two rusty signs, Charlie eventually found the words "THE PASSING HOUSE" carved in stone above a tall oak door.

"What are you going to say?" asked Emma as Charlie reached for the knocker, a large brass hand.

"I'll say 'Where's Billy?' That should be enough," said Charlie.

However, when the door finally opened after several knocks, Charlie's speech deserted him, for the man standing in the doorway gave him such a ferocious glare, it took his breath away.

"What do you want?" the man asked tersely.

Charlie gulped and Fidelio said, "We'd like to see Billy, sir."

"Billy?" the man looked outraged. "Billy?"

"He does live here, doesn't he?" asked Emma.

"Go away," shouted the man. He began to close the door but Charlie put his foot on the threshold. At the same moment, Runner Bean saw a black cat dart across the hall behind the man. With a joyous bark, Runner Bean leaped after it, or rather he tried to, because something slammed into his nose and sent him howling backward.

"What did you do to my dog?" cried Charlie.

Usher de Grey kicked Charlie's foot away and slammed the door.

"He's in there," whispered Emma. "I'm sure he is. Poor Billy."

"He's in there, all right," said Charlie. "That was the man I saw at Bloor's, the man who doesn't like kids."

"Now what?" asked Fidelio.

Runner Bean's anguished howling made it difficult for Charlie to think. Banging your nose on something you can't see is very frightening for a dog, and Charlie didn't know how to describe a force field in animal language. Only Billy could do that.

"I'll think of something." Charlie sounded as cheerful as he could.

They were all reluctant to leave the Passing House while Billy was still trapped inside, but there was nothing else they could do. Another plan would have to be made.

As Charlie stepped out of Crook's Passage, he

looked back. The Flames hadn't moved. They were sitting in a row outside the door of the Passing House. Maybe they held the key to Billy's escape.

Billy had been watching his TV when he heard the dog. At first, the sound was only a series of anguished howls, but then Billy began to recognize Runner Bean's voice and to understand his dog talk.

"Ghost gate!" barked Runner Bean. "Ice wall! Fire wall! Hurting gate! Cat's trick! Pain! Charlie, help!"

Billy jumped up and ran to the window. All he could see through the thick mist was a gray stone wall. His window was locked and he had no means of opening it. He went into the passage outside his room and tiptoed onto the landing. Looking down into the hall, he arrived just in time to see Usher de Grey slam the front door. Billy ran back into the passageway and stood with his back pressed to the wall, hardly daring to breathe. Charlie was outside, but would his visit cause trouble? The thought of more pain made Billy close his eyes in dread.

"Billy!" said a soft voice.

Billy opened his eyes and saw the small black cat at his feet. "Friends," she said in the smallest of voices.

Billy crept back to his room, followed by the cat. Without making a sound, he carefully closed the door.

"Sorry for hurting dog," said the cat. "Clawdia had to show Billy's friend the danger. Had to show Usher's secret wall. Please tell dog Clawdia is sorry."

"I'll tell him if I ever see him again," said Billy.

"My friends are here," the little cat went on. "They stay. They help Billy to leave. Tonight, Billy must be ready."

"Tonight?" Billy shook his head fearfully. And yet the longing to escape was so great, the thought of freedom was so intoxicating, that he began to laugh with excitement.

"Shhh!" hushed the cat. "Not yet."

"Where will I go?" asked Billy. "If I leave here."

"Friends show you."

"Who are your friends?"

"Cats, naturally. Copper coat, orange coat, golden coat."

"The Flames!" gasped Billy.

"Flames, yes. Clawdia will go now."

Billy opened the door, and the black cat stepped into the hallway. "Don't forget," she said. "Tonight!"

"How could I forget?" Billy whispered.

BREAKING THE FORCE FIELD

Billy always ate dinner alone in his room. When he finished, he would take his tray down to the kitchen, and there he would do all the dishes while the de Greys sat at the table, working on their accounts.

On the night that Billy was hoping to escape, he noticed that Florence had a pile of forms before her. She leafed through the papers, licking her thumb and smiling with satisfaction.

Oaths, thought Billy. He realized that somehow he would have to destroy his own oaths if he were ever to truly escape from the de Greys. But where was the bag with the oaths kept? He would have to find out.

Billy dried the last plate and put it in the china cabinet. "Good night, Mom! Good night, Dad," he said. (He found it impossible to call them by their first names, as they had demanded.) "Thank you for my nice dinner," he added.

"What was it?" asked Florence, without looking up.

"A sandwich," said Billy.

"Anything in it?" asked Usher.

Billy had to think hard about that one. "I think it was margarine," he said.

"Has the pain gone, dear?" Florence gave him a cursory glance.

"Yes, thank you, Mom."

"Let's hope you don't get ill again," said Florence, checking off one of the papers.

"Yes. Good night."

Neither of the de Greys paid Billy any attention as he left the kitchen. He walked across the tiled hall, telling his feet to behave the way they normally did, but his head was in such turmoil, he couldn't even remember how he used to walk. Once he reached the stairs, he took the steps two at a time, eager to make preparations for the night ahead.

The de Greys never looked in on Billy at night, but just in case, he wore his pajamas over his everyday clothes. Instead of getting into bed, he crept onto the landing and waited for Florence to leave the kitchen. At seven o'clock, she came out carrying the gray bag. Billy stepped into the shadows as she crossed the hall and went into a small office on the other side. She came back out without the bag.

Billy tiptoed back to his room. Leaving the door slightly ajar, he took off his glasses, laid them on his bedside table, and then got into bed. It was the longest night he could remember. The cathedral clock struck twelve, then one and two and three. Having given up all hope of rescue, Billy fell into a fitful sleep.

While Billy slept, the night clouds rolled away revealing a sky of soft, pearl gray. The city was still swaddled in mist; only the roofs of the tallest buildings could be seen from above, their wet slate shining in the dawn light.

From the mass of yellow leaves that crowned an ash tree, an orange cat emerged. With amazing agility it leaped onto a roof several feet away. It was followed by a yellow cat and then another cat, the color of a dark flame. The three cats sped over the rooftops until they came to an open skylight. One after another, the cats dropped into an empty room at the top of the Passing House.

Usher de Grey was so confident of his force field that he never bothered to lock any doors. The Flame cats had no trouble making their way down through the house, but they were aware that the place was laced with a dangerous magic. For them, however, breaking a force field was as easy as stepping through paper.

The little black cat was waiting for her friends on the landing. "I will fetch the boy," she said.

Billy woke up with a start when Clawdia jumped on his bed.

"Time to go, Billy!" she whispered. He rubbed his eyes and put on his glasses. Then, slipping out of bed, he took off his pajamas. Suddenly, the enormity of what he was about to do made him shiver with apprehension. He looked around the room, at the TV, the computer, the books, and the games, all his if he stayed here forever. He was stepping into the unknown on the word of a small black cat. Could he trust her?

When he saw the Flame cats Billy's nerves were soothed by their comforting purrs and warm colors. Now, he felt he could do anything.

Florence and Usher de Grey slept very soundly, proving that the old saying, "The wicked never sleep," can hardly be true. When Billy and the cats passed their bedroom, they dozed on, happily enjoying the sort of dreams that most people would consider nightmares.

In the cats' extraordinary glow, Billy could actually see Usher's force field. Sparkling blue lines were strung across the hall like the threads of a giant cobweb. The blue lines were especially thick where they covered the doors, and Billy's heart sank when he saw the door to the room where Florence had left the oaths.

The cats leaped neatly down the stairs, and when they reached the first blue strand, they bounded through it, leaving the broken strings hanging limply in the air.

"Come, Billy. It's safe!" said Aries.

Billy ran down into the hall and carefully followed the cats' passage through the force field. "Before I leave I must go into that room." He pointed to the office.

The three cats turned their golden gaze toward the door. It was Sagittarius, the yellow cat, who moved first. Standing on his hind legs, he tore at the threads covering the office door. Billy reached for the handle and the door opened. The gray bag was standing on the floor, just inside. When Billy picked it up, he found that the clasp came undone as soon as he pressed it. Florence obviously relied on her husband's power to guard the collection of oaths.

Billy quickly searched through the papers in the bag, and finding the forms that he had signed, he pulled them out. He was tucking them down his sweater when he felt the cats' eyes upon him. He looked up, realizing what they wanted him to do.

"I should take them all, shouldn't I?" he said. "So they will all be free."

"Yes, Billy," the cats replied in unison. "All."

"Make haste," added Leo. "Soon they will wake."

As he ran from the room, Billy put his forms back in the gray bag, then tucked it under his arm. The Flames were already tearing at the threads that covered the front door. When they had broken every strand, Billy seized the handle. An eerie wail echoed through the house as he wrenched open the door, and the black cat called, "Fly, my friends. He is waking."

Billy lunged through the door with Usher's furious roar ringing in his ears. "The kid's out! Get up! Get up!"

Racing over the rough stones of Crook's Passage, Billy was glad to have the Flames' luminous glow show him the way, but he was still terribly afraid. Where was he to go now? And how would he get there?

"Courage," said Leo, running beside him.

Sagittarius, the brightest, bounded ahead, while Aries brought up the rear, turning his head every now and again to observe the dark alley behind them.

Now they were out on the main road and running toward the cathedral. As they sped across the cobblestoned square, the clock in the great dome chimed five o'clock, and a flock of jackdaws rose, chattering into the dawn sky. Billy looked longingly at Ingledew's bookstore: He knew Emma Tolly lived there, but Leo warned, "Don't stop, Billy. It's not safe yet."

Down to High Street and through the city, Billy's heart was beating wildly. He began to think that if the oaths didn't kill him, then this journey surely would. The mutter of an engine could be heard coming closer, second by second. Without slowing his pace, Billy looked back and saw a gray car emerge from the mist behind him. The de Greys.

"This way!" Sagittarius commanded, darting into an alley.

How they reached the road to the Heights, Billy would never know. He had never been much of a runner, yet he hadn't stopped running since he left the Passing House. Had the cats lent him their strength as they guided him through the foggy streets?

Leo answered his unspoken question. "The Red King's strength, Billy."

When they began the steep climb up to the Heights, they passed a redbrick house with a high wall and tall, barred gate. "LOOM VILLA" said the sign on the gate. Billy was only a few yards away from the house when the gate burst open, and four black dogs erupted onto the road. Instead of running faster, Billy stopped, too terrified to move. The dogs' savage black eyes were fixed on him and their great jaws gaped, revealing long, murderous teeth.

The Flames surrounded Billy, hissing dangerously. The dogs lowered their heads and snarled.

"Keep moving, Billy," said Aries.

Billy shuffled backward, his trembling knees hardly supporting him. Just when he thought they might give way completely, a violent crack of thunder stopped the dogs in their tracks. A bolt of lightning lit the sky, and the black dogs raced for home, howling in terror.

"Now, Billy. Run for your life!" said Leo.

Billy could see headlights creeping through the fog, and clutching the bag of oaths, he ran. The road became steeper, but he didn't slacken his pace. His heart thumped, his head spun, and his legs shook but he was running for his life, and this time he couldn't stop. The car kept coming, closer and closer through the fog. Soon it would be upon them.

Rain splashed onto the road. Thunder rumbled overhead, and Billy's tears mingled with the raindrops coursing down his face. "I can't go faster than a car," he sobbed. "I can't. I can't. They're going to get me."

"No," growled Leo. He looked up as a ball of fire came hurtling out of the thundery sky. It hit the hood of the gray car with an earsplitting crack. The engine burst into flames.

Scarcely able to believe what he saw, Billy turned and sped up the hill. "It was Tancred, wasn't it?" he panted. "Tancred and his storms."

"The very same," Leo agreed.

The road curved sharply, and to Billy, hunched over the bag of oaths, it seemed like a spiral up into the sky. The rain was falling in sheets now, and borne on a sudden gust of wind, came a dreadful, threatening shriek. "You can't win, Billy Raven. Never, never, never." Florence de Grey was still on his trail. But without a car, the race was even.

With a burst of defiance, Billy bounded on up the hill, and as the wind intensified, he opened the gray bag and pulled out a handful of oaths. Holding them into the wind he let them fly away. Never had he felt as jubilant as he did now. He put his hand in the bag and released another sheaf of papers. Another and another, until the bag was empty and the air was full of fluttering, windblown papers. And Billy was sure he could hear the hopeful whispers of the tricked, dispossessed, and penniless people whose names were now being washed away by the rain.

"Good! Good!" the cats cheered.

With a big grin, Billy flung the gray bag into the

storm, and a distant voice called, "Foolish boy! You'll be punished for that! Just you wait!"

It wasn't often that Charlie woke up as early as six o'clock on a Sunday morning. In fact, he couldn't remember a single instance when he had. So he had to bring his watch right up close to his sleepy eyes. The chestnut tree outside his window was thrashing about in the wind and thunder rumbled in the distance. And then the doorbell rang.

Swinging his feet to the floor, Charlie dragged himself over to the window and looked out. He was very surprised to see a familiar SUV parked outside number nine. There, on the doorstep, stood a rather wet and impatient-looking man. It was Mr. Silk, Gabriel's father.

"Hello, Mr. Silk!" called Charlie.

"Ah, Charlie." Mr. Silk scratched the back of his neck as if he were not sure that he wanted to be doing what he was doing. "I've come to fetch you," he said.

"Fetch me?" Charlie was even more surprised.

"It seems —" began Mr. Silk.

He got no farther because the door was abruptly flung open by Grandma Bone. "What?" she said in her rude manner. Today, it sounded even ruder than usual.

"I've come—" Mr. Silk tried again.

Again he was cut short. "What time of day do you think this is?" demanded Grandma Bone.

Fully awake now, Charlie began to throw on various items of clothing. Maybe something had happened to Gabriel or another friend who lived on the Heights. Tancred or Lysander.

Charlie ran down to the hall where Grandma Bone was still lecturing Mr. Silk on the selfishness of waking people on Sunday morning. Mr. Silk was now completely soaked and looking very depressed.

"Ah, Charlie, let's go," he said, turning away from the tyrannical woman.

"What am I to tell his mother?" shouted Grandma Bone.

"Tell her I'm at Gabriel's," said Charlie, rapidly following Mr. Silk. He had noticed a container of Uncle Paton's favorite peanut yogurt poking out of his grandmother's bathrobe pocket, and just to put her in her place, he added, "I bet you got up early so you could finish off Uncle P.'s yogurt."

Grandma Bone shot Charlie a hateful look and slammed the door.

Charlie scrambled into the car, and Mr. Silk drove off. Thunder and lightning accompanied them all the way to the Heights, and with the noise of the engine and the rain drumming on the roof, Charlie had to shout to make himself heard.

"What's happened, Mr. Silk?" he asked.

"Difficult to say." Mr. Silk was very vague for a thriller writer. He resembled Gabriel, with his long face and forlorn expression. They even had the same overlong, floppy hair, though Mr. Silk's was a bit threadbare. He made up for this with a thick, drooping mustache. After some thought, he said, "There's a boy in Gabriel's gerbil house."

"What boy?"

"Little fella, white hair, glasses."

"Billy!" cried Charlie. "So he escaped!"

"Says he's got to see you. Gabriel begged me to come. Well, we couldn't sleep anyway with that storm going on. The storm boy, Tancred, says it'll calm down soon. It takes time apparently once he's got full-blooded thunder on the go. Understandable, I suppose."

"Yes." Charlie was impressed by Mr. Silk's understanding.

Half a mile past the gates of Loom Villa (where four rottweilers were barking their heads off), the SUV passed a wrecked car cordoned off with police signs. The hood had caved in, the paint was scorched, the windshield smashed, and the tires were just charred bits of rubber.

"Wow! That car looks as if it was struck by lightning!" said Charlie.

"It was," said Mr. Silk. "The driver is in the hospital, but his wife was unharmed, except that she seems to have gone completely nuts."

"Good idea for a thriller, huh, Mr. Silk?" Charlie asked.

"Mmm!" the thriller writer pulled his mustache pensively.

Charlie got a brief glimpse of Lysander's house as they passed a pair of tall wrought-iron gates. Lysander's father was the famous Judge Sage and the house reflected his important position.

"The boy is up at our place," Mr. Silk told Charlie. "And Tancred Torsson. We've never had so many visitors this early on a Sunday." He turned the SUV into an extremely muddy yard and pulled up before a dilapidated-looking house.

Charlie jumped out of the SUV straight into a deep puddle. He wished he'd remembered his boots but it was too late now. Mr. Silk pointed to the side of the house where a narrow path led to the field at the back. "They're all in the gerbil house," he said. "Don't ask me why."

"OK." Charlie trudged through the mud toward a large shed where Gabriel spent a lot of his spare time, breeding gerbils. The words "SILK'S GERBILS" had been painted in red across the door. Charlie could hear a low murmur coming from inside the shed, but this stopped as soon as he tried the door, which was locked.

"Who is it?" asked Gabriel.

"Me," Charlie replied.

After a moment's squeaking and shuffling, Gabriel opened the door and Charlie stepped into the shed. He found Tancred and Lysander sitting on a bench beneath a shelf of gerbil cages. The bench was one of the few places where there wasn't a cage, for they lined every wall from floor to ceiling. There were white, black, brown, long-haired, short-haired, large, and small gerbils. The smell was strong.

Billy Raven sat cross-legged on the floor. He looked pleased with himself, and when Charlie came in, he gave him an enormous grin.

"Billy, you're out!" Charlie exclaimed. "How did you do it?"

"The Flames helped me. They broke the force field." Behind his smile, Charlie sensed that Billy was very nervous.

"Thing is, what now?" said Lysander. "Billy said you would know. That's why you're here, Charlie."

"He can't stay here for long," said Gabriel, bolting the door and squeezing in behind Charlie. "That de Grey woman is bound to guess where he's gone."

"I meant to snuff her out!" Tancred smashed his fist into his palm, and a strong breeze swept through the shed, lifting everyone's hair and sending the gerbils squeaking for cover.

Billy put his hands over his ears. "I can't think when they talk like that," he complained. "There are so many gerbils in here, they don't give me a minute's peace."

"What are they saying?" asked Gabriel. "I've always wanted to know."

Billy stared at him, his hands clamped tight over his ears. Lysander lifted one of Billy's hands and shouted, "Gabriel wants to know what the gerbils are saying."

"They say 'Help! Whoops! Here we go again! Watch the kids! That's mine! Get off!'" Billy paused. "Boring stuff, really!"

"Not to me," Gabriel said.

Lysander held up his hand in a commanding manner. "Can we get back to the problem? It isn't going to be easy to find a safe place for Billy — a place where no one will think of looking. Obviously, all our houses will fall under suspicion because we're endowed. Unfortunately, the judge is away or I'd ask his advice."

Gabriel suggested that breakfast would help everyone think, and he left the gerbil house, promising to return with eggs, bacon, and toast.

Peering through a small window between the cages, Charlie watched Gabriel going into a door at the back of the house. "Why do we have to eat in here?" he said.

"To protect Gabriel's family," said Lysander. "They can't defend themselves against — whatever those people are going to send after Billy. And they will send something, believe me. But at least we're all endowed. We stand a chance."

Lysander's words were prophetic, for the morning light that had begun to filter through the small

245

window was suddenly snuffed out, and they were plunged into a murky darkness. Even the gerbils fell silent as a soft tapping could be heard on the roof.

"What on earth . . . ," said Tancred.

The sound intensified until it became a loud drumming. It seemed as though millions of tiny hands were striking every surface of the shed, and it began to groan and shake under the assault.

Desperate to know what was going on outside, Charlie reached for the bolt on the door. He told himself that it might be unwise to open the door, but by then it was too late, and he found himself peeping out.

A swirling cloud of paper rushed toward Charlie, and briefly he caught sight of Gabriel emerging from the house and then being engulfed by the flying paper. He fell to the ground and a breakfast tray slipped out of his hands. It crashed onto the cobblestoned yard, sending food in all directions.

As the paper swept into the gerbil house, Billy Raven sprang up, screaming, "It's the oaths!"

THE BATTLE OF OATHS AND SPIRITS

Charlie slammed the door of the gerbil house, but several oaths were already in. They made straight for Billy and clung to every part of him. Billy screamed, whether in pain or fear, Charlie couldn't tell. But when he attempted to pull the papers off Billy, he saw that each one had a glowing green edge that bit into his flesh the moment he touched it.

Tancred and Lysander were also plucking at the papers and they too were bitten by the vicious spirit, or whatever it was that possessed Florence de Grey's lethal oaths. Over and over, they would pull the papers away, only to have them zoom onto Billy again. They tried tearing the oaths, but each tiny piece would fly back and cling to Billy. They scrunched the paper into balls while it twisted in their hands, biting their fingers and burning their palms. But the crumpled paper always unfolded and returned to the attack.

"We'll have to get them out!" shouted Lysander, as Billy spun around, screaming and tearing at his hair.

"Open the door, Charlie, just a fraction," cried Tancred, "and I'll blast them out."

"Suppose more come in," said Charlie breathlessly.

"We'll have to chance it," Tancred told him.

"There are twelve of them, I counted," said Lysander. "So, come on, let's try it."

Every oath that was torn away from Billy was subjected to a cold blast of air as it was thrust through the tiny gap that Charlie allowed. Charlie would then slam the door shut. This maneuver was not easy, as Tancred needed a lot of room to muster a strong blast, and when Charlie reached for the door, he had to keep well away from the storm boy's swinging arm.

Progress was painfully slow, but at last every oath had been banished, and the four occupants of the gerbil house collapsed onto the bench, safe at least for a while. Their hands were covered in red welts, but Billy's face was worse than his hands. His pallor made the crimson streaks appear even more vivid. Burying his face in his hands, the small boy sank to the floor and began to sob.

"Come on, Billy," said Lysander, patting the small boy's shoulder. "We're OK now."

"We're not. We're not," cried Billy. "And it's all my fault."

"It's not your fault," Tancred declared. "You're right about one thing, though. We are certainly not OK. For a start, how are we going to get breakfast? I'm starving."

Lysander shot him a warning look as Billy's expression began to crumble again.

The oaths covered the window. Squinting through a tiny gap between the papers, Charlie got a narrow view of the yard. There was no sign of Gabriel, but he could see four fried eggs, several slices of toast, and some delicious crispy bacon, all lying in the mud. It was really depressing. He was about to turn away when he caught sight of Gabriel's face looking out from the kitchen window. Gabriel gave a thumbs-up sign and Charlie had a wild hope that a plan to rescue them had been devised.

A cloud of paper suddenly descended, dashing Charlie's hopes, as Gabriel's shocked face disappeared behind the clingy green-rimmed oaths. They covered the kitchen window like a crowd of squealing bats.

"Gabriel can't reach us," Charlie said gloomily. "But maybe those poisonous oaths will wear out after a while. Maybe they'll go to sleep — or die!"

"They'll never die," Billy whispered.

"If storms can't do it, I don't know what can," said Tancred dismally.

A despondent silence settled on the four prisoners. Tancred's stomach rumbled, Billy wiped his tear-stained face with the back of his hand, and Charlie slumped to the floor, feeling helpless.

All at once, Lysander announced, "They will have to be killed!"

Everyone looked at him, and Charlie said, "How?"

"My ancestors," said Lysander. "They are more

powerful than those contemptible oaths. But to reach them I will have to go outside."

Tancred leaped up. "You can't, Sander," he protested. "It would be suicide. There must be a thousand of those things out there. They'll eat you alive or . . . or batter you to death."

"No." The boy smiled. "My African ancestors will protect me." He stepped up to the door. "Tancred, you'll have to help. If those devils try to get in when I open the door, a blast of air at my back should do it. Are you ready?"

How could anyone ever be ready for such a drastic move? Once Lysander's mind was made up, however, he never hesitated. Before Charlie had time to collect his thoughts, the door was open and Lysander was out. Tancred brought his upheld arm swinging down in an arc toward the oaths that were attempting to dart inside. One got in before the door was slammed shut, but as the malicious thing shot toward Billy, Tancred caught it and, with Charlie's help, dispatched it through the door with another blast of air.

"Ouch! Those things are getting stronger," said Tancred, examining his hands. "Look! The cuts are deeper."

Charlie stared at the cuts lacerating Tancred's fingers. They were badly in need of a bandage.

"Here. I've got a hanky." Billy pulled an exceptionally white handkerchief out of his pocket and gave it to Tancred. "Florence said I must always have a handkerchief handy. I suppose she was right."

Charlie bound Tancred's hand, but blood began to seep through the hanky, and Billy moaned, "Oh, no. I hope you won't bleed to death."

"'Course I won't, silly." Tancred hid his hand behind him. "Think of Sander! He's far worse off than I am."

"Sander!" cried Charlie.

All three boys leaped to the window. A moment ago it had been covered in paper, but now it was clear and the horrified onlookers saw that the oaths had gathered into a vast army, intent on attacking the motionless figure in their midst.

The yard was so dark it was as though an early dusk had fallen. But they could see that Lysander had buried his face in his hands, while the green-edged leaves of paper swarmed around him, striking and cutting wherever they could. The mass of paper emitted an angry buzz that grew louder and louder until Billy Raven could stand it no longer.

"They're going to kill him," Billy cried.

"Shh!" hissed Charlie. "Listen."

Very faint at first but getting stronger every second, the sound of drums came rolling through the air.

"Lysander's ancestors are coming," said Charlie.

A smile lit Tancred's face. "Hear that, Billy?"

Billy nodded. Once before he'd seen Lysander's spirit ancestors do battle. He knew that now they stood a chance.

When the sound of drums reverberated in the yard, the oaths appeared to lose their energy. Some

fluttered away from the group, as if they were confused. The sky became inky black, and Charlie wondered
if the ancestors were bringing night with them to
emphasize their radiance.

The drumrolls increased, and the spectators
pressed closer to the window, waiting for the spirits to
appear. More of the oaths were losing their focus.
They floated away from Lysander and drifted aimlessly
into the sky.

A golden mist crept through the dark, and
Lysander lifted his head as the last of the oaths broke
off their assault and hovered uncertainly above him.
Eerie forms began to take shape in the mist: tall figures, robed in white, their hands concealed, until on a
sudden drumroll, every figure pulled out a gleaming
weapon. Spears, swords, and axes were held aloft, and
a mysterious hum rippled through the air.

When the oaths sensed that they were facing
death, they attacked their enemy with a savage fury.
But time and again the papers were slashed. The shiny
green borders would flare briefly and then fade as the

oaths turned to sheets of ash. Some of them, attempting to escape, sailed up into the dark sky. But spirits can fly too, and every escape was cut short with a bright sword or a gleaming spear.

"It's a bit like fireworks, isn't it?" said Billy in a voice of wonder.

Charlie and Tancred had to agree.

No one could have said for sure how long the battle raged, for time seemed to hold its breath until the radiant mist began to fade and the last tall figure vanished.

It was the silence that convinced Charlie they were safe. The drumming had stopped and the angry buzz of paper had died. Lysander jumped into the air with a triumphant shout. "They're dead and gone, you guys. Come on out!"

Charlie opened the shed door a little warily. The leaden clouds had gone and he looked up into a morning sky streaked with blue and gold.

"Come on!" Lysander beckoned.

They expected his face to be covered in wounds,

255

but he appeared to be completely unmarked. Their own cuts too had faded; even the marks on Billy's face had shrunk to the size of tiny threads that were quickly disappearing.

"Powerful medicine," said Tancred, giving Charlie a shove from behind.

As Charlie lurched into the open, he saw that the yard was littered with ash. It must have been an inch thick and it slithered softly underfoot.

"You did it, Sander!" cried Tancred.

The Silks' backdoor opened, and with a loud yelp, Gabriel rushed out to join the others. The four boys ran around the yard, kicking the ash into dusty clouds and rocking with laughter. Charlie's relief was so enormous that he couldn't breathe properly, and his laughter was mixed with short bursts of hiccups.

The hiccups stopped when he noticed Billy, standing alone in the door of the gerbil house. He was smiling, but his big red eyes looked almost as frightened as they had when the oaths were flying at him.

"What is it, Billy?" said Charlie.

Gradually, the laughter stopped, and Charlie and the others walked over to the small white-haired boy.

"You're OK now, Billy," said Tancred, but even as he said it, he and everyone else realized that this wasn't true.

"Where am I going to go now?" Billy raised his troubled gaze to the four older boys.

His question was answered temporarily by Mrs. Silk, who called them all in for breakfast.

There was a great excitement in the Silk household. Gabriel's three sisters kept up a barrage of near-hysterical chatter all through the big and delicious breakfast. What was the flying paper all about? Who burned it? Who was drumming? The battle in the yard had been obscured by a thick mist, and no one in the house could see what had happened. They only knew that it was too dangerous to venture out.

Mr. Silk, who'd been writing frantically in a large notebook, eventually flung down his work and shouted, "Quiet, girls! A man can't think!"

"But what WAS it?" persisted April, the smallest girl.

"It was a phenomenon that must on no account be talked about," said her father. "Even to your best friends."

"Is it something to do with Gabriel's oddness?" asked Mai, the middle sister.

"I've told you before, don't call it my oddness!" shouted Gabriel. He didn't get on too well with Mai.

Charlie wondered how Mrs. Silk managed to keep on doling out perfectly cooked breakfasts and pouring cups of tea that were always exactly the right shade of brown. She darted about the kitchen, humming softly and smiling to herself, and Charlie decided it must be relief that made her look so happy. It can't have been easy having furious oaths and ancient spirits battling in her backyard.

Tancred, who wolfed down his breakfast in record time, asked what was going to happen to the food in the yard.

Mrs. Silk looked up in surprise and June, the oldest of Gabriel's sisters, said, "You don't want to eat it, do you?"

Tancred's friends waited anxiously for his reply, but before he could open his mouth, Mr. Silk said firmly, "The hens will deal with it."

The chickens had run for cover as soon as the oaths appeared, but now they could be glimpsed through the window, happily scratching through the ash. Gabriel remembered his gerbils, and he rushed out to make sure they'd recovered from the attack on their house. He came back saying that all was well except that Rita, his favorite, had unexpectedly given birth to more babies than he could count at a glance.

Lysander needed to get home. He gave a cheerful wave and rushed off, saying, "See you later, guys!"

Charlie always felt safe when Lysander was around. Now he was gone, just when they were most in need of his company and advice. Tancred was a powerful ally, of course, but the stormy boy was a little unpredictable. A decision had to be made about Billy. The Silks' house wouldn't be safe from Florence or the Bloors for much longer.

The telephone rang in the hall and Mrs. Silk went to answer it. "Charlie, it's your mom."

Charlie ran out into the hall and picked up the receiver. "Hello, Mom!"

"Charlie, what's going on?" said the distant voice. "Is Gabriel in trouble? Are you coming back for —"

"Hold on, Mom," Charlie said firmly. "I'm OK. But Billy's in a bit of trouble and we're trying to sort it out. He's run away."

"Run away?" Charlie's message had done nothing to reassure his mother. "But, Charlie . . ."

"I may not be back for a while. I don't know how long this will take."

"How long what will take?"

"Just tell Uncle Paton what's happened, will you, Mom? And please don't worry. I'm OK. Really."

As Charlie replaced the receiver he noticed a white moth sitting on his sleeve. It spread its wings, revealing the sparkling silver tips.

"It's you again," said Charlie.

The moth flew off, but Charlie failed to see where

it had gone. He ran back into the kitchen. "I think Billy and I ought to leave now," he told Mrs. Silk. "Thank you for a great breakfast."

Mrs. Silk said that it was always a pleasure to see Charlie, but she wanted to know exactly where he and Billy intended to go next. Charlie had been wondering about this and he didn't know how to answer her.

"They're coming home with me," Tancred declared. He stood up so suddenly that a breeze floated over the tablecloth, sending sprays of sugar and crumbs into the air. Gabriel's sisters loudly applauded. They begged Tancred to do it again, but Tancred, grinning bashfully, said he couldn't do it, "Just like that!" whereupon a sly little draft caused knives, plates, and saucers to collide with soft clinks and tinkles.

At this point Mrs. Silk became very anxious. "If Billy has been mistreated, someone should be told," she said. "The police . . . or . . . social services." She turned to Billy. "Perhaps you should go back to the academy, Billy. At least you would be safe there."

"Noooo!" Billy vehemently shook his head.

"Leave him be," Mr. Silk advised his wife. "He'll certainly be safe at the Thunder House."

Tancred and his father were both storm-bringers, and there was always a wild wind and a rumble of thunder around their house. It was probably the safest place in the city right then, and Charlie was very relieved that Tancred had taken the decision out of his hands.

"My uncle Paton will explain why Billy can't go back," he told the Silks.

The whole family gathered in the doorway to see the three boys off. It was almost as if they were going on vacation rather than running for safety.

When he reached the gate, Billy suddenly turned back and asked, "What happened to the cats?"

"What cats, dear? I haven't seen any cats," said Mrs. Silk.

"Oh, they must have gone home," said Billy sadly.

By the time they began the long uphill walk, Billy was already exhausted from his run earlier that morning. The other two had to keep stopping while he trudged after them, puffing and wheezing. In the end Tancred told Billy to jump on his back, and he carried him over the rough, winding road that led to the woods at the top.

Charlie breathed a sigh of relief when Tancred's gate came into sight. There were two signs nailed to the gate. One said, THE THUNDER HOUSE and the other BEWARE OF THE WEATHER. As they drew closer to the gate, Charlie heard hoofbeats. He tried to ignore the sound, but when he couldn't stand the tension any longer, he looked back. The road was empty, but the hoofbeats were getting louder.

Tancred turned around, and Billy, peering over his shoulder, said, "It's the ghost horse again. It's following us."

Charlie gave a yell and raced for the gate. He didn't bother to unlatch it but threw himself over and fell onto the stony lane beyond.

"What's got into you, Charlie?" called Tancred.

"It's Borlath!" Charlie whimpered. "He's after me. Hurry up, you two! Please!"

Billy slid off Tancred's back and began to climb the gate. "I don't think it'll hurt you!" he shouted.

"A lot you know!" cried Charlie. He began to rush up the lane.

A wild and deafening neigh shattered his eardrums. The horse must have cleared the gate, because Charlie could hear hooves thudding over the path behind him.

"Run into the woods!" called Tancred. "It can't get you there. At least, not so easily."

Charlie stumbled off the lane. "It's a ghost horse," he moaned. "It'll find me anywhere." He staggered into the trees and leaned against a broad trunk, trying to catch his breath.

There was a deathly silence in the woods. The wind had died down, and every twig, leaf, and blade of grass was still. Charlie closed his eyes. Maybe he was safe. He began to hear Tancred and Billy stumbling through the undergrowth toward him. A warm draft swept across his cheek. Breath? Something wet and whiskery touched his ear.

A deep grunt echoed right through Charlie's body and he slumped to the ground.

CHILDREN OF THE QUEEN

Charlie looked up at the two concerned faces.

"Hey, Charlie. I think you fainted," said Tancred.

"Did I?" Charlie dragged himself upright.

"What happened?" asked Billy, frowning with alarm.

"The horse," croaked Charlie. "It was right here, snorting into my face. It was horrible."

"Well, you're none the worse for the encounter," said Tancred with a laugh. "You probably terrified the poor thing, screaming like that."

Charlie didn't remember screaming. The woods rustled all around him and there was a faint rumble of thunder above.

"There's a moth on your head," Billy observed, staring at Charlie's tousled hair. "It has silver on its wings."

"Really?" Charlie put up his hand but the white moth fluttered away, into the shadows.

"Come on, let's get going," said Tancred impatiently.

"We'll keep to the trees, just in case the de Grey woman comes looking for Billy."

"Or the Bloors," added Billy. "Can I stay in your house, Tancred, for a long time?"

"Long as you like," said Tancred breezily. "Mom would love it. Come on, ten minutes and we'll be there."

They began to walk through the woods, following a well-worn path used by the sheep that grazed the hillside. Tancred led the party, while Charlie brought up the rear. Charlie began to wonder where Billy could go next. The unspoken question hung in the air until a strange solution presented itself. "There's always the Castle of Mirrors," Charlie said, almost to himself.

"What?" Billy stopped in his tracks.

"It's where you belong. Your own castle, Billy."

"Cook told me the Castle of Mirrors belonged to my family," Billy said slowly. "Do you think I could live there until I grow up?"

"Why not? Maybe you could live there in safety forever," said Charlie.

267

Tancred shouted, "Get a move on, you two!"

Billy and Charlie ran to catch up with him. As they drew nearer to the Thunder House, the breeze turned into a blast and the thunder intensified.

"Dad's in good form," said Tancred.

Charlie's smile froze. A huge unseen form galloped past him. He could feel its great weight and its power as it pounded the earth. The others were aware of it now. The boys huddled together while the ghost horse began to circle them, neighing and snorting as it raced around and around the small group.

Leaves came showering off the trees when the creature reared up. They could sense its forelegs thrashing the air, and Charlie thought, *Any minute now, one of those hooves is going to come down on my head, and there'll be no more Charlie Bone.*

And then Billy Raven did something totally unexpected. He stepped off the path and walked toward the ghost horse, grunting gently.

"He's crazy." Tancred clutched Charlie's shoulder.

"Yep!" whispered Charlie. Billy might have a way

with animals, but how could he talk to a monster like Hamaran with Borlath's heart?

Once again, the thunder stopped and the trees became still. There was a long, gentle whinny and then silence. And in the silence, Billy Raven dropped to his knees and bowed his head.

"What the . . . ?" Tancred's voice cracked with horror.

"Shhh!" Charlie grabbed Tancred's jacket.

The white moth had reappeared, and now it was fluttering just beyond Billy, its shimmering silver-tipped wings moving so fast that they seemed to be drawing a shape in the air. The shape gathered depth and something huge began to appear beneath the hovering silver, until there it was: a tall white horse with a noble head and flowing mane.

Charlie gasped and backed away, pulling Tancred with him.

"It doesn't look vicious," Tancred said in Charlie's ear.

"It isn't," said Billy.

"How do you know?" Charlie demanded. "Did it talk to you?"

"Yes." Billy looked over his shoulder and smiled at the boys. "It's OK, really. It's . . . She's the queen."

"QUEEN?" said Tancred and Charlie.

"Queen Berenice," Billy told them. "She was the Red King's wife."

"You mean . . ." Charlie's mind was in turmoil. He tried to remember what Manfred had said about the experiment: a gravestone marked with a "B," the bones of a horse buried beneath it, and the heart in a casket.

"Not Borlath," he murmured, "but Berenice." A smile crossed his face and he moved closer to Billy. "That stupid old man got it wrong again."

Tancred, following cautiously, asked, "How did she get here?"

"Old Ezekiel brought her to life. It wasn't Borlath's heart, it was the queen's. Queen Berenice."

They were now standing directly behind Billy, who slowly got to his feet.

"She's been following us," said Billy. "She says

we're her children and she wants to protect us. Some-one brought her here from the otherworld, but her spirit kept fading, taking her back, until your wand kind of steadied her."

"My wand?" Charlie was mystified. "I thought Manfred had destroyed it, unless . . ." He looked at the white moth, its wings just visible as a tiny glint between the horse's ears.

"They say that wands can take a different form," said Tancred, "if they have to."

"Oh." Charlie blinked. Tancred knew more than he had realized.

The white horse began to grunt, softly this time, but with a flowing, almost-human sequence of sounds. Billy listened intently, and when the horse was quiet at last, he told the others, "She heard us talk about the Castle of Mirrors and it frightened her. She saw the island where it was built and knew what would happen there."

"So she knows where it is," Charlie said thought-fully.

"I suppose so." It was obvious that Billy had no idea of the castle's terrible history.

"Charlie, please tell me that you're not going to do what I think you're going to do," pleaded Tancred.

Charlie grinned. "It was just a thought." But the thought was growing.

The three boys stood in silence and watched the stately creature cropping the grass. It was hard to believe that she had been a queen, almost a thousand years ago. Old Ezekiel had made a mistake, but what he had done was miraculous all the same. He was still a powerful magician, and before long he would find Billy and take him back to Bloor's, unless . . . The thought in Charlie's mind grew into a plan. And the plan somehow became the only solution. Charlie knew in his heart that finding his father was foremost in his mind, but Billy's safety was a close second.

"Ask her if she'll take us to that island," Charlie said to Billy.

"Charlie!" Tancred protested. "You can't!"

"I think we have to."

Billy was eager to try. He dropped to his knees again and began to grunt softly to the mare. She raised her head, her ears back, and her large eyes rolled fearfully.

"She doesn't like the idea," Billy whispered.

"Tell her about my father," urged Charlie. "Tell her you have to find somewhere safe."

Billy began again, and this time he added a plaintive whinny to his language.

Suddenly, the mare reared up. With a squeal of terror, she careened off through the trees. They listened to the thud of hooves receding until they faded altogether, and the only sounds were thunder and windblown trees.

"That's that, then," said Tancred. "Let's get to my place."

"No," said Charlie. "She'll come back."

"You're joking, right? That mare is one scared animal, Charlie. She'll never take you to the Castle of Mirrors."

"She will," Charlie insisted. "She thinks we're her children. She's got to protect us."

Billy didn't like arguing with boys like Tancred, but as he looked from the storm boy to Charlie, he said timidly, "I think Charlie's right."

"Have it your own way," said Tancred, "but I'm off." As he strode away, he called back. "I'll bring you some food in a bit, if you're still here, which I suspect you will be."

"Do you think Tancred's right?" Billy asked Charlie.

"No." Charlie sat down and made himself comfortable against a wide tree trunk.

There was a loud crack of thunder followed by a sudden downpour, and Billy squeezed in beside Charlie.

"Tancred's angry," said Billy.

"He'll get over it," Charlie told him.

But, if anything, the storm got worse. Wind surged through the trees, sending leaves and dead branches clattering into the undergrowth. Uprooted nettles, brambles, and dry grass whistled all around Charlie and Billy as they huddled under the broad oak, shielding themselves with their arms. After what seemed like hours of battering, the weather calmed down and the boys fell asleep, worn out by their extraordinary morning.

Charlie woke up to see Tancred striding toward him with a large tray. "I knew you'd still be here," said Tancred, setting the tray down beside the tree. Charlie beheld plates of roast chicken, vegetables and gravy, and three bowls of plum pie and custard. Mrs. Silk's breakfast seemed hours ago, and the smell of the feast before him was enough to make a hungry boy yelp with joy. Which Charlie did, rousing Billy, who fell sideways into the grass.

"That was some storm," Charlie muttered as he bit into a chicken leg.

"Sorry. Dad and I had a fight," said Tancred. "He said you two ought to be eating at a table, not crouching in the woods like fugitives. So I said I wouldn't eat with him if he was going to be like that. He almost exploded, but Mom said boys would be boys, and she remembered Dad and her having a feast in the woods in their long-ago younger days. That calmed him down."

When all the plates and bowls had been scraped clean, Tancred asked if Charlie and Billy were ready to go home with him. "It's quite obvious that mare is not going to come back," he said. "She's probably galloped back into the otherworld by now."

Charlie licked a last, delicious morsel off his fingers and replied, "No. She will come back."

"God, you're stubborn, Charlie Bone," said Tancred, getting to his feet. But this time he seemed more resigned than angry. "What am I going to do with you?"

"Call my uncle Paton," Charlie told him. "Try and explain what's happened. Everything. And say I'll probably be staying the night with you, just in case Mom gets worried."

"I'll do my best. But I'll come back at dusk, and if you two are still here, I'll drag you up to the Thunder House, whatever you say. You can't stay in the woods all night."

"No," said Billy in a small voice. "Because Asa Pike will be around."

Charlie had forgotten Asa. "We won't be here," he said firmly. "The queen will come back."

"OK. We'll see." Balancing the tray on his spiky yellow hair, Tancred pranced off through the trees, and Billy actually managed to laugh for the first time that day.

For the next few hours, the two boys played I Spy, chased leaves, climbed trees, and dozed. But as the shadows lengthened, Charlie's heart began to sink. He realized he had been hoping for too much. What had he expected? That a fragile family bond could hold fast through a thousand years?

We're still the children of the Red King, Charlie thought desperately. *So we're the queen's children, too.*

For Billy, the disappointment was finally too much. He slumped down the path, sobbing, "She's not coming, is she?"

Charlie could only shrug. "And she's got my wand," he said, trying to make light of the situation. "If that's what the white moth is."

Dusk began to fall very fast now. The woods grew damp and chilly, and Charlie knew he would have to make a decision. When he saw Tancred's pale head approaching in the distance, he called, "OK, Tanc. We're coming."

Billy jumped up, happy to be leaving the dark woods at last. But Tancred suddenly stopped and said in a low voice, "Charlie — behind you!"

Charlie turned very slowly, expecting to see the gray wolflike form that Asa took at dusk. But it was not Asa. It was the queen.

"She came back," breathed Billy.

The mare's coat was a startling white in the dusk. She stood facing them, her feet planted firmly on the path, her noble head turned slightly to watch them with a large, dark eye. Charlie was glad to see the white moth glinting in her long mane.

"Talk to her again, Billy," Charlie said quietly. "Tell her how much we need her."

Billy walked up to the mare, and dropping on one knee, he told two stories in a humming, neighing, lyrical voice: the story of his dead parents and his lonely life, and the story of Charlie's lost father. And as the child talked, Charlie watched the horse's face. He was sure that he saw a tear fall from her shining brown eye.

When Billy had made his last, frantic entreaty, the mare lowered her head and neighed softly.

Billy turned to Charlie. "She'll do it. She says her fears are unreasonable when matched against our happiness."

Charlie was taken aback. "She said that?" And he looked at the mare, wondering how he and Billy were going to climb up on her back and once there how they would stay on.

To his surprise, Tancred had thought ahead. When he finally walked into the clearing, Charlie saw that he was carrying a huge saddle and several long leather straps. "Dad's," said Tancred. "He used to ride hurricanes, don't ask me how."

"You believed she'd come back after all, didn't you?" said Charlie.

"I thought if she did, you couldn't go galloping off without all this stuff," said Tancred, grinning.

The white mare allowed them to saddle her up, helping in every way she could, and when this had been done, Tancred lifted Charlie onto her back and then Billy, who squeezed behind Charlie, holding him tight around the waist.

"This is it?" said Charlie, hardly able to believe what was about to happen. "'Bye, Tancred. And thanks."

"Good luck," said Tancred, his gruff tone unable to disguise a slight uneasiness.

The mare began to trot through the trees, but as she gathered speed, Charlie shouted, "Tancred, did you speak to my uncle?"

"He wasn't there. I told your mom you'd be staying the night with me."

"You've got to speak to my uncle. Swear you will, Tancred!"

"I swear!" cried Tancred. He waited until the white mare was out of sight and then he ran home.

Darkness fell fast and Tancred didn't see the gray beast crouched in the undergrowth, watching and listening.

Just for a second, Charlie caught himself wondering if he should have given this adventure a little more thought before leaping into the dark — or onto a horse's back. But it was not in his nature to fret over past mistakes, so he clung to the reins and prepared to enjoy the ride of his life.

Once she was out of the woods, the mare kept to the narrow path that led to the top of the Heights. From here, the city lay before her like a distant constellation. The Red King and Queen Berenice had often come riding on this hill, and she knew exactly where their castle lay. Even in this new world of lights and noise and tall, shining buildings, she could still see the outline of the castle walls, behind the big gray house that held the troubled children from her endowed lineage.

The city throbbed with its painful past. The queen

could feel it as she walked on the surface. It saddened her, for she had spent many happy years in the Red Castle.

In the months before her tenth child was born, a dreadful sickness had swept through the country. The queen was struck with it, and although she fought the sickness, she grew so weak that when her daughter Amoret arrived, she knew she would never live to protect her or the other, more vulnerable of her children. But now she had two of her children back again, and she would use the strange new chance that she had been granted to help these brave boys.

For almost a thousand years Queen Berenice had lived in the land of the dead — the otherworld — and from there she had brought certain powers into this new life that neither she nor her favorite mare had possessed all those years ago. These powers enabled her to climb the steepest cliff, to clear the widest chasm, and to fly with ease over the boiling surf.

They traveled under a full moon, and all the way they kept to the coast, a route the queen knew well.

Charlie was aware that he and Billy had a charmed life that night. They entered a world even stranger than the places he had found when he traveled into pictures. There were no roads or houses, lights or noises in this land: It was ancient, wild, and empty.

Several times, Charlie fell asleep, but when he woke he was always astride the mare, with Billy's sleepy head against his back and the white moth shining before him, like a tiny crown between the horse's ears. As far as he knew, the mare never stopped — not once — until she trotted into a wide bay where the beach sparkled with shells and silver sand.

The mare gave a soft whinny and Billy said, "We're here."

"Here?" Charlie looked about him. All he could see was the shining ocean and the beach; behind them a tall cliff rose into the darkness.

"It's out there!" Billy slid off the horse and ran to the edge of the water. "There!" he pointed.

"I can't see anything." Charlie slipped his feet out of the stirrups and jumped onto the beach. "Where?"

He searched the dark horizon and saw far, far out a mysterious glimmer, like the reflection of stars on water. "I think I see it now," he said. And he wondered if someone in that distant castle was lighting a candle. His father, maybe.

The mare neighed, a loud, urgent sound.

Billy said, "She says we mustn't go out there now. We must wait for morning."

"And how are we going to get there?" Charlie asked himself. But he was too tired to think anymore. Sleep weighed heavily on his eyelids and his legs were about to buckle under him.

They slept in a cozy hollow at the base of the cliff, and the mare stood beside them, shielding them from the night wind.

They awoke to a blue sky and a sea that was clear and calm. But where was the island? The horizon was lost in mist. The boys took off their socks and shoes, rolled up their jeans, and walked into the sea, peering at the tantalizing haze. The water lapped at their knees and Charlie's stomach rumbled. He couldn't help hoping that if they ever reached the elusive castle, his father might have the means to make them a nice hot breakfast. On second thought, even a cold one would do.

At the moment, things weren't very promising. The distant glimmer of last night could have been anything: a passing ship, a falling star, a mirage? Charlie's feet were beginning to feel numb. He waded back to shore with Billy splashing behind him.

They sat on the shell beach, rubbing their wet feet with their socks. Charlie was surprised to see that Billy's face was shining with excitement. He thought he ought to warn him that the situation wasn't entirely hopeful. "Suppose we never find the castle?" Charlie said.

Billy didn't lose his smile. "I haven't seen the sea for ages. In fact, I can hardly remember it."

This hadn't occurred to Charlie. All the same, he had to bring Billy back to earth. "We might be in the wrong place." He glanced at the white mare cropping the grass on the cliff, and lowered his voice. "I mean, it was almost a thousand years ago when she . . . was alive. She could have got it wrong."

"I don't think she did." Billy cleaned his glasses and squinted at the sea.

Charlie looked up. The mist was beginning to rise, and there on the ocean, an island was revealed. A distant, beautiful, blue island with a glittering crown. A castle of shining glass.

When she saw the island, the white mare's scream was almost human. Her hooves sent sprays of shells into the air as she raced across the beach, leaped over a rocky outcrop, and disappeared from view. But her voice could still be heard, calling to them as she galloped away from the sea.

"She says she's not leaving us," said Billy, "but her heart won't let her look at the island where her children died. What does she mean?"

Charlie decided that it was time to tell Billy the true history of the Castle of Mirrors. But would Billy want to go there once he knew what had happened to Prince Amadis?

THE ENCHANTED CAPE

"**W**hat! The QUEEN!"

Manfred stepped back to avoid his great-grandfather's flying spit. Even so, a large glob of it fell on his nicely polished shoe. Asa, cringing beside him, managed to stifle a giggle.

This was turning into one of Manfred's more unpleasant Mondays. The weekend had been bad enough, with that little squirt, Billy Raven, escaping from the Passing House and Usher de Grey's near-fatal accident. Not to mention the loss of the oaths and Florence going crazy. Her screams, when they had to lock her in the cold room, still rang in his ears. Hopefully, she'd cooled down by now.

On top of these misfortunes, Asa Pike had come creeping in with the news that the great experiment hadn't worked exactly as they had thought. Instead of a warhorse with a brutal heart, they had brought back to life a white mare with the heart of a loving mother queen.

"Look on the bright side, Grandfather," said Manfred, gingerly pushing the spit off his left shoe with the toe of his right. "After all, it's quite an achievement."

"I didn't WANT the QUEEN!" screamed Ezekiel. "I wanted Borlath."

"Well, you've got the queen," Manfred said flatly. "Or rather, Charlie Bone has got her, and now he and Billy are well on the way to the Castle of Mirrors."

"Well on the way," echoed Asa, looking unnecessarily pleased with himself.

"It's your fault," blazed Ezekiel, pointing a gnarled finger at Asa. "You found the gravestone; you brought me the heart."

"I didn't know whose it was," whined Asa. "There was just a 'B' on the grave. No one told me the queen was called Berenice."

"Ugh!" growled Ezekiel.

Asa grew bolder. "I've done well," he insisted. "I followed Paton Yewbeam, and I found that Crowquill man. I spent hours hiding in the Silks' filthy yard, and then crouching in that damp wood, and now my bones ache something awful. If it wasn't for me, you wouldn't know where Billy had gone, would you?"

"All right!" yelled Ezekiel. "Take the day off."

"I don't want the day off," Asa muttered peevishly. "I just want recognition."

"You've got it." Manfred nudged Asa in the ribs.

"They're getting above themselves," grumbled Ezekiel. "The whole bunch of them. Lysander, Torsson, Gabriel Silk — it's got to be stopped. Send me the Tilpin boy!"

"Joshua?" Manfred raised an eyebrow. "What can he do?"

"You'd be surprised, Manfred," said his great-grandfather. "But you'll soon find out. Now buzz off, both of you."

Manfred objected to being treated like a child. He deserved better. With a dark scowl he marched off down the many corridors and stairways that led from his great-grandfather's room, while Asa shuffled in his wake, whining.

"What does he want Tilpin for?" Asa complained. "He can't do anything. He's too small, and he's had no experience."

"We know he's got magnetism," Manfred retorted. "I suppose it depends what he does with it. Could be interesting."

"Hmff!" Asa sniffed.

Manfred caught Joshua just as he was coming out of the green coatroom. Assembly was over and the children were about to go to their first classes.

"Mr. Ezekiel wants to see you," said Manfred, grabbing the small boy's shoulder.

"Oh?" Joshua gave Manfred one of his extraordinary gap-toothed smiles, and once again Manfred felt the peculiar tingle that made him return Joshua's smile even though a moment ago smiling had been the last thing on his mind.

"Do you know how to find Mr. Ezekiel's room?" Manfred asked kindly.

"Yes, sir. It's in the west wing, right at the top."

"Good lad. Off you go, then. Better hurry."

"Yes, sir."

It was very gratifying to be called "sir." Manfred wore his smile every step of the way across the great hall, but it faded abruptly when he skidded on a piece of apple peel and almost lost his balance.

"AAAAAARGH!" roared Manfred.

The hall was now empty, except for Dr. Saltweather, who was stepping slowly down the main stairs with a newspaper under his arm and a baffled expression on his face.

"It's that Vertigo girl again," Manfred shouted at Dr. Saltweather. "She's dropping apple peels all over the place. Something's got to be done about it."

"Not my department," Dr. Saltweather mumbled. "I'm head of music." He sauntered off, looking even more agitated than before.

Manfred gave a groan of irritation and made for his office.

Dr. Saltweather was now walking down the corridor of portraits. He was so worried, he had forgotten where he was supposed to be going. His newspaper carried a rather unsettling report. Two people had vanished from a small town in the northeast. Normally, this sort of news would cause Dr. Saltweather a mere flutter of concern; he had a kind heart and even the misfortunes of total strangers affected him. But today's news was altogether more disturbing.

The two men in question were a headmaster called Tantalus Wright and a postman whose name was Vincent Ebony. This could have been a coincidence, of course, but it was the men's peculiar habits that caused Dr. Saltweather to find their disappearance too sinister to be mere coincidence. The headmaster's special subject was medieval history and he suffered from narcolepsy. In other words, he fell asleep without any warning, in the most unusual places, which caused the unfortunate man's students a great deal of mirth.

Dr. Saltweather opened his newspaper and reread the small article inside the back page. "Mr. Vincent Ebony is a cheerful man with a great sense of humor. He laughs readily at the silliest jokes and is often to be heard singing Gershwin's *Bess You Is My Woman Now.* Mr. Ebony's wife, Bess, was too upset to comment."

Both men had disappeared at the end of August near the small town of Yorwynde. Tantalus Wright, an avid hiker, never returned from his Sunday walk, and Vincent Ebony's van had been found abandoned at the edge of a small forest. There was no sign of the postman. The two men had been missing for three weeks.

"It can't be! How can it? Two in one? Two in one!" Dr. Saltweather ambled on, shaking his head. He could hardly discuss the matter with the headmaster, as it was Dr. Bloor who had insisted on Tantalus Ebony's appointment. It was difficult to know exactly who was who in Bloor's Academy — or who was what, when it came to it.

"Morning!" Cook brushed past Dr. Saltweather in the dark corridor. "You look troubled, Doctor."

"Yes." Dr. Saltweather turned quickly and watched Cook hurry on up the corridor. He realized that she was the very person he could confide in. There was no doubt in his mind that Cook was on the right side, though he hardly knew what he meant by that.

"Cook!" Dr. Saltweather called softly. "Could I have a word?"

Cook looked around, surprised by the doctor's furtive tone. "Of course, Doctor." She walked back to him.

Dr. Saltweather smoothed out the back page of his newspaper and held it out to Cook, pointing at the small column near the bottom. "What do you think about that?"

Cook quickly scanned the article and gasped. "What do I think?" she said tremulously. "I think it means trouble, Dr. Saltweather. Very bad trouble, especially for certain people in this city."

"Like whom?" The doctor was intrigued.

"Like Charlie Bone and his uncle," said Cook.

"Ah." Dr. Saltweather stroked his chin. "Charlie wasn't in assembly today, nor was little Billy Raven."

"I've had word about him," said Cook, "but this" — she tapped the paper — "this is extremely serious. I must make a phone call immediately."

"But, Cook, how can it be?" said Dr. Saltweather, now more baffled than ever. "Two people in one. How did it happen?"

"Believe me, it can do that sort of thing," said Cook, hastening back in the direction from which she'd come.

"IT?" called Dr. Saltweather.

"Yes, 'IT,'" Cook replied, scurrying faster. "I'll explain another time. But right now, I must make a call. Thank you, Doctor, thank you. We have reason to be very, very grateful for this information." Her voice trailed off as she disappeared around a corner.

Dr. Saltweather suddenly remembered that he should be attending a meeting in the Wind room with Mr. Paltry and Tantalus Ebony. The head of music was late for his meeting, but when he got to the Wind room, Tantalus Ebony wasn't there.

"He's not in school," said old Mr. Paltry, picking his teeth with a matchstick. "Didn't you notice? He wasn't in assembly."

"No. No, I didn't." Dr. Saltweather felt foolish,

anxious, and confused all at the same time. "I wish you wouldn't smoke," he said to the elderly flutist. "It sets a bad example."

"I don't smoke." Mr. Paltry slipped the match into his pocket.

"I can smell it, Reginald," said Dr. Saltweather. "No wonder you're short of breath these days." He gave a sigh of irritation. "We'd better get on without Mr. Ebony."

A breathless Cook hurried into the kitchen and picked up the receiver of a phone situated on the wall beside the swinging door. The kitchen staff was chattering together in the background, and Cook had no fear of being overheard. She quickly dialed a number and listened to the phone ringing at number nine Filbert Street.

"Yes?" said an irritated voice.

Cook deepened her voice and, speaking like an old man, said, "I would like to speak to Mr. Paton Yewbeam."

"He's not here," said Grandma Bone.

"Mrs. Jones, then," said Cook. "She'll do."

"What's this about?" demanded Grandma Bone.

"Er . . . it's the dry cleaning. . . ."

"Not my best coat? Black with a velvet collar." This was shouted so loudly, Cook had to hold the receiver away from her ear.

"No, no. The article in question is red and . . ."

"Maisie, phone! Your clothes are in trouble." The receiver was dropped onto a table and Cook heard footsteps receding on a tiled floor. A moment later, Maisie's anxious voice said, "Yes? What's happened?"

"Maisie, it's me, Cook. But don't let on," said Cook in her normal voice. "I wanted to speak to Mr. Yewbeam, but apparently he's out."

"Not just out," said Maisie, lowering her voice. "Gone. Amy and I are very worried. He got news about Charlie, and then he and . . . and, you know, that Mr. Crowquill took off very early this morning."

"Dear, oh dear." Cook didn't know what to make of this. "And have you any idea where they've gone?"

Maisie put her mouth right over the receiver and whispered, "Castle of Mirrors."

"Worse and worse. I fear someone else is on the way there, too. Have you any means of contacting Mr. Yewbeam?"

"None," said Maisie. "He left his cell phone behind."

A voice beside Maisie said, "Why are you whispering to the dry cleaner?"

"Wasn't. Lost my voice. Tragedy with red cardigan." Maisie's voice became too faint for Cook to hear, but then it suddenly returned. "Thank you so much for informing me," she said to Cook. "I'll come by to pick up what's left of it later. Good-bye."

Cook replaced the receiver. "Nothing to be done," she muttered.

"I'd say there was quite a lot." One of the kitchen assistants came tripping up to Cook with a tray of burned pies. "We'll have to bake some more."

"You'll have to bake some more," snapped Cook. "I didn't burn them."

• • •

Fidelio Gunn was becoming more anxious by the minute. Gabriel had whispered something to him in assembly, but he could hardly make out what it was. All he heard were the words, "Charlie . . . a castle . . . and Billy Raven." Fidelio couldn't imagine what had happened to Charlie. It wasn't like his friend to rush off somewhere without telling him.

"Fidelio, you're not concentrating," said Miss Chrystal, who was accompanying him on the piano.

Fidelio lowered his violin and studied a music score on the stand before him. "Sorry, Miss Chrystal. I lost my place."

"What's the matter?" Miss Chrystal swung around on the music stool. "You played this piece almost perfectly last week."

Miss Chrystal was a very young teacher. She had blond hair and the sort of pretty features that almost invited children to confide in her. She kept their secrets and had never been known to betray any of them.

"I'm worried about my best friend," Fidelio blurted out.

"Charlie Bone?"

"Yes. He's not in school and I don't know what's happened to him."

"Dr. Saltweather may have heard something. I'll let you know what I find out during lunch break, shall I?" Miss Chrystal smiled encouragingly.

"Thanks, Miss Chrystal." Fidelio settled the violin under his chin and prepared to play again.

The lesson was not a success, and as soon as the bell rang, he rushed out rather rudely and tore off to the coatroom to hang up his cape. He was just about to go outside when he saw Dorcas Loom approaching the door to the Music Tower. She had a blue cape bundled under her arm.

Fidelio was suspicious. "Whose is that, Dorcas?" he asked.

She gave a little start. "Oh, it's Mr. Pilgrim's," she said, recovering her composure. "It was found in the library, so I'm taking it up to the music room."

"But Mr. Pilgrim has left."

Dorcas shrugged. "So what!"

"So . . . ," Fidelio hesitated. Dorcas' sly expression bothered him. She had a reputation for bewitching clothes. Could she have tampered with the blue cape?

"Never mind." Fidelio stepped out into the garden.

Gabriel was nowhere to be seen, but Fidelio spied Tancred talking to the new boy, Joshua Tilpin. Fidelio ran up to them. "Tancred, can I have a word in private?" He glanced at Joshua.

Tancred patted Joshua's shoulder and said, "Run along, Josh. And thank you for finding that book."

Joshua beamed at Tancred. "Anytime, Tancred. See you later." The small boy sauntered off on legs that looked as though they couldn't support a bird, let alone a boy.

"He's weird," Fidelio remarked lightheartedly.

"Not at all," said Tancred. "He's a good guy. Very helpful."

Fidelio changed the subject. "I wondered if you know what has happened to Charlie?"

"As a matter of fact, I do. Let's walk a bit."

Fidelio followed Tancred up to the castle walls,

where he found Emma and Olivia sitting on top of the log pile. Olivia appeared to have an endless supply of apples, because here she was, peeling again with the small silver knife that she carried everywhere. Emma was watching her friend with a frown that had become permanent lately.

"These two know what's happened," said Tancred, perching on one of the lower logs.

"I'm always the last to know anything these days." Fidelio sat on a log halfway up.

"That's because you're not endowed," said Olivia. "Not that I am. And not that I'd want to be."

Fidelio ignored her. "Tancred, tell me please, where's Charlie gone?"

Tancred took a breath. "It all started on Sunday morning when Billy Raven escaped from his new parents." He went on to tell Fidelio everything.

"Phew!" Fidelio glanced at the looming red walls. "That's what all the fuss was about. It woke me up. Dogs barking, cars honking, police sirens, thunder — that was you, I suppose," he said to Tancred.

"Guilty!" Tancred put up his hands with a grin. "But Sander saved the day. If it wasn't for him, I don't think I'd be here."

They could see Lysander arguing with Asa Pike on the other side of the playing field, and Tancred said, "Asa's really got it in for Sander today. First, he said Sander's tie wasn't straight, then he said he was being too noisy, which he wasn't, and now look at him."

"I've got a bad feeling about today," said Emma quietly.

Fidelio knew what she meant. Maybe it had something to do with Charlie's absence. "What's all this about a castle of mirrors?" he asked.

"My auntie read about it in a book," said Emma. "Hundreds of years ago, one of the Red King's children set the castle on fire, with his brother's family still inside. But one of them escaped, and that was Billy's ancestor. The walls of the castle turned to shining glass. Imagine!"

"And Charlie thinks he'll find his father there," Tancred added.

Olivia suddenly jumped up and flung her apple into the bushes. "I wish Charlie was here," she said, striding away from them.

Fidelio felt the same way.

That night, the atmosphere in the King's room was distinctly chilly. It was a chill that seeped right through to the bone and Emma, for one, couldn't stop shivering. She shook so much that her pen kept dropping out of her hand. The third time she dropped it, the pen rolled right across the table, and Emma was sure that Inez or Idith had pushed it. The twins kept staring at Emma with their blue china-doll eyes, and she found it almost impossible to concentrate.

Joshua Tilpin had taken Charlie's empty seat beside Emma, and he leaned over the table, picked up her pen, and handed it back to her. He gave her a little smile that tugged at her until she was forced to smile back. But Joshua wanted more than a smile; he wanted her to fly. Emma suddenly imagined herself a great hawk, swooping over her friends, attacking their heads, their hands. . . . But why would she do such a terrible thing? She looked away from Joshua. He gave her the creeps.

Gabriel, sitting on the other side of Emma, whispered, "Are you OK, Em?"

Emma nodded.

"Quiet!" said Manfred. "No whispering."

Inez and Idith turned their cold gaze on Gabriel, Asa's yellow eyes hardened, and Dorcas Loom gave a secretive smile.

Emma glanced along the line beside her. Gabriel, Tancred, and Lysander were bent over their books. Their gloomy frowns made her feel even more uneasy.

When homework was over, the endowed children began to file out of the King's room with Manfred at their head. Emma waited for Gabriel, who was taking longer than usual to pack up his work. The same thing was happening to Tancred and Lysander. Books dropped, others wouldn't close. Pens rolled away and paper fluttered out of their hands.

"Something's wrong," said Emma.

"You can say that again," groaned Lysander.

"We're outnumbered," Gabriel said. "Four to five, six, if you count Manfred."

The three boys managed to gather everything together at last, and Emma walked with them toward the dormitories. As they were crossing the landing, Gabriel turned away from the group and began to run down into the hall.

"Where are you going, Gabe?" called Lysander. "Matron'll get you!"

"I'm allowed to do half an hour's practice in the Music Tower," said Gabriel. "Mr. Ebony gave me special permission on Friday." He pulled a note from his pocket. "So Matron will have to shove it."

This brought a smile to his friends' faces, but all three felt inexplicably uneasy as they watched Gabriel cross the hall to the door in the Music Tower.

Gabriel too had a sense of foreboding, but he loved to practice on the grand piano, and it was precisely because he had been feeling so troubled that he could hardly wait to lose himself in music.

It was a long climb to the top of the tower, and when Gabriel reached the music room, he had to sit on a stool to recover his breath. As he lifted the piano lid, he noticed a blue cape on a chair beside the window. Surely, it had to be Mr. Pilgrim's. Gabriel had always been very attached to Mr. Pilgrim. The strange teacher was a brilliant pianist, and although he made very few comments, Gabriel had always been aware of Mr. Pilgrim's warm approval.

Where was the piano teacher now? What had happened to him? Gabriel seldom used his endowment. It could affect him badly if he put on the clothes of someone who had suffered grief or pain. But this time Gabriel's curiosity got the better of him, and he felt compelled to put on the cape.

As soon as he pulled the hood over his head, reality began to slide away, and Gabriel was imprisoned in a darkness so deep and dreadful he couldn't escape from it. He tried to tear the hood away, but his arms were useless, and he was forced to endure the horror until he fell senseless to the floor.

THE WALL OF HISTORY

On a silver-white beach far away from his friends' misfortunes, Charlie found himself in a difficult situation. Billy had become angry and frightened when he heard the story of Prince Amadis. With his head down and hands thrust deep in his pockets, the white-haired boy paced the beach, kicking at sand and shells. "Why didn't you tell me?" he cried accusingly. "Why didn't you tell me about my guardian and the book and all those terrible things that happened — out there?"

"I'm sorry, Billy. My uncle didn't think it would be safe for you to know. And then, when we met the queen, somehow it was all too late." Charlie was keeping half an eye on the sea. The tide was coming in fast, and soon there would be no way off the beach. They were in a small bay with walls of dangerous-looking rocks on either side and an almost vertical cliff behind them. There was another problem. How would they reach the island?

Ignoring Billy for the moment, Charlie began to search the rocks and the base of the cliff for a boat. Why there should be one in such a secluded place, he hadn't considered. Slowly and steadily the sea crept over the sand.

"Charlie!" shrieked Billy, suddenly aware of the fast-approaching water. "What's happening?"

"The tide's coming in." Charlie was investigating a deep cave. It was so dark, he couldn't see where it ended. If only he had a flashlight. But he hadn't even brought a box of matches. A tiny light swept over his head and fluttered to the back of the cave. It was very faint, but it enabled Charlie to make out what looked like a boat, lying on its side at the top of a steep incline. The light moved across the cave, revealing a black wall glistening with water.

"Charlie! What are we going to do?" came a panic-stricken voice.

"Come and help," called Charlie. "I've found a boat."

Billy was beside him in a moment. "How did you find it?"

"There's a light." Charlie peered at the hovering shape. It had wings tipped with silver. "It's the white moth."

"Your wand," said Billy, "and look, it's sitting on something."

"An oar," cried Charlie. "There are two of them."

It was a small boat, but it took all their strength to heave it down the sloping floor of the cave and out on to the beach. By the time they got there, the water was lapping at the mouth of the cave.

Pulling off his socks and shoes, Charlie rolled up his trousers and told Billy to do the same.

"Where are we going?" asked Billy.

"Where do you think? To the island."

"N-n-nooooo!" moaned Billy. "I don't want to. I won't. There'll be ghosts out there after what happened. Please don't make me."

"Don't be an idiot," said Charlie touchily. "There's nowhere else to go. We'll drown if we wait any longer."

The boat was already beginning to float as they pulled it down the beach, and Charlie ordered Billy to jump in before it was too late. Still whining, Billy scrambled over the side while Charlie held the boat steady, and then Charlie was in, too. Sitting opposite Billy, he fixed the oars into the oarlocks and began to paddle away from the cliff.

"Can you row?" asked Billy, clinging to his narrow seat.

"Like a champion," said Charlie. "My great-grandpa lives by the sea."

"Oh!" said Billy, with a hint of admiration.

It was true. Charlie had become an excellent oars-man during his visits to the sea with Uncle Paton. But he'd never covered such a huge distance as the one he was now attempting. He rowed against the tide and the sea got rough. Now and again a huge wave would spill over the side and Billy would shriek with terror. Trying to hide his own fear, Charlie advised Billy to keep his eyes shut until they were safe.

"Will we ever be safe?" Billy's pathetic voice was beginning to get on Charlie's nerves.

"If you can't cheer up, just shut up!" he barked.

Realizing his life was in Charlie's hands, Billy didn't say another word. Charlie's arms were already aching so badly that he thought they would drop off before he got to the island. Every time he looked over his shoulder, the blue-gray shape with its crown of glass looked as distant as ever. If anything, it seemed to be receding and Charlie began to doubt its existence. Maybe it was a mirage that they would never reach — a cruel trick that kept pulling them farther and farther away from the mainland and out on to the empty ocean.

Charlie decided he wouldn't look back again until he had counted up to five hundred. He had a short rest, took a deep breath, then saw the white moth resting on his sleeve. Remembering that his former wand needed instructions in Welsh, Charlie said, "*Helpi vee!* Help me!"

He wasn't sure what to expect, but nothing miraculous happened. Giant waves still rocked the boat and broke over the bow, sending sprays of water over Charlie's back. But long before he had counted to five hundred, the boat thudded against a rock, and this time, when Charlie looked over his shoulder, they were there.

Steering carefully around the rock, Charlie jumped out, instructing Billy to sit tight while he pulled him into shallow water.

Billy's eyes were open now, and he couldn't wait to get out of the boat. With a loud splash, he landed beside Charlie, up to his waist in water.

Relief made both of them giggle. They pulled the boat out of the water and up onto a grassy bank, shaking with laughter and shivering with cold.

"We'll dry our clothes in the castle," said Charlie. "I don't want to arrive in just my underwear."

"It's not as if the king will be there," Billy remarked with another giggle.

It was just as well their shoes were dry as the ground was pitted with stones and thistles. According to *The Book of Amadis*, the fields around the castle had once been filled with well-tended crops. But now, coarse grass grew almost waist high. It was like moving through a prickly sea.

The ground began to slope up to a rocky hill dotted with small misshapen trees. Rising above the trees, the blazing glass walls of the castle cut into the blue sky in strange, jagged points. If there were any windows in the mysterious building they were made of mirrored glass, for nothing resembling a window could be seen.

The boys began to walk through the leafless windblown trees while the sun warmed their backs and dried their clothes. Closer and closer, they moved toward the castle. Higher and higher. Charlie found that he was trembling with apprehension. A lump had formed in his throat and he couldn't trust himself to speak.

All at once, Billy raced up to the castle. He touched the shining walls and said breathlessly, "It really is made of glass."

Charlie drew up beside him. "But where's the door?"

They scrambled around the castle, searching for a way in, but seeing only themselves reflected in the mirrored walls. The castle was far larger than Charlie had imagined. He realized that they had only reached the outer walls. Inside there must be a large courtyard and then the keep. He could just see the top of a tall glass tower some distance from the walls.

They had almost reached the point where they had started when Billy, a few meters ahead of Charlie, suddenly disappeared.

Charlie stumbled forward crying, "Billy, where are you?"

"Here!" came a voice.

Almost at his feet, Charlie noticed a hole that had previously been covered with coarse scrub. He knelt down and, peering inside, could just make out Billy's pale face smiling up at him.

"It's OK," said Billy. "There's a passage and I can see a light at the end."

Charlie climbed into the hole and slid into the

darkness. It was very exhilarating flying over such a shining, slippery surface, but landing on hard rock at the bottom was a bit of a shock.

"Ouch!" Charlie stood up and banged his head on the low ceiling. "Ouch again!" He was standing in a tiny underground space with barely enough room for two.

"Look, look!" Billy demanded. "A passageway."

Charlie turned sideways and saw a shadowy gap in the rock. He leaned down and looked inside. A narrow tunnel led toward a distant gleam of light. "That's not a passageway, it's a tunnel," said Charlie.

"Same thing."

"It's not. We'll have to crawl."

"Let's crawl, then." Billy dropped to his knees and began to crawl along the tunnel. His reluctance to visit the castle had vanished and he was now even more enthusiastic than Charlie.

They were halfway down the tunnel when Charlie began to hear the sound of a piano. His heart beat faster and yet he hesitated before climbing out of the tunnel.

He was afraid of what he might see. When he finally emerged from the dark, he found himself in a vast courtyard, covered with shining stones. The music came from a square tower in the center. A flight of narrow steps led up to an arched door in the tower; both the door and the steps were made of coarse black glass.

The steps were as rough as sandpaper and easy to climb. Billy went first and when they reached the top, he knocked politely on the door.

The music stopped but no one appeared. Charlie cautiously pushed the door and it swung inward. Together, the boys stepped into the room beyond.

Charlie's first sight of the man inside was a fragmented reflection, for the room was walled in rectangles of misty glass and its occupant stood behind him. Very slowly, Charlie turned. He saw a man of medium height with dark hair and large green eyes. He had a long, aquiline nose and a wide mouth. His skin was sallow and he looked as if he had spent a long time indoors. There was something familiar about the man and it gave Charlie a surge of hope.

317

The stranger smiled tentatively. "What have you brought me?" he asked.

"Nothing." Charlie was puzzled. "Were you expecting something?"

"Sometimes they send food." The man sat down on a rickety-looking chair and sighed. "A boy brings it from the mainland."

Aware that his father had lost his memory, Charlie asked, "What do they call you, sir?"

"I am called Albert Tuccini but, of course, that is not my real name."

"Do you . . . do you know your real name?"

Albert Tuccini shook his head. "I cannot help you there."

Charlie took a step closer to the man. "I think I know you, sir."

The man lowered his head. "Many people know me. I was a famous pianist."

"Then why are you here, sir?" asked Billy.

"Ah." Albert Tuccini put a finger to his lips. "It's not

safe for me outside. I do not belong here, you see. I have lost my country, my home, and my name."

Charlie thought he detected a foreign accent in Albert's speech, but he told himself that this could be explained by the man not knowing who he was. He went up to Albert Tuccini and touched his shoulder. "I think I know your real name, sir. Maybe I can help you to remember."

"Yes?" A little gleam of hope lit the man's sad, green eyes.

"I think your name is Lyell Bone."

"Lyell Bone," the man repeated. "It is a good name."

"And I'm Charlie, your son," said Charlie in a rush.

Billy pulled his sleeve. "You don't know that," he said in a low voice.

"I do," said Charlie. "I'm sure of it."

The man looked puzzled. "Son?" he said doubtfully. "It's not possible."

"Yes, yes!" cried Charlie, utterly convinced that this was indeed his father. "And now that I've found you, everything's going to be all right. I'll take you home, and you'll meet Uncle Paton again. Remember him? Paton Yewbeam."

"Paton?" the man repeated. "I remember Yewbeam. It was Miss Yewbeam who brought me here. Miss Eustacia Yewbeam. It is she who sometimes brings food."

"Of course!" Charlie was so excited he could hardly keep still. "There are three Miss Yewbeams. They're my great-aunts, and I know they made you disappear."

The man said, "Well, well," and shook his head. "Please, will you call me Albert for now? I am used to it."

"Just for now, then," Charlie agreed.

Billy suddenly said, "I can't live in this place! Not if the Yewbeams come here."

Charlie realized that for Billy, the situation was as bad as ever. "We'll find somewhere else," he told Billy, "soon as we can."

But while they had been talking, there had been a dramatic change in the weather. A northerly wind had begun to howl around the castle, and flurries of hail beat upon the glass walls. A journey across the sea would be too dangerous. They would have to wait until the storm died down.

Albert offered to give the boys a meal. Lifting the lid of a large oak chest, he took out several cans and emptied them into a saucepan. A small paraffin stove stood in the corner of the room and Albert proceeded to heat the food. When this was done Billy and Charlie were handed two bowls of baked beans and two spoons.

"I will use the saucepan," their host said cheerfully, dipping a wooden spoon into the remaining beans. "Food from a can can be very good, yes?"

"Yes," said Charlie, wondering if his father lived entirely on beans.

The boys sat on a straw mat that partially covered the hard glass floor and Mr. Tuccini sat on the only chair. While he ate, Charlie looked around the mirrored room. It was sparsely furnished. Against one wall was a mattress with a pile of blankets on top of it. A battered suitcase stood beside the mattress, and Charlie assumed it held all its owner's possessions, for there were none to be seen, except for a few books, some plates and spoons, and a pile of paper sitting on a round table. Beneath the table was a large bowl, a jug, and several jars. A windup gramophone had been placed on the floor just inside the door.

On one side of the door, a flight of steep steps led farther up the tower. Billy had been staring at these steps while he ate; in fact, he couldn't take his eyes off them. "Where do they go?" he asked, nodding at them.

"They lead up to the walls of history," said Albert. "I have been there but the walls tell me nothing. Sometimes, I hear laughter and singing, a word or two that I cannot understand and — sounds that I do not wish to tell."

"Ghosts?" asked Charlie.

"Maybe," said Albert evasively.

"I would like to go up there," said Billy.

But when they had finished their meal, the boys' eyes began to close and soon they were fast asleep.

When Charlie woke up, the mirrored room sparkled with reflected candlelight. He was lying under a blanket with Billy beside him, still sleeping.

"You were tired," said Albert, looking down at Charlie. "You have had a long journey."

"Very long," said Charlie. "I'll tell you about it if you like."

"I would like it very much. To hear a voice is so good." Albert came and sat at the edge of the mat.

Before Charlie described his journey with Queen Berenice, he felt that Albert should know something about the children of the Red King and Bloor's Academy. Albert turned his head a little when Charlie mentioned Bloor's, as if the name struck a chord somewhere. But after this, Charlie's listener sat very still, regarding Charlie with a look of thoughtful concentration.

"I suppose it all sounds a bit difficult to believe,"

said Charlie when he reached the part where the white moth had discovered the boat.

"Nothing is improbable to one who cannot remember his own life," said Albert with a rueful smile. "And see, there is your moth."

Charlie saw the moth sitting close to Billy's white head.

"It was there all the while you slept," Albert told Charlie, "as though on guard."

Billy woke up and automatically felt for his glasses. He could see very little without them and he always felt lost until they were perched firmly on his nose.

"I thought I'd been dreaming," said Billy, sitting up. "But it's all true, isn't it?"

"It's true. We're in the Castle of Mirrors," said Charlie.

Billy immediately looked for the stairway beside the door. "And I was going to go up there, wasn't I? Really, it's more like I feel that I've *got* to go up there." He threw off his blanket and stood up, still gazing at the stairway. It seemed to draw him like a magnet.

"I'll come with you," said Charlie.

Albert handed Billy one of the many candles that stood in empty cans all around the room. "You will need this," he said. "It's dark up there."

"My ancestors lived here," said Billy proudly, "and Charlie thinks I might be able to see them. I was frightened yesterday, but not anymore." He marched over to the stairway and began to climb. Charlie followed more slowly.

The steps were unevenly spaced and rough underfoot. Charlie found them hard to climb. The stairway wound upward, becoming steeper and narrower all the time. Charlie lost sight of Billy, but he could hear his light footsteps hastening up the tower. The candlelight grew fainter as Billy drew ahead; soon Charlie only heard the tap of Billy's feet to guide him. "Billy, I can't see!" he shouted.

Billy had reached the walls of history. He was hardly aware of the shout from below, and Charlie had to grope his way up the steps and into the extraordinary room at the top. Here, the mirrored panes of glass that

formed the wall reflected Billy's white hair, his gleaming glasses, and the flickering candle in a hundred
different places. When Charlie stood beside the smaller
boy, his reflection looked faint and shadowy.

"They're coming," Billy whispered. He stood en-
tranced, staring at the glass wall.

Charlie began to make out indistinct forms drifting
behind Billy's reflection. "What can you see?" he asked
softly.

"People," said Billy in a hushed voice. "A whole
family. A man in — sort of armor — but his helmet's
off. And a blond lady, laughing. They're sitting at a
table and — eating, yes, it's a feast. They're hungry
and happy. One of them is like me — just like me.
Can you hear them, Charlie?"

"No. Nothing."

"I can hear names. And someone singing."

"What names?" asked Charlie.

"The blond lady called the man Amadis — and she
called the boy like me Owain. And then Amadis said,
'Again, Amoret. I love that song.'"

"Amoret!" cried Charlie.

"Shhh! You'll frighten them away."

"Amoret?" said Charlie, lowering his voice. "Are you sure he said Amoret?"

"Yes," Billy whispered. "The lady singing is Amoret. She has black hair and she's very beautiful."

Charlie stared at the walls of history, stared and stared, willing himself to see someone, anyone who could draw him in. At last, he began to hear distant singing and he found himself floating toward a pale face framed by dark curls.

"Charlie!" cried Billy. "You're not going in, are you? Don't! Don't! You'll never get out!"

THE BLACK YEW

Charlie struggled like a swimmer underwater. Traveling toward a reflection was very different from entering a painting or a photograph. Amoret's face kept disappearing. It was almost as if she were trying to send him back.

But Charlie wouldn't let go. He fought his way forward, pushing the heavy air aside, kicking at the bonds that held him back. At last, he broke into a room where a woman stood clutching two children. Prince Amadis had gone and Amoret was looking straight at Charlie.

"Go," cried Amoret. "Whoever you are, you must go!"

And now Charlie became aware of the terrible sounds outside the room. The boom of rocks on a heavy door, the hiss of arrows, the screams and moans of battle. He floated out into the courtyard, and in the midst of a panic-stricken crowd, he saw a small white-haired boy with a raven on his shoulder.

The boy darted toward a well and climbed inside. The next moment the castle walls burst into flames and Charlie was surrounded by a wall of fire.

"Help! Help!" Charlie screamed.

Something held him down. He couldn't escape, couldn't breathe.

There was an earsplitting crack, followed by the sound of splintering glass. It reminded Charlie of Uncle Paton's accidents, and he immediately felt reassured. Was he safe at home?

"Charlie! Charlie, come back!" called a distant voice.

Charlie blinked and found himself looking at a cracked mirror with lights dancing on every tiny pane. Broken glass lay all around him, glittering like tinsel.

"Charlie?" Billy stood before him, holding a candle. "Are you back?"

Charlie blinked again and shook himself. "Yes, I'm back."

"Mr. Tuccini had to break the glass. We thought you were trapped in the wall of history."

"It seemed the only way to get you out." Albert Tuccini peered down at Charlie. "It is a strange thing you do, this traveling. Not always good, I fear."

"No, not always," Charlie admitted. "But I just had to go in this time, because my ancestor Amoret is in there, too. She must have been in the castle when it was set on fire, before it turned to glass. But where were her children?"

"It is not possible always to find an answer," said Albert a little sadly. "Come. You have experienced some bad things. You must rest."

"The wall of history is broken, and it's all my fault," said Charlie ruefully.

"Only the surface," said Albert. "The walls are thick. They can withstand a lot more than my old shoe." He held up a black shoe, which he proceeded to put on his left foot, lacing it tightly before approaching the perilous staircase.

When Charlie descended into Albert Tuccini's room, dawn light was beginning to steal through the glass walls. The storm had gone and Albert announced that it would be a fine day. If they left soon, the tide would take them safely into the bay.

"You will come with us, won't you?" begged Charlie.

Albert spread his hands. "I dare not."

"But why? We'll keep you safe," Charlie declared. "You must come back, because of Mom — and everything."

"I have a wife?" Albert looked stunned.

"Of course. How do you think I got here?" said Charlie indignantly. He began to feel a rising panic. He'd found his father only to leave him in a place where he might never see him again. If Grandma Bone got to know about Charlie's visit to the island, the Yewbeams were sure to move his father somewhere even more inaccessible.

It was Billy who convinced Albert that he must come with them. "We can't row the boat on our own," he said, his eyes huge with anxiety. "We need you, Mr. Tuccini. Charlie's not strong enough to row all the way back again."

Albert scratched his curly hair. "Very well. Maybe

it is the right thing for me to do." He led the boys out of the tower and across the courtyard to a door set in the glass walls. One push and a panel of glass swung open. When they had all stepped out, Albert closed the panel. Now it was completely indistinguishable from the rest of the wall. "It can only be opened from the inside," Albert told the boys. "To enter one must use the chute."

A vision of Aunt Eustacia sliding down the chute popped into Charlie's head, and he grinned to himself.

As they walked back to the shore, Charlie told Billy about the white-haired boy he'd seen climbing into the well. "That's how he survived," he told Billy. "He climbed out after the fire, and somehow he got to the mainland and traveled all the way to the middle of Europe with his raven. That's where your name comes from. And your guardian, Christopher Crowquill — his ancestor was your ancestor's brother."

"Maybe I can live with Christopher Crowquill," said Billy hopefully.

Charlie was silent. Poor Christopher was in as

much danger as Billy. He couldn't possibly look after him. "Uncle Paton will know what to do," Charlie mumbled.

Albert Tuccini strode ahead of the boys. He told them that he walked to the shore every day. "For exercise, you know," he shouted back to them. "To fill my lungs and keep my limbs in shape."

Luckily, the storm had blown the boat farther inland rather than out to sea. Albert and the boys rolled up their trousers and took off their socks and shoes. They pulled the boat into the water, and while Charlie and Billy perched on one seat, Albert sat opposite and took up the oars. His back was toward the tall cliffs on the mainland, so he didn't see the two figures standing on the distant beach.

Charlie saw them first. His heart gave a lurch. Was it the Yewbeams? Billy saw the figures too and he clutched Charlie's sleeve. "They've come to get me," he whimpered. "I should have stayed on the island."

"You wouldn't have been any safer," Charlie told him. "Calm down, it might not be them."

Albert looked over his shoulder. "People. Can you see who they are, Charlie? Do you want to return to the castle?"

Charlie screwed up his eyes and stared at the beach. "No," he said slowly. "I think — yes, yes, I'm sure I know who it is." For one of the figures was beginning to come into focus. A tall man with black hair and a black coat. "Yes!" cried Charlie. "It's my uncle Paton. I don't know who the other person is, but he's very small and kind of hunched. I don't think he can be dangerous."

Charlie's excitement got the better of him, and he bounced up in his seat, tipping the boat sideways.

"Whoa!" cried Albert. "You almost had us in the water, Charlie Bone!"

Helped by the incoming tide, they were now fast approaching the beach. Charlie couldn't wait to see his uncle's face when Albert stepped ashore, for Lyell Bone had been Uncle Paton's best friend, and surely Paton could help him remember who he really was.

"Uncle Paton!" Charlie called. "Guess who I've found!"

Paton waved and shouted. "I see you have Billy Raven with you. And here is Mr. Crowquill."

"No, no! You don't understand." Charlie couldn't stand the suspense.

Albert looked back at the beach, but Uncle Paton gave no sign that he had recognized him. The boat bumped onto a sandbank and Albert and the boys climbed out, splashing through the shallow water as they pulled the boat onto the beach.

Charlie couldn't wait any longer. "Look, Uncle Paton, I've found my father."

Uncle Paton regarded Albert with a puzzled frown. Eventually, he said, "Charlie, this is not your father."

Charlie was so shocked he couldn't speak.

"They call me Albert Tuccini," said Albert, extending his hand. "I am very pleased to meet you."

Uncle Paton introduced himself and Christopher and they all shook hands.

Charlie felt as though there were a lead weight on his chest. It caused him so much pain he couldn't think, couldn't move. The immense cloud of disappointment muffled the voices around him. He was vaguely aware that Christopher Crowquill was hugging Billy. And he saw Uncle Paton listening to Albert and gazing over the sea to the Castle of Mirrors. His uncle must have persuaded Albert not to return to the island, because the next moment the happy group was moving up the beach.

"Charlie, are you all right?" Uncle Paton looked back and waited for him.

"I . . . I . . . yes," said Charlie miserably. He walked up to his uncle.

"You've had a terrible disappointment. I'm so sorry, Charlie." Uncle Paton squeezed his shoulder.

"It's OK. I was being silly. I knew it couldn't really be him."

"One day it will be," said Uncle Paton.

Charlie watched his uncle and Albert push the ·boat into the cave. And then they were all climbing the wall of rocks into another bay where a narrow path wound up to the top of the cliffs.

Christopher Crowquill led the way, with Billy behind him. Next came Uncle Paton, followed by Charlie. Albert Tuccini brought up the rear. It was a perilous climb, and when they were halfway up, Uncle Paton said, "You should have seen us coming down, Charlie. We were on our bottoms most of the time."

Charlie managed a halfhearted smile. He looked back at the Castle of Mirrors. It was shrouded in mist. Soon it would be invisible. But its precious secrets would still be there, hidden in the wall of history, and one day Charlie would return to find them.

By the time they had reached the top of the cliff, the tide was high, and looking down, Charlie saw foaming waves crashing against a barrier of jagged black rocks.

Albert Tuccini had been watching Charlie anxiously. He put a hand on Charlie's arm and said, "I am sorry that I am not your father."

"That's all right," said Charlie lamely.

They were walking along the cliff top to the road where Uncle Paton had parked his car. As they turned away from the sea, a bird gave a sudden shriek and flew into the sky. Peering ahead to see what had frightened the bird, Charlie saw a dark shape standing directly in their path.

Uncle Paton slowed down. "What the . . ." He shook his head. "A tree." He strode out again ahead of the others.

When they drew near the tree, they saw that it was squat and curiously misshapen. Its crooked branches bore clusters of thin, blackened needles, and the bark of its gnarled trunk was riven with scars.

"A black yew." Paton's voice was choked with dawning horror.

Before their eyes, a gnomelike face twisted out of the rough bark. The branches shriveled, scattering their needles like dark rain, and the writhing trunk slowly assumed the form of a tall man. It was Tantalus

Ebony. He stared at the motionless group, his thin lips curled into a malicious smile.

Charlie couldn't believe his eyes. Was Tantalus Ebony a shape-shifter?

The man spoke. "We meet again, Paton Yewbeam."

"What . . . ?" Paton began.

"Come, come, Paton. Don't tell me you haven't been expecting this moment. I warned you, didn't I, that if you harmed my Yolanda you would pay for it with your life?" The voice was familiar, and yet it seemed to come from deep underground. "You KILLED MY DARLING!" the shape-shifter suddenly roared.

"Yorath," Paton said fearlessly, "your daughter was a monster."

The shape-shifter gave a scream of fury and came running full tilt at Uncle Paton. Charlie could see what was going to happen. Careless of his own life, Tantalus would take his uncle over the cliff. Charlie clung fiercely to Paton, but his uncle pried away his clinging hands and stepped forward.

In a sudden instant, a small gray body flew at Tantalus. For a moment, they wrestled together, and then amazingly, Christopher Crowquill was forcing the shape-shifter toward the cliff. It happened so fast that no shouts, no movements were quick enough to stop their headlong rush toward the cliff's edge — and over it!

There was a shout, a scream, and then silence.

Paton ran to the place where the two figures had disappeared. He spread his arms as Charlie and Billy leaped forward. "NO!" he commanded, forcing them back. But Charlie had already seen the boiling sea and the dark rocks. There was nothing else, except for a black bird bobbing on the waves. A crow? A raven? Or a shape-shifter?

"The dear man gave his life for me," Paton said huskily.

"Why?" cried Billy. "Why did he do it? He was my only relative. My guardian. Now there's no one again."

"There's us," said Charlie.

"Why? Why?" Paton shook his head. "It makes no sense." He squared his shoulders and seemed to pull himself together. "We must leave here. I'll alert the coast guards when we've put some distance between us and this awful place. Nothing more can be done."

In stunned silence, they walked on until they came to Paton's car. Charlie and Billy scrambled into the back, while Albert took the passenger seat.

While he drove, Uncle Paton explained the shape-shifter's attack to a bewildered Albert Tuccini. "He is so old he has no form of his own and has to borrow the shape and sometimes the minds of other creatures. His daughter was just as bad. She killed my mother, and then tried to do away with someone very dear to me."

Charlie whispered, "Miss Ingledew?"

Billy shuffled away and huddled in the corner, a picture of misery.

"What a fiend this Yolanda must have been," said Albert.

"I electrocuted her," Paton said flatly.

If Albert was shocked, he didn't show it. Maybe some of his memories were coming back to him. Memories that were so bad, nothing would ever surprise him again.

After they had been traveling for some time, they stopped at a café on the edge of a small town. The day was warm and sunny and Uncle Paton chose to sit at one of the tables outside. He gave Charlie a list and enough money to pay for four lunches. Billy, who seemed to have recovered a little, followed Charlie into a low-beamed room, lit by several soft lights.

"Just as well your uncle didn't come in," said Billy, nudging Charlie's elbow as he read out the list to a purple-haired woman behind the counter.

Charlie gave Billy a warning look, and Billy said in a crushed voice, "I didn't give anything away, did I?"

Charlie grinned at the purple-haired woman, and she smiled back in a surprised way before disappearing through a curtain made of beads.

When Charlie and Billy went back to their table,

Uncle Paton was in a public phone booth across the road.

"He is telling the police about the accident," said Albert. "It's a terrible thing."

"One bad thing and one good thing, really," said Charlie without thinking.

Billy shot him an injured look. Albert said nothing. A few moments later, a girl in a very short black dress appeared with a tray of sandwiches, water, orange juice, and coffee. Uncle Paton returned from the phone booth, saying he had done his best to explain what had happened, but the police seemed to think it was a hoax.

"I don't know what else I can do," said Uncle Paton with an uneasy glance in Billy's direction. "As for Alice, how am I going to tell her? She'll be heartbroken."

"Like me," said Billy, gazing at the ham sandwich he couldn't eat.

"Billy, dear boy, I don't know if this will help, but your guardian cared very, very much for you. He did what he did for a good reason. In fact, I believe he sacrificed himself for you. For seven long years, he longed to see you. He would not lightly have given up an opportunity to be with you."

In a weak voice, Billy said, "Oh."

Albert Tuccini remained quiet during the meal. There was a strange, faraway look in his eyes, and he seemed hardly aware of the others. When the sandwiches had been eaten (Charlie ate Billy's), Albert announced that he was going inside to find the men's restroom.

Several minutes passed. When a quarter of an hour had gone by and Albert still had not returned, Uncle Paton became anxious and Charlie was sent to look in the restroom. There was no one there.

Uncle Paton frowned when he heard the news. "No one? Are you sure?"

"More or less," said Charlie.

Paton stood up. "I'll have a look."

"Do you think you should? There are lots of lights in . . . ," Charlie began.

But his uncle was already striding through the

door of the café. Charlie prayed that he wouldn't have an accident. A few moments later, he heard a man's voice shout, "Sue, the lights have all gone out in the men's restroom. There's an awful mess in there. Glass everywhere."

Uncle Paton came hurrying out. He looked flushed. "Bother!" he muttered. "Still, I'm sure no one can point the finger at yours truly."

He had been followed by the purple-haired woman, who now looked extremely irritated. "Are you Mr. Paton Yewbeam?" she asked.

"Er, yes," Uncle Paton said nervously.

"That guy left a note for you." She handed Paton a folded note and walked off, grumbling that she had enough to do without having to carry notes and clean restrooms.

Uncle Paton unfolded the note. His expression became very grave as he read it. "I can't say I'm surprised. Poor man."

"What does it say?" begged Charlie.

His uncle read the note aloud.

"Dear Mr. Yewbeam,

I have so enjoyed knowing briefly you and Charlie and Billy. But now we must part company. Do not look for me, I beg you. It is better this way. Maybe we will meet again in happier times.

"Your humble friend,

Albert Tuccini (so-called)"

"Where will he go?" asked Charlie. "If he doesn't know who he is?"

Uncle Paton gave a shrug and tucked the note in his pocket. "I believe he is a gifted pianist, Charlie. We must hope that he can find a life for himself, somewhere in this world."

They walked back to the car and began another long journey south, toward Filbert Street and Bloor's Academy.

Christopher Crowquill's sudden and dreadful departure had put everything else out of Charlie's mind, but now the memory of his journey with Queen Berenice came flooding back and he couldn't imagine how he could have forgotten to tell his uncle.

"You didn't ask how we found the island," he said, leaning over Paton's seat.

"Your friend Tancred told me about the white horse, if that's what you mean," said Uncle Paton. "I couldn't get him off the phone. He told me everything: oaths and ogres, spirits and storms. That lad can go on, can't he? Not that I wasn't interested. You two have certainly been through the wringer these past few days."

"Wringer?" asked Billy.

"Squeezed, mangled, wrung out," Uncle Paton explained.

"Mangled," said Billy quietly. "Yes, I feel mangled."

"Boys, I should . . ." Uncle Paton hesitated, and then he said, "Never mind." Charlie wondered what his uncle had been going to say. His voice had held a note of warning, but perhaps he felt that they had been through enough today.

There was a long silence and then Charlie said, "The queen ran away when she saw the island. I wonder where she went."

At the mention of the queen, Billy sat up and a smile crossed his face. "She said she wouldn't abandon us. I think we'll see her again. In fact, I know we will. It's like she's a kind of parent."

Charlie was glad to hear Billy sounding so hopeful. He wished he felt the same.

A tiny point of glimmering light moved down his sleeve, and leaning forward, Charlie said, "Uncle Paton, I've found my wand. Or rather it found me. It's turned into a moth."

"I'll be darned. What's next?"

The moth's company was comforting to Charlie, who just then felt in great need of comfort. "You won't tell Mom what I thought, will you?" he asked his uncle. "About my dad?"

"No, Charlie. I'll keep that to myself."

LOSING THE BALANCE

It was dark when they arrived in the city. Uncle Paton didn't drive straight to Filbert Street, as Charlie expected. He parked, instead, beside the familiar and very noisy building where Fidelio's family lived. Gunn House.

"What are we doing here?" asked Charlie.

Uncle Paton turned around in his seat. "It seemed the best solution," he said, looking at Billy.

Billy had been silent for most of the journey. He had even given up wondering where he would go or where he would be safe. Maybe he had expected to live at number nine, although with Grandma Bone around, it would have been impossible to hide him for long. Now, all at once, Billy grasped what Uncle Paton was saying.

"Do you mean that I'm to live here?" said Billy.

"I can't think of anywhere better," said Paton. "As a matter of fact, Mr. and Mrs. Gunn have already approved the plan. You'll hardly be noticed in a house that holds

seven children already. It was Mr. Crowquill's sugges-
tion." Paton's voice softened. "And a very good one,
too. You were never out of his thoughts, Billy."

It was then that Charlie guessed why Christopher
Crowquill had saved Uncle Paton's life. Christopher was
already ill, anyone could see that. He was an easy victim
for the Bloors. Not so for Uncle Paton, who was endowed
with a deadly talent. Christopher had saved the only
person he knew who could protect Billy Raven.

Billy already looked happier. "Yes, it is a good idea.
I've stayed with Fidelio before."

As soon as they got out of the car, the noise from
Gunn House came surging toward them. Musical
instruments of every description were being banged,
blown, scraped, and pounded. Mr. Gunn's loud bass
and Mrs. Gunn's powerful contralto competed with
their children's instruments, and the whole building
shook with sound.

"Good thing the house is detached," said Uncle
Paton. He pressed a knob beside the front door.

Immediately, a recorded voice boomed, "DOOR!

DOOR! DOOR!" Obviously a bell would never have been heard above such a racket.

Fidelio's older brother, Felix, answered the door. "Charlie Bone!" he exclaimed. "Fidelio's been worried sick about you. Where've you been?"

"It's a long story." Charlie stepped into the house, closely followed by Billy.

"Billy Raven! So you were together all the time," said Felix, banging the door shut.

"Hold on," said Charlie. "My uncle is still outside. Do you mind turning off the lights?"

"Good grief! Mr. Yewbeam!" Felix hurriedly switched off the hall light. "Oh, parents! Lights!" he shouted. "Mr. Yewbeam's here!" He opened the front door and Uncle Paton stepped into the dark hall.

Mr. and Mrs. Gunn continued their duet in the kitchen, while Felix bellowed, "Lights, parents! Lights! Paton the power-booster is here."

Charlie couldn't see Uncle Paton's face, but he knew his uncle was blushing because of the way he cleared his throat.

Still singing, Mrs. Gunn poked her head out of the kitchen door. "What, what, what, what, what, what, what, what?" she trilled in the scale of C major.

"YEWBEAM, MA!" yelled Felix. "Mr. Yewbeam. Lights."

"Heavens!" sang Mrs. Gunn, turning off the kitchen light.

This brought a musical bellow from Mr. Gunn as he stumbled over the deaf cat, and a yell from the cat whose tail had been stepped on.

"So, Billy's been found," said Mrs. Gunn when she saw him cautiously entering the kitchen. "Welcome, Billy, you'll be safe here, my love. So many children, so much music. You'll be well hidden."

The three visitors sat at the kitchen table, and while they ate a selection of Mrs. Gunn's exotic sandwiches, Felix gave them the news from Bloor's Academy. Felix had recently obtained his music degree and was about to embark on a world tour with his group when he'd been summoned to Bloor's to fill in for a music teacher who'd mysteriously disappeared. "Name of Ebony," said Felix.

"We know," said Charlie.

"Couldn't resist the offer," Felix added. "The pay's really good."

"I bet," said Uncle Paton. "So what's been going on?"

"What hasn't?" said Felix dramatically. "Gabriel Silk's in a coma. Left the school."

"What?" cried Charlie. "How did it happen?"

"Something about a cape," said Felix. "But your other friend, the stormy one . . ."

"Tancred? What's happened to him?" Charlie dropped his sandwich and the cat pounced on it.

"Gone berserk," said Felix. "It keeps raining on his friends. Fidelio's been soaked several times, so's Lysander, and that girl Emma Tolly has had a really bad time. Her fingers were struck by lightning."

"Not her fingers!" Charlie could hardly believe it. What could possibly have happened to Tancred to make him torment his friends in this way? Charlie had been thinking about taking the rest of the week off from school, but that was out of the question now. He had to find out what was going on at Bloor's. Cook's words echoed in the back of his mind. *"I'm the lodestone, Charlie. I keep the balance. Once that has gone, we're lost."*

So, what had happened to Cook?

"Three against six," Charlie said to himself. "Seven if you count Manfred."

"What's that, Charlie?" said Uncle Paton.

Charlie looked up. "I've got to get back to Bloor's."

"Not tonight, dear boy," said his uncle. "The lights will be out. They probably won't even open the door."

"Tomorrow, then," said Charlie. "As soon as possible. I'll walk if I have to."

"No need for that," said Felix. "I'll give you a lift."

When Charlie and Uncle Paton got up to leave, there was an unpleasant noise under the table and Mr. Gunn sang, "Pusskins has eaten a parsnip again!"

Charlie was relieved to see Billy join in the laughter. He was definitely in the right place — at least for now.

As soon as Charlie walked into number nine and

turned off the hall light, Grandma Bone shouted at him from the living room. "Don't bother to tell me where you've been. I know. You stupid boy."

"Cut it out, Grizelda," growled Paton.

Charlie was grabbed by Maisie, who drew him into the candlelit kitchen clasped in a bear hug. His mother joined in the hug, and when Charlie had been almost suffocated, he was allowed to sit at the table and drink a mug of cocoa.

Naturally, Amy and Maisie wanted to know everything that had happened, but Uncle Paton insisted that Charlie be allowed to go to bed while he told them about the Castle of Mirrors.

Charlie's eyes were closing as he climbed into bed. The last thing he saw before he fell asleep was the soft glow of the white moth as it settled on his bed-side table.

Felix Gunn was as good as his word. He turned up in a small, rather battered French car, just as Charlie had finished his breakfast.

"Who's that?" Grandma Bone demanded, as Felix whisked Charlie off to Bloor's.

"None of your business," said Maisie.

But, of course, Grandma Bone was bound to find out. Whether it was Felix's visit that drew her attention to the Gunns, Charlie would never know. Perhaps the Bloors had never seriously considered the Gunn family as Charlie's allies, until Fidelio's brother arrived outside number nine. But once the Bloors began to take an interest in Gunn House, the consequences were disastrous.

Charlie could feel the tension in the air as soon as he walked into assembly. Fidelio gave him the thumbs-up sign from the stage, but everyone else stared at him suspiciously. He felt as though he'd grown horns. "And I've only been away for two days," he said to himself.

Charlie finally caught up with Fidelio during the first break.

"I don't know who's been spreading the rumors,

but there have been some wild stories going around about you and Billy," said Fidelio, as they walked across the grass together. "People were saying that you'd been expelled."

"I'd better tell you the truth," said Charlie.

Fidelio suggested they keep walking as there were eavesdroppers everywhere. In a few minutes, they were joined by Lysander. Charlie had never seen him look so downhearted. It was he who had found Gabriel lying senseless under a blue cape.

"I was worried when he went up to the music room," Lysander told Charlie. "Especially when Fido had seen Dorcas Loom taking a cape into the tower. As soon as I found Gabriel, I told Dr. Saltweather. He called the ambulance."

"You told the right person," Fidelio said gravely. "If you'd told Matron, poor old Gabe might never have made it to the hospital."

It was a sobering thought.

"There was a kind of earthquake that night," Fidelio

added as an afterthought. "A great rumble underground. But in the morning everything looked normal."

"Underground?" said Charlie, frowning.

"And now look at Tancred." Lysander pointed across the field. "Tancred and that little squirt."

Charlie saw Tancred and Joshua sharing a joke with Dorcas Loom of all people. Joshua's sweater was plastered with dead leaves.

"But how . . . ," began Charlie.

"Magnetism!" Lysander spoke through gritted teeth.

"Joshua?" Charlie was incredulous.

"You'd be surprised," Lysander said grimly. "My mom knows all about it. You don't have to be strong or handsome or even clever. Some people have just got it. They can twist you around their little fingers."

"But Tancred," said Charlie in disbelief. "He was helping us. How could he turn — just like that? I mean, it didn't happen to you."

"I was prepared," said Lysander. "But magnetism is a powerful endowment. You must have felt it, Charlie. When Joshua smiles at you, there's a kind of tug that makes you want to be his friend, in spite of yourself."

"I have felt something," Charlie admitted. "But I won't let him get to me."

Lysander nodded in his wise and thoughtful way. "And nor will Emma."

"Emma's stronger than she looks," said Charlie. "But Tancred. How could Tancred let himself be so — so taken in?"

Lysander sighed. "Tancred's a good guy, but he's just the tiniest bit vain. Joshua played on that. And now Tancred's putty in his hands."

"I can't believe it," said Charlie. On the other side of the grounds, someone screamed. One of the smaller new girls had been knocked over by a large log. Idith and Inez stood smirking, a few meters away.

"It was them," said Lysander. "They're evil, those two."

Olivia and Emma had seen the boys and were just approaching them when a cloud burst right above the girls' heads. As they ran forward, the rain moved with them, and the three boys turned and raced for the trees. Charlie caught a glimpse of Tancred's smiling face and Joshua Tilpin rocking with laughter.

"He did it on purpose," cried Olivia as she bounded for cover. "Glad you're back, Charlie. Maybe you can do something about Tancred."

Charlie didn't know what he could do. He looked around the circle of faces. It was good to know there were a few friends whom he could still rely on. And then he noticed Emma's hands. The tip of each finger was bandaged. Only her thumbs had escaped the lightning or whatever it was that had injured her.

"Was that really Tancred?" Charlie stared at the bandages.

"I don't know," said Emma. "One minute I was standing by the log pile, talking to Liv, and the next there was a clap of thunder, a flash, and everyone screamed and rushed indoors. I felt a kind of stinging in my fingers. . . ."

"And I looked at her hands," said Olivia, pointing at Emma's fingers, "and they were bright red."

"They're better now." Emma waggled her fingers. "And I can't prove it was Tancred."

"It was him all right," Olivia insisted. "You've got to do something, Charlie!"

"Me?" said Charlie as everyone looked at him.

"You can begin by telling us where you've been," said Lysander.

"OK."

Charlie gave his friends a brief description of his ride on the shell beach and then the extraordinary Castle of Mirrors. There was a gasp of horror when he told them about Tantalus Ebony and Christopher Crowquill. No one knew what to say until Fidelio uttered a small grunt and said, "Just like that? It's too horrible."

Charlie didn't tell them that he had believed Albert Tuccini to be his father. His disappointment was still too painful.

"It's horrible, all right," said Lysander. "But only too possible. We all know Albert Tuccini, don't we? He came to give us a piano recital during spring semester. Don't you remember?"

It all came flooding back. "Of course," said Charlie slowly and sadly. "And the face at the window in my great-aunt's house, and the piano at the top, after the fire. It was Albert Tuccini all the time, not . . . not someone else."

"Those Yewbeam aunts of yours!" Lysander raised his big, brown eyes to the sky. "They're criminals, Charlie. They've been taking advantage of that poor pianist, pretending to help him but all the time making money from his concerts. What a bunch of horrors."

"You can say that again," said Charlie with a grimace.

Tancred's mischievous shower had stopped by the time break was over, and the five friends were able to run into school without getting any wetter.

Charlie decided that he must find Cook. Only she was wise enough to advise him now. But when she didn't appear at lunchtime, Charlie was afraid that even Cook had fallen prey to the sinister forces that were creeping through Bloor's Academy.

Snack time was Charlie's only chance to get into the kitchen, so while Fidelio kept watch, Charlie slipped around the counter and entered the noisy kitchen.

"What do you want, young man?" asked one of Cook's assistants, a thin young woman with a red face and fluffy hair.

"I'm looking for Cook," said Charlie.

"She's not been well, love. She went to lie down."

"Oh." Charlie wasn't sure what to do next. Cook's secret rooms lay behind an insignificant broom closet. None of the kitchen staff knew of their existence. Maybe Cook was upstairs in the chilly room where the Bloors thought she slept. Charlie had a strong feeling that she would have gone to her cozy underground apartment.

"Thanks," he said to the assistant. He made for the door into the cafeteria, but as soon as the woman's back was turned, he bent double and shuffled quickly behind one of the counters. He had to wait until another assistant moved toward the sinks;

then he dashed to the broom closet, wrenched open the door, and leaped inside, closing the door behind him.

A small peg at the back of the closet served as a doorknob, and when Charlie turned it, a door opened into a dark passageway. Charlie closed the second door. He was now standing in utter darkness. Cook usually had a soft light burning in the passageway. Not today. Charlie's uneasiness turned into a foreboding feeling.

Groping his way along the wall, he stumbled down two steps, then inched forward until he could feel a small closet. He opened the door and stepped into what had once been a cozy living room. Today, it was unrecognizable. For one thing, the floor sloped alarmingly. All the furniture had fallen over and now lay in a mess at the lower end of the room.

The feeble light from an overturned lamp showed Charlie a figure lying flat on the floor in front of the cold black stove. The dog, Blessed, sat beside it.

"Cook!" cried Charlie.

Blessed turned his mournful gaze on Charlie, as he rushed over to them.

Cook looked dreadful. Her gray hair had turned completely white. Her usually rosy face was drained of color and she appeared to have lost a great deal of weight.

"Charlie," moaned Cook. "You've come back."

"What's happened, Cook?" cried Charlie.

"The balance has gone. I told you, didn't I? We must keep the balance."

"But I thought that you kept the balance. You said you were the lodestone," said Charlie wildly.

"I can't keep it if you're not here, can I?" Cook spoke in a thin, resentful voice. "You and Billy, both gone, and that awful boy, that magnet, taking over."

"Sorry," Charlie mumbled. "I took Billy to the Castle of Mirrors."

"So I heard. Alice Angel has told me everything. That poor Mr. Crowquill. Mind you, I knew there was something fishy about Tantalus Ebony. Help me up, Charlie."

As Charlie pulled her to her feet, Cook said, "I was feeling so bad I thought I'd have a nap. The stove went out when all that happened" — she indicated the jumble of furniture at the end of the room — "and I couldn't get it going again."

The floor sloped so badly Charlie had difficulty in keeping his balance, let alone holding Cook upright. While she clung to the mantelpiece he quickly fetched a chair and pushed some newspapers under the front legs. When the chair was reasonably steady, Charlie helped Cook to sit down.

She sank back and patted her chest. "Aaah! That's better." Blessed shuffled close to her chair. "This old dog has kept me company, bless him." She stroked the dog's wrinkled head.

"When did all this happen?" asked Charlie.

"Monday night. After they found poor Gabriel. I can't say I was surprised, with you gone and the Torsson boy behaving badly."

"I thought I was doing the right thing, taking Billy to the Castle of Mirrors," said Charlie.

"Don't give me that, Charlie Bone," Cook said angrily. "You weren't thinking of Billy. You made yourself believe you'd find your father. You threw reason to the wind, didn't you? Once again, you rushed off without a thought for anyone else."

Charlie gave a huge sigh. "I did want to help Billy. Really. It's just . . . well, I wanted to find my dad, too."

Cook stared at him for a moment. "I can't blame you, Charlie," she said gently. "I'm sorry you didn't find your father."

Charlie avoided Cook's eye and looked at his feet. "So what can I do now?"

"I honestly don't know. We need another endowed child. Someone who can put friendship before self-interest. Someone who'll work with us, Charlie. Maybe then, things will balance out."

"I think I know who might be endowed," said Charlie. "But they won't admit it."

"Well, whoever it is, they'll need a powerful talent to turn things around this time." Cook got to her feet and smoothed her wrinkled apron. "You'd better get back now, Charlie. Blessed and I will follow at a slower pace."

When Charlie finally managed to make a break for the kitchen door, he found Fidelio sitting alone, while the fluffy-haired kitchen assistant wiped down the empty tables. "And where have you come from?" she barked at Charlie.

"He went to look for a cloth," said Fidelio, who had made a disgusting puddle of crumbs and orange juice on his table.

"Boys," grumbled the woman. "My girls don't make this kind of mess."

"Glad to hear it, ma'am," said Fidelio. "Good afternoon." And he dragged the speechless Charlie out of the cafeteria.

"So what's going on?" Fidelio whispered harshly as the two boys walked along the corridor of portraits.

"Cook's in a bad way," said Charlie gloomily. "And I've got to find someone who can turn everything around."

"An impossible task," groaned Fidelio.

They had almost reached the hall, and seeing Manfred striding down the staircase, Charlie whispered, "Maybe not."

Homework in the King's room that night was even more unpleasant than Charlie expected.

"Good of you to join us, Bone," said Manfred when Charlie walked in.

Charlie took a seat beside Emma while six unfriendly faces watched him from the other side of the table. Tancred sat alone, Charlie noticed, so there was still a hope that Joshua hadn't entirely won him over. On the other side of Emma, Lysander was keeping his head down. He bent over his work, refusing to look anyone in the eye.

The twins began the trouble: Charlie's books were sent flying off the table and Emma was hit by a pencil case. When Lysander's exercise book was ripped down the middle and hurled to the ceiling, he lost his temper.

"Cut it out, you trash!" he yelled at the twins, flinging a book at them.

The twins ducked together. They didn't cry out or scowl or even frown. Their faces were completely blank.

Manfred barked, "Next time you open your mouth it's detention for you, Sage."

Lysander made an ambiguous sound and sat down.

Joshua was smiling at Tancred, and in the next few minutes, Charlie, Emma, and Lysander were the victims of a small downpour that soaked their hair and their work. Surprisingly, Manfred came to their rescue.

"Stop that, smart aleck," Manfred barked at Tancred.

Somehow, Charlie survived the evening and then another whole day. But on Thursday night he lay awake, long after lights-out, trying to decide what his next move should be.

He heard a car door slam. There were muffled footsteps in the courtyard below. Charlie ran to the window and looked down. Manfred and Weedon were dragging a small white-haired boy toward the main doors.

Billy had been found.

OLIVIA'S TALENT

Felix Gunn was dismissed from Bloor's Academy. Before he went, however, he managed to relay the grim events of Billy's capture to Fidelio and Charlie.

In the middle of the night a wolf — or something like it — had jumped through the open window of one of the bedrooms. The Gunn children were not easily frightened. In fact, they were a brave and daring bunch. They had attacked the beast with anything that came to hand. Cellos, music stands, drumsticks, and even a French horn had been used to beat the snarling, creeping, dreadful creature.

But by the time Mr. and Mrs. Gunn had come to their children's rescue, Billy Raven had run howling out of the front door — straight into the arms of Manfred Bloor.

"Flushed out," said Fidelio, "like a poor rabbit."

No sooner had Fidelio spoken than Manfred stood

in the doorway of the blue coatroom, where Felix had been relating his grisly tale.

"Felix Gunn, you've been dismissed," Manfred said coldly.

"So I have." Felix made a little bow. "Good-bye, boys. And good luck. You'll certainly need it." He picked up his guitar and hummed his way across the hall to Mr. Weedon, who was obliged to unlock and unbolt the heavy doors.

"Stop gaping, you two," snarled Manfred. "Get to your classrooms."

Charlie and Fidelio obeyed without a murmur.

Billy didn't appear in school. He wasn't seen until Friday afternoon when everyone was dashing out to catch the school buses. Charlie happened to look up just as he passed the staircase, and there he was, a small figure standing in shadow at the far end of the landing. Charlie raised his hand, but before Billy could respond, Manfred shooed Charlie through the door.

• • •

When Charlie got home, the Friday tea party was already in progress. Grandma Bone was absent, so the atmosphere was considerably lighter than it had been the week before. However, Charlie caught Uncle Paton looking slightly pensive between mouthfuls of his pistachio ice cream. At length his uncle explained that he had been to see Alice Angel. When she heard about Mr. Crowquill's brave sacrifice, she had become extremely distressed. She had closed her store, put her house up for sale, and was, this very weekend, preparing to leave the city forever.

"But she can't!" cried Charlie, a spoonful of ice cream held in midair. "She's the only one who knows how to save us."

"I dare say you know what you mean, but we don't," Uncle Paton said dryly.

Charlie had deliberately put his terrible week to the back of his mind while he enjoyed his treats, but now he realized that he would have to explain himself.

When Charlie's three relatives heard about Billy's

capture, Tancred's defection, and Cook's upturned room, they pushed the remains of their delicious meal away from them, declaring that their appetites had fled.

Maisie was all for Charlie leaving the academy immediately. Amy kept murmuring, "No, no, no. It's too much." Uncle Paton stood up and paced the kitchen, pummeling the fist of his left hand into the palm of his right. Suddenly, he wheeled around and said, "What makes you think that Alice Angel can help?"

"She knows about someone's endowment," said Charlie. "Someone who might be able to turn things around for us."

"Who?" Paton demanded.

"I think it's Olivia, but I'm not absolutely sure," Charlie replied.

"Then find out, dear boy," Paton commanded. "Tomorrow, first thing, or Alice will be lost to you. What are your plans?"

Charlie admitted that he didn't have any.

"Hmmm." Uncle Paton paced again. He began to issue instructions while he was on the move. "This is what you must do, Charlie. Tomorrow morning you will meet Emma at the bookstore. Together you will visit Emma's friend Olivia and persuade her to accompany you to Alice's house. It's merely a stone's throw away from the Vertigo place, I gather."

"What about Runner Bean?" said Amy. "Charlie always takes him for a walk on weekends."

"We'll get the Gunn boy to do that," said Uncle Paton. "I will phone the Gunns when I have arranged things with Julia — Miss Ingledew. Are you clear about all this, Charlie?"

Charlie nodded, then yawned. "I will be tomorrow."

"Moth!" cried Maisie, taking a swipe at Charlie's shoulder.

"NO!" shouted Charlie and Uncle Paton in unison.

"Goodness." Maisie's hand dropped to her side. "What a fuss about a little moth."

"It's my wand," said Charlie quietly.

"Silly me. I should have guessed," said Maisie huffily. "Why can't it sort out your problems, Charlie? That's what wands are supposed to do, aren't they?"

"It does help me." Charlie gently lifted the moth from his shoulder. "But not in an obvious way. It has to choose to."

"Pardon me for asking a silly question," said Maisie with a smile.

On Saturday morning, Fidelio and Runner Bean turned up at number nine.

"I don't think this was Uncle Paton's plan," said Charlie, as Fidelio and Runner Bean headed for the kitchen.

Maisie was delighted to see her old friend Runner. A meal of scraps was quickly provided for him, while Charlie and Fidelio ate hard-boiled eggs.

Grandma Bone came downstairs just as the three-some was leaving the house. "Not that dog again," she yelled.

Runner Bean lunged at Grandma Bone's ankles,

and there was an undignified scuffle before Charlie managed to get the big dog through the front door.

Emma was waiting for Charlie at the bookstore, so at least that part of the plan had worked. But whether Fidelio and Runner Bean were supposed to join them on their walk to Olivia's house, Charlie wasn't sure.

"We're backup," said Fidelio, before Charlie could voice his doubts. "And Runner can sniff out any lurking, spying, hairy beasts."

When three children and a dog arrived at Olivia's house, Mrs. Vertigo looked anxious. "We've never had an animal that big in our home," she said.

"He's OK, Mom," Olivia called from the top of the stairs. "Let him in."

"If you say so, Liv." Mrs. Vertigo stood aside while the group filed into the house and up the stairs to Olivia's room. It was rather tight. Olivia's bed, the floor, and the chairs were covered in clothes, shoes, hats, beads, and wigs in various colors.

"I've had it with all this stuff," Olivia declared. "I'm giving it all away."

"You can't," said Charlie, regarding the mounds of colorful clothes. "You're not — not you without all your . . . your . . ."

"Disguises?" Fidelio suggested.

"I don't want to be disguised anymore," said Olivia. "I'm not an actress."

"You are, you are!" Emma insisted.

Olivia shrugged. "Why are you guys here, anyway?"

Her four visitors sat on the bed, and Charlie explained the situation at Bloor's and why they needed to know if Olivia was endowed.

Olivia sat in a chair and listened impassively to Charlie. It was only when he described Billy Raven's desperate plight that he noticed her face soften a little and he felt a glimmer of hope.

"Couldn't you just visit Alice Angel," Charlie urged, "before she leaves the city? She's feeling really down because of Mr. Crowquill. Imagine, she kept him going all through the terrible time he was in prison, and now he's gone."

"It wouldn't hurt just to see her, Liv," said Emma.

Olivia frowned. She got up and looked out of the window. "I could go over the wall," she said.

Before she had time to change her mind, the others coaxed her downstairs and out into the garden. Olivia and Charlie climbed the wall while Emma, Fidelio, and Runner Bean waited in the Vertigos' garden.

Charlie knocked on Alice's backdoor but there was no response. He looked through the windows; all the downstairs rooms appeared to be empty. Olivia went to the front of the house and pulled the bell chain. No one answered the door. She noticed the FOR SALE sign by the gate and ran back to Charlie.

"She's gone!" cried Olivia. "Now I'll never know."

"Hold on, Liv, she can't have gone." Charlie was peering through a window at the side of the house. "I can see two suitcases in the living room. And a rain-coat on the back of a chair."

"So she's somewhere in the city, but where?" Olivia now seemed desperate to find Alice Angel. She ran back to the wall with Charlie in tow, and they both climbed back to the other side.

"Well?" said Fidelio, while Runner Bean barked enthusiastically.

"Not there," said Charlie.

"How are we going to find her?" Olivia wrung her hands dramatically.

"The shop's been closed, so she won't be there," said Charlie.

"We'll have to scour the city," said Fidelio.

"It's too big," Charlie objected. "We could search for days and never find her."

"I think I can help," said Emma quietly. "What does this Alice Angel look like?"

They all stared at Emma, and Olivia said, "She has a lot of white hair and a beautiful face."

Charlie made an inspired guess. "She might be carrying some flowers, white ones."

"I've got the picture," said Emma. "Now, do you mind going indoors, all of you. Because I don't like doing what I'm going to do in public." She looked at her bandaged fingers. "I think Joshua got Tancred to injure my fingers on purpose."

"So that you couldn't fly." Olivia looked concerned. "Don't hurt yourself, Em. If it's too painful — just don't. You might fall."

Emma waved them away. "It'll be OK."

They trooped indoors and stood by the French windows, trying not to look into the backyard but finding it impossible not to take the occasional peek. Emma was hidden by the shrubbery, and it was only when a small brown bird flew up into the apple tree that they knew she was on her way. They watched the bird soar in the sky and said, "There she goes. If anyone can find Alice Angel, it's Emma Tolly."

Emma's wing tips gave her trouble to begin with. She hovered uncertainly over Filbert Street but finally regained her balance when she sailed into a cloud above the cathedral. Taking advantage of the warm autumn temperature, she drifted across the city, her sharp bird eyes taking in every detail of the busy citizens striding, ambling, and running below her. She even flew above Bloor's Academy and the castle ruin.

She saw Billy Raven walking across the ground with Blessed at his heels and would have liked to stop and talk to him, but time was precious.

The bird, Emma, was about to fly away from the ruin when she saw something that caused her to lose her concentration, and she began to drop toward the earth.

Deep in the ruin, tall ivy-covered walls surrounded a green and secret courtyard. In the center stood a tree with red-gold leaves. A sound came from the tree, music of a kind that Emma had never heard. Alighting on a wall, she saw a white horse grazing beneath the tree. Emma had no doubt that the tree and the horse belonged together and that they were a part of a world that was altogether different from her own.

The horse looked up when it saw the bird. "Child," it said. "My child."

"I fly," said Emma.

"May fortune fly with you," said the horse.

A surge of hope carried Emma into the sky. Her wings no longer ached and she felt profoundly happy.

With renewed energy she continued to search the city, until she came to the park at the end of Filbert Street. Below her, a white-haired woman sat alone on a bench. Her head was bent over a bouquet of white flowers on her lap.

Emma gave a sharp cry and the woman looked up. She had a beautiful but sad face. Emma wheeled around and flew back to Olivia's garden. Her three friends were still gathered around the window when she ran up the path, a girl again, crying, "I've found her. I've found her. She's in the park."

Four children and a dog raced down to the park, through the gates, and across the grass to the bench where Alice Angel sat alone. When she saw Olivia, Alice's sad face broke into a smile. "Olivia, have you come to say good-bye?"

"I've come to say I'm sorry," Olivia blurted. "I'm sorry for everything, for not believing, and for your friend who's gone."

Alice brought the white flowers up to her face and breathed in their scent. "I wanted to put these on his grave, but of course, he doesn't have one. Poor Christopher."

"I'm sorry, so sorry," cried Olivia, almost beside herself with remorse.

"You've come to see me. It's not too late." Alice stood up. "And you, Charlie, was it you who brought her here?"

"It was all of us," said Charlie. "My friend Fidelio" — Fidelio made a bow — "but mostly it was Emma. She found you."

"Ah!" Alice gave Emma a knowing look, then she carefully placed the flowers on the bench and turned to Olivia. "So you're ready to accept your inheritance?"

"I suppose I am," said Olivia.

"And who would you like to see what you can do?" asked Alice.

"My friends, of course," Olivia replied.

"No one else?" Alice said gravely. "You can choose whom to show your revelations."

"Can I?" Olivia's eager face began to look serious. She regarded a cyclist whizzing around the cycle path, two boys playing football, and a woman walking her dog. "Well, right now I only want my friends and you to see what I can do — oh, and Runner Bean, of course."

"Very well! Think of something, anything. Think very, very hard. See it in your mind, every facet of it."

"Hang on, I'm not going to turn into what I see, am I?" Olivia asked.

"No," replied Alice.

"OK. Here goes." A frown of concentration creased Olivia's brow, and then the familiar, mischievous gleam came into her eyes. Everyone stood very still, even Runner Bean, who seemed to have grasped the gravity of the situation. After a minute of total silence, Alice said, "Now, Olivia, look over your shoulder!"

Olivia looked. Everyone followed her gaze. In the middle of the park a huge murky cloud appeared. Gradually it assumed an indistinct, wobbly shape.

"No," said Alice. "You haven't quite got it, Olivia. Relax! You're trying too hard."

Olivia smiled and half-closed her eyes. The wobbly shape hardened into something horribly real.

Fidelio yelled first, and then Runner Bean gave a terrifying, primeval howl. Charlie's mouth dropped open but he was too scared to make a sound. He knew that what he was seeing wasn't real, but it looked real, it smelled real, and it sounded real. A huge dinosaur, a *Tyrannosaurus rex* by the look of it, stood a few paces away from them. Its vast mouth was open, its breath horrendous, and its blood-curdling roar a sound you only hear in nightmares.

Still howling, Runner Bean was the first to move. He tore off toward the park gates with three children yelling and screaming behind him. When the cyclist saw them he shouted, "What the . . . ?" and fell off his bike. The two boys picked up their ball and ran for the trees, crying, "Is it a ghost?" The small dog leaped into a trash can and its owner proclaimed that the world had gone mad.

"Children, stop!" called Alice. "It can't hurt you."

From a safe distance, they turned and looked back at the dreadful creature. Peals of laughter ran across the park as Olivia rocked back and forth, unable to stop herself. Alice put an arm around her shoulder and spoke softly.

Olivia nodded. She stopped laughing and looked over her shoulder. Behind her the awful image lost its shape. Gradually it faded into a cloud of particles that floated into the sky, like a shower of dead leaves.

Olivia clapped her hands and did a little dance. Before her friends had recovered from the first illusion another took its place. A feast served on glittering silver plates was laid upon a long table. And there was the Mad Hatter, the March Hare, and the Dormouse, half inside a teapot.

Next a rainbow arched over the park, and when this had faded, a knight in shining armor galloped across the grass on a huge black stallion, with feathers in his bridle and a scarlet cape embroidered in gold. Charlie could hear the pounding of hooves, the creak of leather, and the jangle of spurs.

Olivia danced around Alice with her head back and her arms thrown wide open. "Look what I can do," she cried. "Look! Look! Look!"

"Very impressive," Fidelio whispered to Charlie. "I don't know about her, but I'm exhausted."

Runner Bean sank to the ground with a moan and covered his eyes with a large paw.

Alice spoke to Olivia again, and when the knight and his horse had left the scene nothing took their place. Olivia flung herself on the grass sighing, "Phew! I overdid it, didn't I?"

Alice smiled fondly at her. The others approached a little warily, but Runner Bean stayed right where he was, his eyes still covered with a paw.

When they were all sitting comfortably on the bench and trying to shake themselves back to reality, Olivia asked Alice why it had taken so long for her to find out what she could do. "And how did you know about it? And why the apple?"

Alice considered the flowers on her lap. "It's difficult to put it into words," she said. "I always knew that one day I would see someone who would need my help to find themselves. It's a strange endowment, you may think." She looked at Charlie sitting beside her.

Charlie said, "They're all strange. All the endowments."

Alice gave him a grateful smile. "That's true. To cut things short, I was asked to decorate a room for a certain baby's christening." She glanced at Olivia. "The baby's mother was so pleased with my flowers, she invited me to join the party. I had no idea that it would be one of the most important days of my life. They brought in the baby and everyone clustered around, cooing and chattering and calling to you, Olivia."

"Was I a beautiful baby?" Olivia asked.

"To tell the truth, you were a bit tubby, but" — she looked sternly at Fidelio and Charlie who couldn't restrain a giggle — "but as soon as I saw you, Olivia, my heart missed a beat. I wondered what was happening to me. Later, they lay you in a lovely white crib, and when I gazed down at you, I knew that you were special. I also knew that it would take twelve long years for you to accept your inheritance."

"How did you know?" Olivia asked earnestly.

"This will sound really peculiar," said Alice.

"We don't mind," said Charlie. "Everything is peculiar."

"Well, there is an apple tree at the end of my garden. It's mine because it grows there, but it's also yours, Olivia, because a branch hangs into your garden. There were thirteen apples on the branch that day and . . . and . . ." Alice paused, and then in such a quiet voice that they all had to lean very close to her, she continued, "a voice in my head said, 'In the thirteenth year of the apple, may she accept her inheritance with grace.'"

"Oh!" said Olivia, as though struck by a sudden thought. "I was twelve at the beginning of the semester. So I guess I'm in my thirteenth year. And the apples . . . they wouldn't be peeled until I believed, until I accepted."

"That's about it," said Alice. "I hope you're happy, Olivia."

"Well, yes, of course I am. But I feel a bit odd, because I was never one of them." She gave Charlie a regretful grin. "And now I don't know what I'm going to do with this bizarre talent."

"I'm sure your friends will help you find out." Alice looked at Charlie.

Fidelio, who had lost his habitual smile, suddenly asked, "Are you a witch, Miss Angel?"

Alice laughed. "I suppose I am. But I am a white witch." She paused and added gravely, "Children, I don't want to alarm you, but you should be warned — where there is a white witch, there is always another of a darker nature."

"Who is it?" said Charlie.

"I'm afraid I have no idea." Alice stood up. "And now I must leave you," she said in a businesslike tone. "I have a train to catch."

"You're really going?" cried Olivia.

"I have fulfilled my destiny — at least one of them." Alice gave a contented sigh. "You're on your own now, Olivia. But I'm sure you'll cope very well."

Olivia leaped up and hugged her fiercely. "Thank

you," she said. "Thank you for being my guardian angel."

"It has made me so happy," said Alice.

Emma asked, "Before you go, can you tell us, will that other witch, the dark one, follow you?"

Alice gave a little shrug. "I have no way of knowing that. Good-bye, my dears, for now."

They watched Alice Angel walk away and disappear through the park gates. She didn't look back, and her disappearance was just that, a melting into thin air, as if she hadn't really been there at all. And yet the flowers still lay where she had left them.

"I'll give them to Mom," said Olivia. "She loves white flowers."

Charlie's thoughts had already returned to the problems at Bloor's, and he was beginning to devise a scheme for Olivia. "I think we should keep your talent a secret," he told her. "Does everyone agree?"

Fidelio said, "A secret weapon!"

"You mean no one should know except us?" asked Emma.

"No one," said Charlie.

"Suits me," said Olivia. "But how am I going to help?"

"Have you been in the King's room lately?" asked Charlie.

"Lots of times, when I've had detention," Olivia replied.

"Good. The first thing we've got to do is make Joshua Tilpin look repulsive, so repulsive," went on Charlie, relishing the vision he was beginning to conjure up, "that Tancred will be repelled by him. In fact, it would be just as well if all the endowed were repelled by him."

"I've got an idea," said Fidelio. "We all know what Tancred's afraid of."

"Spiders," said Emma.

"Spiders," Charlie agreed. "Second thing is to scare the living daylights out of Ezekiel Bloor. I'll have to work on that one."

"Oh, yes!" cried Fidelio, punching the air. "This is going to be good. This is going to be very, very good."

THE WARRIOR

Uncle Paton said it would be foolhardy to use the Filbert Street house for a meeting. Ingledew's would be far better. Olivia's newfound talent must remain a secret. No one would think it unusual if they saw her enter the bookstore. Emma was her friend and they often spent the weekend together.

On Saturday evening, Charlie and Uncle Paton set off for Ingledew's. Grandma Bone paid no attention to them. She had the upper hand, so she thought. Charlie and his troublesome friends had been taught a lesson. Billy Raven was once again in the Bloors' power, and Charlie was in hers — more or less.

Fidelio insisted on being in on the plan, and when Charlie and his uncle walked into Miss Ingledew's cozy back room, Fidelio was already there, sitting on the sofa between the two girls. Charlie squeezed in beside Olivia, and Uncle Paton took one of the

armchairs. Miss Ingledew brought in a plate of cookies and sat on the arm of Paton's chair.

The meeting began.

"Timing is the most important aspect of this plan,"
said Uncle Paton. "Are you clear about that, Olivia?"

Olivia said, "My watch is never wrong," and she
held out her wrist, so that everyone could admire her
large silver watch with its trendy hologram face.

"Very fine," Uncle Paton remarked, "as long as you
consult it at the right time."

"Yes," said Olivia meekly.

"And now you must be absolutely clear about
everyone's position in the King's room. Charlie,
describe the room as it usually looks when you are all
doing your homework."

Charlie described everyone's position as best he
could.

"It's up to you and Emma to make sure they all
keep their places, so that Olivia can visualize them,"
Uncle Paton said sternly. "Right?"

"Right," said Charlie and Emma.

Uncle Paton then went on to outline the next part of the plan.

An hour later, the meeting broke up. Felix Gunn arrived to take Fidelio home, while Charlie and Uncle Paton walked back to Filbert Street. Olivia was to spend the night with Emma. She needed to look at some of Miss Ingledew's illustrated history books.

"I hope the Bloors won't guess what we're doing," said Charlie, as he and his uncle mounted the steps of number nine.

"Charlie, they'll never guess," said Uncle Paton confidently. "Not in a thousand years."

Charlie found it hard to act normal on Monday. Fidelio's excited swagger made him nervous. "We're supposed to look depressed," he told his friend.

"You, maybe," said Fidelio. "But I'm not one of the endowed victims. Anyway, I always act like this."

There was one other person who Charlie had to alert. Lysander hadn't been at the meeting, but

Charlie felt he had to warn him about what might happen. Unfortunately, he couldn't get Lysander on his own until after dinner when they were climbing the stairs to the King's room. Charlie deliberately knocked a pile of books out of Lysander's arms, and they tumbled down the stairs.

"What did you do that for, clumsy?" grumbled Lysander, as he bent to retrieve the books.

Charlie leaned down to help him. "I've got to warn you," he whispered.

"Warn?"

"Shhh!" hissed Charlie. "Something's going to happen to Joshua in a minute. Tancred will be scared out of his wits, but it's not real, OK? It's just an illusion."

"What . . . ," began Lysander.

"Are you two going to move or shall I walk over you!" Dorcas Loom glared at them from the bottom of the stairs.

"Cool it, Dorc," said Lysander, gathering up his books.

The two boys leaped up the stairs, followed by Dorcas, who was puffing like a steam engine.

Charlie took a quick look around the King's room before he sat down. He was relieved to see that everyone was in the exact place that he had described to Olivia. Asa's face was covered in bruises, he noticed.

Charlie glanced at Emma beside him, but she refused to meet his eye. Probably, she didn't dare to. Everything now depended on Olivia.

The clock ticked, as it always did. The Red King looked down from his portrait, as he always did, and yet — was it Charlie's imagination, or did the king's eyes look brighter tonight? And was there an added sparkle in his crown?

"The king can't help you, Bone," said Manfred in a withering tone.

Charlie dropped his gaze. Asa snickered, and Joshua beamed at Tancred. A large raindrop fell on Charlie's open book, and then another. He pulled his book away and a puddle formed on the table in front of him. Charlie dabbed at it with the sleeve of his sweater.

Lysander said, "Cut it out, Tanc!" He was rewarded by a blast of air that blew all his papers into his face.

Come on, Olivia, thought Charlie. *Do it now!*

Emma's pen began to leak. Ink spread across a page of her beautifully neat handwriting. There was ink on her hands, on her cape, on her face. Idith and Inez were staring at her.

Emma stared back. "Stop it!" she cried.

Dorcas burst out laughing and nudged Joshua. Suddenly, she drew away from him. Charlie watched a huge black spider crawl over the top of Joshua's head. Another one crept over his shoulder. Tancred leaped up, screaming. He ran for the door while Manfred shouted, "Torsson, have you gone mad?"

Joshua's smile began to fade. Both his sleeves were covered in spiders. He stood up and tried to shake them off. By then everyone had seen the spiders. The King's room was filled with screams. Everyone rushed for the door. Joshua tripped, and the twins ran over him as he lay groaning on the floor. A mighty wind rushed around the room as

Tancred's trembling fingers fought with the door handle. At last, the doors were opened and nine children erupted into the passage.

Manfred tried to keep his composure, but at length even he was swept up in the panic.

Tancred was now completely out of control. Wind and rain rushed through the building. Thunder crashed overhead and lightning zipped past the windows. Homework was terminated while the staff ran around with rags, mops, and buckets.

Charlie raced down to the cafeteria. The room was in darkness, but far below him, he could hear a deep rumble. The floor of the cafeteria shuddered; tables and chairs slid across the floor banging against each other. And then there was silence.

Charlie was about to go into the kitchen when Cook emerged, holding a candle.

"Is that you, Charlie?" She peered into the darkness.

"Yes, Cook. Are you OK?"

"Right as rain. I don't know how you did it, Charlie,

but the balance is back. My floor's all nice and straight."

"Phew. That IS good news."

"Isn't it?"

"Excuse me, Cook, but there's something I've got to find out."

"Run along then, bless you!" said Cook.

At the height of the commotion, a loud banging could be heard on the main doors.

Mr. Weedon, confused by the pandemonium, forgot himself and unlocked the doors. A tall figure walked into the hall.

"I wish to see Mr. Ezekiel Bloor," the stranger demanded.

"You can't do that," Mr. Weedon shouted above the wind. "It's forbidden."

"Don't be silly." Uncle Paton strode past Weedon and entered the door to the west wing.

Olivia, peeping into the hall from the purple coatroom, consulted her watch.

• • •

Ezekiel and Dr. Bloor were enjoying a glass of port in the very room where Billy Raven had been forced to sign his oath. The two men were oblivious to the noise in the main part of the school. They sat close to the window, which framed a magnificent sunset. At the other end of the long table, Billy Raven's white head was bent over his homework.

Dr. Bloor leaped up when Paton came through the door. "What the devil are you doing here, Yewbeam?" roared the headmaster.

"I've brought some papers for you to sign," said Paton.

"Papers?" screeched Ezekiel. "What papers?"

"They concern Billy Raven. I want you to give him permission to spend his weekends wherever and with whomever he chooses."

"You're mad," sneered Dr. Bloor.

"Not at all." Paton laid two papers before them. "Sign here. And here." He pointed to the bottom of both papers.

"And what on earth makes you think we'll sign this rubbish?" said Dr. Bloor, pushing the papers away.

Paton stroked his chin. "Dr. Bloor, your grandfather recently made a little experiment."

A shadow crossed Ezekiel's face and he licked his lips.

"What of it?" said the headmaster.

"I thought you would like to know that it was a success — except for one thing. The creature — for want of a better word — is now under my control."

"What? How . . . ?" Ezekiel tried to lift himself out of his chair.

"Prove it!" said Dr. Bloor.

"Very well." Paton opened the door.

There was no doubt about it. Olivia's imagination was marvelous indeed. Framed in the doorway stood a gigantic black warhorse. Lifting its great head, it gave a terrifying bellow and began to enter the room. The warrior on its back had to bend his head as they passed through the seven-foot doorway. When he raised it again, Ezekiel Bloor slumped forward in a dead faint.

Paton regarded the armored warrior with admiration. He wore a tall silver helmet with an awesome-looking nosepiece, and the lower part of his face was covered by a thick black beard. His ruddy cheeks were smeared with blood, as was his suit of gleaming chain mail. In his hand he carried not an elegant sword, but a large and very bloody axe.

"HAAAA!" roared the ghastly warrior, raising his weapon.

Billy emitted a terrified squeal, but Paton, turning to him quickly, gave a large wink.

Dr. Bloor, on the point of losing consciousness, said weakly, "Where do I sign?"

Paton, somewhat surprised by the speed of his success, produced a pen and held it firmly between Dr. Bloor's trembling fingers. "Better sign twice. Your grandfather appears to be out for the count."

With a face the color of a bleached sheet, the headmaster managed to sign both papers before dropping the pen and collapsing onto the table.

"Ouch!" said Paton as Dr. Bloor's head hit the table

with a thump. "Thank you, Prince, you may go now!" He waved at the ghastly apparition, and the warrior and his horse gently faded.

"Wh-what was that?" Billy stammered.

"An illusion," whispered Paton. He patted Billy's head. "See you on Friday, Billy."

Charlie was waiting in the hall when his uncle returned from the west wing. Paton held the papers aloft. "All's right with the world," he declared triumphantly. "It worked."

"Hooray!" cried Charlie, regardless of the rules. There was after all so much noise in the building, who would notice a few words spoken in the hall? "I must find Billy and tell him the good news."

"He knows, dear boy. He knows," said Uncle Paton.

THE CAPTIVES' STORY

On Saturday morning, Paton Yewbeam sat in his car outside the city hospital. It was a dark thundery day, but this had nothing to do with Tancred Torsson, who was at that very moment watching a soccer game with his friend Lysander.

Paton wore his dark glasses as usual, but an article in his newspaper caused him to jump so violently that the glasses slid down his nose and fell into his lap. Paton was reading about a place he'd known as a child, a place he had come to remember with horror.

This is what he read:

CELEBRATIONS WERE HELD IN THE VILLAGE OF YORWYNDE YESTERDAY. ON TUESDAY MORNING, HEADMASTER TANTALUS WRIGHT AND POSTMAN VINCENT EBONY WALKED INTO THEIR HOMES AFTER AN ABSENCE OF THREE WEEKS. THEY TOLD US THAT

THEY HAD BEEN HELD CAPTIVE IN YEWBEAM CASTLE, A PLACE RENOWNED FOR ITS TROUBLED PAST.

THE TWO MEN HAD LIVED IN A STATE OF SEMI-CONSCIOUSNESS, UNABLE TO MOVE OR SPEAK. BOTH CONFESSED TO HAVING FELT AS THOUGH THEIR MINDS WERE BEING USED. THEY EXPERIENCED STRANGE DREAMS IN WHICH THEY WERE SURROUNDED BY CHILDREN IN COLORED CAPES.

"Ye gods!" Paton brought the newspaper closer to his face.

MR. WRIGHT SAID THAT THEY SEEMED TO HAVE BEEN HELD IN A STATE OF SUSPENDED ANIMATION AND, THEREFORE, DID NOT SUFFER FROM THE LACK OF FOOD OR WATER. HE ALSO SAID THAT FOOTSTEPS COULD BE HEARD ABOVE THEM. ONCE OR TWICE, A VOICE CALLED OUT, AND SOMETIMES THERE HAD BEEN A TUNEFUL HUMMING. HE WAS CONVINCED THERE HAD BEEN A THIRD PRISONER IN THE BUILDING.

ON TUESDAY MORNING, MR. EBONY AND MR.

WRIGHT HAD BEEN INEXPLICABLY RELEASED. "IT JUST CAME OVER US," SAID MR. EBONY. "WE COULD MOVE, WE COULD TALK. WE GOT TO THE DOOR, AND THEN WE WERE OUT. I DON'T KNOW IF THE OTHER GUY GOT OUT, THOUGH."

POLICE HAVE SINCE MADE A THOROUGH SEARCH OF THE CASTLE, BUT NO ONE HAS BEEN FOUND.

Paton lowered the paper. "Ye gods!" he said again.

Inside the hospital, Charlie, Billy, Fidelio, Emma, and Olivia were making their way to the ward where Gabriel was recovering.

"Five children?" said the nurse on duty. "No. That's too many. Three at the most."

"We'll wait outside, shall we, Liv?" said Emma.

"'Course," said Olivia. "I'm not sure I want to see a load of sick boys, anyway." She looked almost her old self in an orange velvet skirt, silver top, and hair discreetly highlighted in pink.

"Come on, then," Charlie said to the two boys.

Gabriel was sitting up, but he looked thin and peaked. He gave a weak but delighted smile when he saw his friends. The three boys approached the bed. Fidelio was the most relaxed. "How are you doing?" he said, grasping Gabriel's white hand.

Charlie just grinned. Hospitals made him nervous. They were too clean, too tidy, and too quiet.

Billy was having trouble with his pockets. The moment he'd been released from Bloor's Academy on Friday, he'd insisted on getting Rembrandt from the Pets' Café. Charlie had told him to keep the rat well-hidden or they'd find him in Grandma Bone's soup. So Billy had a rat in one pocket and a gerbil in the other.

The gerbil was Mrs. Silk's idea. She thought it would help Gabriel's recovery. "He'd just love to know what his gerbil says," she told Billy.

Billy shuffled close to Gabriel's bed and put the gerbil on the oh-so-white sheet.

"Rita!" Gabriel exclaimed, lifting the gerbil to his cheek. "I love you, Rita!"

Rita gave several loud squeaks.

"Tell me what she's saying, Billy," begged Gabriel.

Billy was in a quandary. Rita seemed to be swearing. Among other things, she was saying, "Where am I? Who got me into this mess?"

"She says she loves you, too," said Billy.

"Oh, Rita, you're the best gerbil in the world!" cried Gabriel.

There was a sudden scream from the boy in the next bed. "Nurse! He's got a rat! There's a rat in here!"

"WHAT?" said a very stern voice.

Billy grabbed Rita, and the three boys ran out of the ward, while shouts of "Rat!" "That's disgusting!" "Where? I want to see!" followed them out into the corridor.

But louder than all the shouts was the sound of Gabriel's laughter.

JENNY NIMMO

I was born in Windsor, Berkshire, England, and educated at boarding schools in Kent and Surrey from the age of six until I was sixteen, when I ran away from school to become a drama student/assistant stage manager with Theater South East. I graduated and acted in repertory theater in various towns and cities.

I left Britain to teach English to three Italian boys in Amalfi, Italy. On my return, I joined the BBC, first as a picture researcher, then assistant floor manager, studio manager (news), and finally director/adaptor with *Jackanory* (a BBC storytelling program for children). I left the BBC to marry Welsh artist David Wynn Millward and went to live in Wales in my husband's family home. We live in a very old converted water mill, and the river is constantly threatening to break in, which it has done several times in the past, most dramatically on my youngest child's first birthday. During the summer, we run a residential school of art, and I have to move my office, put down tools (typewriter and pencils), and don an apron and cook! We have three grown-up children, Myfanwy, Ianto, and Gwenhwyfar.

CHILDREN OF THE RED KING BOOKS

BOOK #1: *MIDNIGHT FOR CHARLIE BONE*

Ten-year-old Charlie discovers that as a descendant of the Red King, he has magical powers that he must learn to use at the mysterious Bloor's Academy.

"A MYSTERIOUS BOX, A MISSING GIRL . . . AND VARIOUS VILLAINS ALL FIGURE INTO CHARLIE'S EXCITING, FAST-PACED ADVENTURE TALE, WHICH HAPPILY IS THE FIRST BOOK IN A PLANNED QUINTET CALLED CHILDREN OF THE RED KING."

— *BOOKLIST*

BOOK #2: *CHARLIE BONE AND THE TIME TWISTER*

It's up to Charlie to help Henry Yewbeam, a young time traveler from 1916, return to the past. Will Henry ever see his home again? Not if his evil cousin Ezekiel can help it!

"CHARLIE BONE IS A LIKABLE CHARACTER WHOM KIDS WILL TURN TO FOR A FIX AFTER THEY'VE FINISHED THE LATEST HARRY POTTER FOR THE FIFTH TIME." — *SCHOOL LIBRARY JOURNAL*

BOOK #3: *CHARLIE BONE AND THE INVISIBLE BOY*

Charlie discovers an invisible boy named Ollie in the attic of Bloor's Academy. Can Charlie and his friends make Ollie visible again?

". . . IT'S A WILD ROLLER-COASTER RIDE OF A STORY . . ."

— *SCHOOL LIBRARY JOURNAL*